The KEY

BY
MALCOLM JOHN BAKER

Published by
Malcolm John Baker Publishing

The Key
Copyright © 2021 by Malcolm John Baker

ISBN   (Paperback)   978-1-954168-89-3
        (Hardcover)   978-1-954168-90-9
        (eBook)   978-1-954168-88-6

Acknowledgments

I want to thank Jefferson of First Editing for his
work in editing the book and his inspiration for
the project. As always, he has done a first-class job
interpreting my British into American English.

I would also like to thank Emma Smith of Chapters Media
for her untiring help in the publication's production and,
particularly, for the cover of this book. Excellent job, Emma.

Lastly, I would like to thank all those first responders,
doctors, and nurses who have taken all these risks during the
COVID-19 pandemic to help the whole world. Especially
Dr. Mercedes Madar, my partner and Lady of the Manor of
Hougun, who is in the emergency room every day looking
after the sick. You all do a fantastic job Merci. Thank you.
Let's hope that everyone gets the vaccine
quickly; I had mine two montsh ago.

Other books by Malcolm John Baker

Revenge Is Mine
From a Jack to a king
Daylight Robbery
Which is the Clone
Annabelle
The African Duke

Merlin Series.
Merlin's Secret
Merlin's Shakespeare Encounter
Merlin's French Encounter
Merlin's American Encounter

Coming soon.
The Land of the Giants

Malcolm's websites are.
www.malcolmjohnbaker.us
www.malcolmjohnbaker.com
email m-baker12@sky.com

PROLOGUE

It had been a surprisingly warm day, unusual especially for Alaska in June 1900, so Don did not bother to use the sleeping bag that night; he could not see to get it in any event, as he had been to the beer tent in Nome. He lay down on top of the bag and looked up at the canvas roof of the tent, hallucinating about how he would be received by his wife when he arrived home unannounced. The image of his beautiful dark-haired Sophie appeared on the canvas, and he blew her a kiss. In reality, the image was that of ten years ago, when she was younger, but he lived happily in his fantasy.

Alcohol affects people in diverse ways; some go out like a light. Others, like Don, are the opposite; it keeps them awake. Don tried to get to sleep, but he was still awake after half an hour, even in his drunkenness. His heart beat faster, his whole body vibrated, and his mind races as he thought of his family back home, his wife and three children, bless their souls.

I knew I should not have drunk so much, but how many men have said that over the years? How long it has been since I left San Francisco. I wonder what Sophie is doing now. Is she thinking of me? Probably not. Don hadn't been able to send her any money as he had promised. He felt a tear form in his eye, he knew he had ket her down, but the gold is not here in any quantity. *One has to live*, he told himself.

He closed his eyes. *I am wasting my time in this gold rush mania. I should be at home in San Francisco with my dear family; there is no gold in my claim area in any event.* He had to admit to himself, although some people had managed to scrape together a few flakes of gold from the beach. As he drifted off to sleep, he decided to end this madness and leave for California in a few days.

An unfamiliar sound suddenly awakened him. Opening his eyes, through the mist of reality, he saw a monster poised over him with a nine-inch Bowie knife. Its eyes are blood red, and its hair seemed to have grown into snakes. The monster brought down the knife aimed at Don's heart, but Don managed to grab at its arm just in time and turned himself sideways, but the knife plunged into his bicep. Blood pours out from the deep wound.

Don rolled off the sleeping bag and onto the cold, hard earth, now red with his blood. His mind is active now, and he feared for his life. The monster had turned into Chuck. The knife had cut deep into his muscle, rendering his arm useless.

Chuck fumed at his failure; his heart is racing, and his face burned. He had wasted the easy option, so now it would be the hard way. He slashed at Don, stabbing him in the chest and stomach. Don began bleeding profusely from six cuts, and the earth around him turned to red mud.

The effects on Don were severe. He seemed to be paralyzed, and his eyes blurred as the alcohol took hold again, or was it something else? He could not think straight. He certainly could not get off the ground; in fact, he could not move at all, despite trying hard. He suddenly realized he is dying as the blood drained out of his body.

What is going on here? He wondered. He'd thought Chuck was his friend, but his mind was fading fast. As he sank into oblivion, his last conscious thought was an image of Sophie holding out her arms for him, beckoning him to come forward. The image slowly faded, like he was drifting down a long dark tunnel as he passed out and died.

Three days earlier, on May 30, 1900, a stranger calling himself Chuck Smith arrived in Nome, Alaska's makeshift gold mining village, looking for Don Wicker. After finding out from the mining reception where Don's tent was, he headed over to it. Several men were talking nearby, and he joined in the conversation. These miners were very sociable and happy to greet the newcomer, who pretended to be there to make his fortune from gold. He had a different objective, though.

All of the others thought *Fat chance of making a fortune from gold mining.* They'd all originally had the same idea, but time is a great learner.

Don said to the stranger, "Do you have a tent?"

"Not yet. I thought I would buy one later from the stores when they open up," the stranger responded.

"Don't worry about that. Why not stay with me for the time being to make sure you like it here? I have plenty of room. The weather is ferocious, you know," said Don.

He was lying about his tent's size, which could barely hold two people, but he welcomed the company.

That was just what the stranger wanted to hear. "That is very kind of you. I am truly grateful. Did you say your name is Don? I forget names so easily. Sometimes I think I am getting old. I am Chuck, by the way."

"Come with me, and we'll get you settled in," said Don, and they left to go to Don's tent.

On June 2, Don Wicker was about to go drinking at the bar tent with his new guest, Chuck. Before they left, he saw his small family heirloom chest with his two trinkets. Don caressed the chest, kissing it tenderly. He could finally admit to himself that his gold mining prospect had been a failure. Though he had found a small quantity of gold, it was not enough to live on in the manner he had promised his dear wife.

He promised himself that he would give up mining and return home to Sophie, the love of his life, in a few days, as soon as he sorted things out. At least he would have one surprise for her.

He didn't know why, but he suddenly thought that he should put his special key in the chest, the one that held his treasure. *Why do I need to do that? Is it on impulse or due to a premonition?* After putting the key inside, he placed the chest next to his bedding and left with Chuck for the bar tent.

Chuck had been waiting impatiently, lost in thought about what he had to do. He questioned whether he was cut out for this, and his heart was racing.

The bar tent was situated at the back of the beach, where everyone camped there could easily reach. There was nothing to do in this godforsaken hole at night but drink the time away and maybe watch the attractive young girls ply their wares.

Chuck made sure that Don got drunk, but he stayed sober for the grim task at hand. He explained that since he was Don's guest, he would buy the drinks that night. Then he would purchase two pints of beer, but every time, he got the bartender to fill his glass with apple juice. The color was the same, and the apple juice tasted better than the beer, he decided. At midnight, the barman, wanting to get to bed, announced, "Time, gentlemen." There was no rush to leave, but the drinkers gradually left and headed back to their tents for the night. A few of the lucky ones took one of the young ladies with them, but they knew it would cost them a quarter.

Don and Chuck were no exception, and they eventually returned to their tent. The beer might taste awful, but after the first glass, the alcohol set in, and it soon tasted good. Don was so intoxicated that he could hardly walk, so Chuck held him up, which was not easy, as Don was a large man and Chuck was much smaller.

The murder was harder than Chuck expected. Once Don was dead, he realized his task was done, although blood was still pumping from Don's cuts, the last action of his failing heart. Chuck moved back to take stock of the situation. His heart was slowing down now, as no one had appeared at the tent entrance, but he knew he had to get far away as quickly as possible. No point in taking risks.

There had not been much noise other than a few grunts and puffs. No one was coming to the tent to investigate, and he peered through the door flap to make sure. He did hear another miner going back to his tent from the bar, but the miner was drunk. Chuck listened to the man's drunken singing and thought he would be no trouble. After peeing on a tree, the miner left for his tent.

Chuck gathered up his few belongings and let out an enormous sigh of relief. He had done what he'd set out to do, even though it had taken him two days to pluck up the courage.

He rechecked the tent flap to make sure no one was around. It was quiet, not a soul in sight; the peeing drunk had gone off to his tent. Chuck made sure Don's body was out of sight of anyone passing by and lay the sleeping bag over him. He then slowly slipped out of the tent. All the miners were now settled down for the night, and silence prevailed. The corral was a short distance away, and Chuck soon found his horse. He quickly saddled it and rode off into the night.

The local policeman made his usual rounds of the tents in the morning to ensure all the inhabitants were safe. He stood on the high ground next to the beach; in front of him stood an array of at least a hundred tents. Men were slowly exiting their tents now that the sun had risen. Most had slept off their drunken stupors, but a few were moaning about the ache in their heads as one kicked the ground in frustration.

The ladies who had spent the night with their clients had already left to go back to the brothel built of timber just off the beach. The policeman looked forward to the new town to be built in the area. At present, only a few wooden houses were lining a single street. One of them was his, and next door was a lot with a sign announcing that the town hall would be built there.

The officer wondered whether it would ever be built; the gold rush was beginning to peter out and had not produced the wealth that the miners had expected. One day he thought we might even have roads leading to other parts of the country. Leaving his thoughts, he knew there is nothing he could do personally, so he turned back to the tents; they are his concern. One is still closed. *That's Don's*, he thought as he walked down to it. *Don is up late this morning; he must have had too much to drink last night.*

He called at the tent flap, "Is everything all right, Don? It's time to get up and go to work, or you'll never make your millions." *Fat chance of that*, he thought, but nevertheless laughed as he said it. There was no reply, so he called out again. Still no response, he opened the canvas and saw Don's body in a pool of dried red blood.

CHAPTER ONE

It was a dull winter's day late in January 2021. Cloe Taylor and John Smith were at Mason and Mason's Auction House preview day on Nashville's edge of town. Mason and Mason is an old, established business; their brochure claimed they'd started in 1821, but no such claim could be confirmed as there were no records in those days. No one actually cared, though, as they were the only auctioneer in the district.

They operated in a single-story prefabricated building on the edge of town and held auctions of furniture and artifacts on the first Tuesday of each month; they had thought about going into property auctions but decided that the time was not right.

Cloe and John had six lots entered into this forthcoming auction, so they came on preview day to see them on display. By the time they reached the venue on John's Harley Davidson, it had started to drizzle, the sort of rain where you get much wetter than you think, but as they had come in their leathers, they did not worry and trotted to the front door.

John loved his Harley. He didn't normally ride it in the rain, and after he wiped the water off, he placed a cover over it to keep it dry. He spent hours polishing the bike, much to the annoyance of Cloe, who said, "You could be better spending your time cleaning the house."

"I'll do it later," John would respond, but he never did, and Cloe knew it, but she loved him to pieces. She was so happy that they had gotten together after her first marriage had failed, and their relationship had brought all these adventures and financial rewards with it.

The auction hall is an ample, open space inside the building. The walls and ceiling were in the Tudor style, with exposed timbers. John remarked that he liked this style of construction, but it fell on deaf ears with Cloe.

Lining the walls were dozens of tables, all displaying the lots for tomorrow's auction. At one end was the auctioneer's desk, with a sign reading, "Charles Mason." It was empty today, but tomorrow it would be a hive of activity. To the left of the auctioneer's chair was the recorder's chair. Again, it was empty today, but the young lady had come in for a while to make sure her chair was well-positioned to see all the bidders tomorrow. There are also several company clerks to ensure no one walked off with any lots on display.

The room's center was taken up with some comfortable armchairs, which would be auctioned off tomorrow, and fold-up chairs for the widely expected attendees. Numbers were always high for these monthly auctions. They were as much social gatherings as a means of purchasing items. Most of the buyers were local people who knew one another and that the management served cheap champagne to encourage the bidding. Coffee was also sold from a café at the rear.

While John went to find their lots, Cloe perused the other lots alone. She considered herself to be clairvoyant and thought that any lot of interest would make itself known to her. It had worked in her favor in the past. After walking along the whole line, she was about to give up when she saw a small wooden chest sitting at the front of one of the tables.

The box looked like one of those pirate treasure chests, like the one they'd found containing Drake's treasures last year, but this one was in miniature, complete with two metal bands. It shone like a brand-new penny. As her eyes fixed on it, it pulsated, becoming brighter and then darker. When she touched it, it became warmer? She rushed off to find John, and not wanting anyone else to hear, she whispered, "Come with me. I've something to show you."

John was keen to stay where he views other items, but he went with her, and she pointed out the chest to him.

"It's just a chest, like the one we got rid of recently," John said, wondering what the fuss was over.

"I know but look at it. It's pulsating and is brighter than it was two minutes ago. Oh, it's stopped now, but it was calling to me," Cloe said. There were no keys to the chest, and it was locked. Choe picked up the chest and gently shook it; she heard a rattle. "There is something inside," she said. "Can you hear the rattle?" She shook it again. "There's definitely something inside, John. Can you hear?" There seemed to be only one thing inside, and it clonked from side to side when she turned the chest over. John thought she had gone mad, but he had to admit that Cloe was psychic, and he knew that she would want to buy it tomorrow.

They had six lots in the auction; these were the last few items from the haul from the Mexican adventure the previous year. A friend had told John to make sure that their lots were at the table's front on preview day. "Watch out for prospective bidders moving them around to conceal them," he had said. This was good advice, thought John, because two of their lots were at the rear of the table and out of sight. He picked them up and swapped them for the chest that had taken Cloe's fancy.

After an hour, they left the preview; there had been a good attendance, with people picking up things and holding them up to the light; John had thought, *What difference does that make?* The rain had stopped when they got outside. John removed the cover from his bike and wiped it down again in a loving way just to make sure, and then they got on.

The couple rode home on the Harley-Davidson Road King Special. The bike was brand new, the first new one John had ever had; usually, he bought second-hand. However, this year, he'd had the money to splash out after the success with the treasures they had found last year in the Caribbean.

It had been six months since John and Cloe's last encounter with danger after discovering Sir Francis Drake's hidden treasures. They had missed out on Blackbeard's treasures, but as John had said, "You can't win them all." That had been quite an adventure, involving a sunken Spanish galleon and an underground Mayan city, all of which had produced considerable financial rewards.

They had sold off all the gold they'd acquired from the sunken Spanish galleon, and they now had large bank balances. John had met Cloe in Homestead, Florida, two years ago. *Oh, boy, that fishnet body stocking was outstanding*, John often thought. They had purchased a new and larger house in Nashville together, a timber-clad property with a rear swimming pool. They lived happily as a couple and talked about marriage, although they'd decided to leave that over for the time being. "You must be very sure," Cloe had said, hoping that John would say, "I'm sure," but no, he'd just nodded in agreement. They both had previous unhappy marriages, so she had to make sure, and John agreed.

John was an informer for the FBI, and he did other tasks for Agent Josh Young, things that, for political reasons, the FBI could not do themselves. He had been doing that for fifteen years now. Before that, he'd been a petty criminal but had gotten caught in a bank raid. He'd made a deal with the FBI: they would drop the charges in exchange for this present arrangement, which had worked out splendidly for both parties. John had a tracking chip in his neck so Agent Josh Young could trace him if he got in trouble. It had been needed on several occasions, although initially the chip had been put in for one job, he'd asked that it be left in for his safety.

They still had six articles left from the Mexican haul, small figurines from the Mayan dynasty, which would be going up for sale at the auction house tomorrow. They'd chosen a local one as they did not want to bring too much attention to the sale, even if it meant getting less money.

The next day was the day of the auction. Ten o'clock, the program said, so they left the house at nine to make sure they were early and got a good seat; it was only five miles to the auction house. Today the weather was much brighter, and they enjoyed the ride. As they drove into the auction room's forecourt, a Channel 5 television truck was parked in the parking area. Cables ran from the truck to the interior of the building.

The auction hall was set up as John and Cloe walked in, and standing in the center was an attractive lady interviewer holding a microphone and talking to the video she is making.

"Good morning. This is Gloria Rowbottom, reporting from Mason and Mason's auction house, which today celebrates its centenary. I am with Charles Mason, the auctioneer for today's event, and he has agreed to tell us of today's proceedings."

The interview went on for five minutes, at which time the auctioneer said, "You will have to excuse me, as I need to get to the rostrum now."

The auction staff took up their positions, and Gloria moved over to the auction tables. As the cameraman panned down the tables, Gloria made various comments that John and Cloe could not hear, as her microphone was switched off now. She stopped at the small chest that Cloe was interested in and studied it, picking it up and holding it to the light as though that would tell her something.

Cloe said, "I hope that interviewer is not interested in my piece." John did not comment, but he sniggered under his breath.

"Here is an exciting item, a small replica of a smuggler's chest. I wonder what price that will go for," Gloria said into the microphone as the cameraman zoomed in on the chest. Off-camera, she said to the cameraman, "I want to watch this piece and see who purchases it. I don't know why; it's just one of those feelings you get now and then." The cameraman nodded.

A few people had also come early, but not as many as John had expected. He hoped more would arrive soon; he wanted to get rid of his lots today, as storage space was at a premium. He and Cloe chose seats where he had a good view of who was making bids.

Cloe said, "I won't be a moment; I just want to register with the sales team," and she left. John did not want to register; he had no intention of buying anything, but he knew what Cloe was is after. She returned a few minutes later with a card displaying the number 165.

The television interviewer was talking to punters as they walked past the tables. She said to one buyer, "May I ask you what lot you are interested in, madam?"

The lady replied, "I am looking for some wall coverings, but they do have some interesting artifacts today as well." Gloria thanked the lady and moved on.

The start time was now less than half an hour away, and the hall began to fill up. "Quite a big gathering. That's good," said John as the start time neared. Their items were lots six to twelve on the auction catalog. The chest that Cloe liked was number sixteen, but John was hoping to dissuade her from buying it.

The auctioneer took the stand at nine forty-five; he was a well-built man of about fifty years, with graying hair and dressed in a dark gray suit with a fancy waistcoat. Cloe thought he was attractive, but she did not mention this to John. With his bold chest, the auctioneer looked as though he had a powerful voice, which he would need for this job, as he had to project his voice forcefully to encourage bids.

The young lady recorder took her chair as well; a large book to record the sales sat in front of her. John had noticed her, of course, as she was very attractive. Everyone was now ready to go. A few people were still coming into the hall, but they had to stand at the back, as the hall was now full.

At precisely ten o'clock, the hall was packed; people were even standing at the sides and the rear. John was interested in how the first six lots would go, and he was delighted with the turnout; it was good for his lots to have such a large number of potential buyers.

He and Cloe were glad they had chosen the chairs they were sitting in; they were comfortable armchair lots. Once the auction started, bids came from all over the room. John thought that the auctioneer made up some of the bids. He had also heard that this was a widespread practice, but all the lots sold at what seemed good prices.

The auctioneer started the proceedings by using a microphone for the benefit of the television people. Usually, he did not need it. He said, "Good morning, ladies and gentlemen. Today I am proud to announce that this is our hundredth year in business, and we are honored to welcome Channel 5 to join us. They will be filming the events and interviewing people. If anyone is with someone they should not be with, you might like to leave now," he joked, which brought a round of laughter. Suddenly there was a stamping of feet on the concrete floor.

Everyone went silent and turned to where the noise had come from. The auctioneer turned to his recorder and whispered, "There is always one comedian, isn't there," and the laughter started up once again.

"We had better get on with the proceedings," the auctioneer said, and he sold the first six lots quickly. It was now time for John's six lots. The first one sold for ten thousand dollars, a reasonable price, thought John. He noticed that only three people had bid on this lot. The other lots were sold for reasonable prices as well. He had twice made bids to bolster the price on one lot but had withdrawn before the auctioneer had brought down the gavel. The total proceeds added up to a hundred thousand dollars, minus the commission of eighteen percent. John had a big smile on his face at that result.

"John, you cheated just then by putting in bids on your own lots," said Cloe.

"I know, but it worked; we got the price up substantially. All's fair in love and war," John said, laughing.

"Okay, let's go," he said to Cloe with a smile, knowing that she would want to stay for the chest.

"Hold on, John. Can we just see what the chest goes for? It's the fourth lot now," she said.

John thought, *Oh, dear, she really does want that chest.*

The next three lots went unsold; then the chest came up. As the clerk lifted the little chest high in the air, the auctioneer announced, "This chest came in a collection from Alaska. There are no keys, I'm afraid, but it looks like an ordinary lock. I am sure many keys will fit. I think it dates from about 1850. It came to light recently when the family of a retired police officer in Nome, Alaska, found it in their deceased uncle's possessions. I have no reserve on this item, so a bargain is there for the taking to the right buyer. Who will start me off at, say, ten dollars?" The clerk twisted his body so the whole audience could see the chest.

Gloria signaled to her cameraman to start filming again, and the camera whirled.

There were no bids. "Come on, now. Someone must see the potential of this small item; it would grace any mantel. There is no reserve. How about five dollars, then, as you all appear to be mean today?"

Someone from the back of the room called out, "Five dollars." The auctioneer was relieved, but Cloe was not; she thought she might get it for five.

Gloria now took more interest. She said to her cameraman, "Zoom in on the events that follow. I have a feeling there is another bidder out there." He taped everything that followed for this lot.

"Thank you, sir. That is five dollars from the man at the rear left side. Who's next for ten?" the auctioneer said in his loud voice. It was always a relief to get the first bid in. *We are on the way now*, he thought.

The bidding continued, with raises of two dollars each as two more punters joined in. The audience was clearly not keen on the chest, and the bidding soon slowed down. In the end, only two people were interested. They bid the price up to twenty dollars, and then one dropped out.

"Any more bids? This is a very interesting antique. There is no reserve, so I must sell," said the auctioneer.

The cameraman turned the camera on Cloe as she held her number up and called out, "Twenty-five dollars!" The price jump surprised the auctioneer, who was quiet for a second. The same friend had also told Cloe that if you want to shut out another bidder, raise your bid over the standard.

Gloria whispered into the microphone, "This lady has pushed up the bid to twenty-five dollars. She clearly wants the item badly."

"Thank you, madam, a new bidder. Do you want to increase yours, sir?" he said to the original bidder, but the man declined, shaking his head. Cloe's strategy had worked.

The auctioneer then said, "For the third and final time, then, are there any further bids?"

Silence

"Going, going, gone." The auctioneer brought down his gavel with a loud bang. "Sold to the lady with number 165, and I hope it brings her happiness." John thought he said that last part a little sarcastically.

As the cameraman zoomed in on Cloe, Gloria said, "The lady won with her bid. I will try to get an interview with her in a minute."

Cloe smiled, delighted with herself, and said, "We can go now." She and John left the hall and went to the office to pay the twenty-five dollars for the chest and collect it. The cashier thanked them and said, "Your money from your sales will reach your bank in about a week."

Gloria rushed over to Cloe. "Hold on one minute, please, madam."

Cloe stopped, instinctively brushing her dress down and pinching her cheeks to make them red.

Gloria repeated, "Hold on a moment, please, madam." She was panting when she finally reached Cloe. "I must be getting old, or maybe I need some more exercise," she joked. "Thank you. My name is Gloria Rowbottom. I'm with Chanel 5, and we are doing a feature on this auction house. It's their centenary, you know. I am interested in the chest you just purchased. I wonder if we can come home with you while you open it. I understand there is no key."

Cloe looked at John questioningly. "I have no objection," he said. Then, always out for a buck, he added, "Do we get paid?"

"I'm sorry, sir, but there is no payment. I might be able to get you some tickets to any of the station's shows."

"In that case, what can I say but of course. You'd better follow us back home."

CHAPTER TWO

John and Cloe ride home on the Harley. Luckily, the chest was small and fitted in the pannier, except it caused a leather bulge. Cloe placed the chest on the sideboard when they got home, and they all looked at it in amazement. John was bemused; it did not go with their furniture at all.

Their sideboard is modern, and the chest is nearly two hundred years old. The television crew arrived shortly after John and unloaded their equipment, came into the house, but first knocked on the door.

"Well, are you going to break it open? We don't have a key," John said to Cloe. The crew began filming, but Gloria did not say anything at this stage.

"I don't know. It doesn't look like a complicated lock, does it? I've got a large box of old keys in the closet; let's see if one of those might fit. I can't stop thinking that the chest is talking to me. Is that possible?" Cloe left the room to find her box of old keys.

"Honestly, I think anything is possible with you, darling. You are clairvoyant," John called after her, laughing.

Gloria said off-camera, "It's funny you should say that because I had that feeling as well."

Five minutes later, Cloe returned with her hefty box, and she took the lid off to reveal hundreds of keys inside. Rummaging through the box, she cast aside all those keys that were too big or too small, and also those of the Yale type. That left her with about fifty keys, and she tried each one very carefully. The chest was old and fragile, and she did not want to break the lock. At about the fifteenth attempt, she found a key that moved the mechanism slightly, but it is rusted and sluggish.

John said, "Here, let me try, you have to tempt the key like a lady." To which Cloe laughed, but she gave him the key.

John inserted the key but first spraying it with WD40 that he had in the sideboard. That worked, and the latch slowly moved over.

"Yippee! That one worked," Cloe said with delight.

"You sound surprised, you with little faith." Said John, and he smiled at the camera, thinking he would like to be on the stage.

The cameraman had been filming while Cloe and John tried the keys, and Gloria watched with interest. She signaled to Cloe that she was turning on the microphone, and then she said into it, "This is marvelous. This chest has not been opened for over a hundred years. What are we going to find? Let's see what is inside the chest, viewers." She dramatized.

Cloe opened the lid very slowly, and it squeaked. "The hinges are rusted. I am afraid the box might break," she said.

John said, "Hold on, don't force it. Here let me use the WD40 again." John sprayed the can on the hinges. It seemed to help. John was interested now in finding out what was inside, his curiosity is catching upon him. He thought it is like opening Christmas presents when you are a kid.

Cloe opened the lid, revealing a piece of paper. She took it out; it looked its age. It was very dried out, and the paper almost crumbled. All the moisture from the paper had gone, but it was still in readable condition for that age. Gloria said to the cameraman, "Can we please zoom in on the paper?"

"It appears to be an old Alaskan gold mine claim, issued in Nome, Alaska," John said, holding the paper very carefully. "We need to put some moisture back in the paper with a kettle later.

He read it in detail. "It is. The claim was issued to a Don Wicker in February 1899."

John was getting more interested now. "The antiquity of this is mind-boggling." He now realized it might be worth more than he had thought earlier. He turned the form over very carefully. On the back was written in pencil:

The finder is welcome to this claim.

I hope it brings you more pleasure than it did me.

I've come to my senses and going home to my lovely wife.

Signed Don Wicker

Dated 1st June 1900.

Cloe and John looked at one another in amazement. The TV crew was also amazed, and Gloria said off-camera, "This will be very interesting to our viewers, a mining claim."

Everyone was speechless for a few moments. Finally, Cloe said, "Wow, what do you make of that? We have to check this out. I wonder if the writing being in pencil makes a difference. We are the finders, after all."

John replied, "Yes, a gold mine claim for twenty-five dollars, a bargain" he is getting in the mood now, laughing out loud. "Sorry about that, Gloria." He says.

Gloria said 'Don't worry about me, I want you to be just natural," and then to the camera, "Hello, viewers. I am now at the home of the purchasers of that chest we just saw at the auction. Having found a key that fits, Cloe has opened the box. Inside was a mining claim for Nome, Alaska. This is intriguing, viewers. I will follow the events here as they unfold as long as the owners allow me to, so keep watching. Don't go into the kitchen yet for that cup of coffee, or you might miss the excitement."

Gloria said off-camera, "Thank you for your help and cooperation. We have everything we need. Now we need to get back to edit the takes and enter this feature for the six o'clock news. If we need any more details, we will contact you. I would like to follow up on what happens if you agree."

"By all means," said Cloe. "I think you had a connection to the chest like I did."

"I did. I know you will investigate this further. I only wish I could be part of it, but I am leaving Channel 5 next week and going to ABC 7 in San Fransisco. If you get an outcome, please contact me there, and I will take it up again."

"I will. It's been a pleasure to meet you, but make sure you edit out any bad scenes of me," Cloe said with a smile.

"Don't worry. I'll make sure you look good," Gloria said, and she and her crew left the house.

"I am glad they have gone," said John. "Let's get back to the chest." Inside was the item that had made the noise; in their excitement, they had almost forgotten it. Cloe picked it up; it was a pebble. She looked closely at it. It was light brown and perfectly round, with flecks of colors through it, reminiscent of a child's glass marble.

"I wonder what the significance of that is?" Cloe said. "There must be one; otherwise, why would Don Wicker put it in his chest?"

"A pebble," repeated John. "Why on earth would anyone keep a simple pebble?"

"Because it has some significance."

"Hey, wait a minute. There is also a key in here. I didn't notice it at first. it was under the paper." John picked the key up. "I wonder what this is for?" He turned it over several times. It looked like a small Yale key but was much too small to be a door key.

Cloe looked at it. "Hmm, I didn't realize they had Yale locks in 1900. It's tarnished from being so long in the chest but look. There is a number etched on this side." She took it from John and polished it so she could read the number. "One fifty-seven," she said. "But where is it for."

"No idea, but I think the Yale lock was invented in the mid-1800s," said John as he got an envelope to put the key in.

"Where has this chest been over all these years, and why did someone else keep it? It must have a significance to that person as well," he said in amazement; thinking deeply, he imagined all types of scenarios. "Perhaps Don Wicker lived for many years after. It may have just been sitting on his shelf and was cleared out on his death. Or maybe he gave it to someone who tried to find gold there. Who knows?

'No, John, the auctioneer said it came from a retired policeman's estate in Nome," said Cloe.

"Oh, yes, I forgot that. Perhaps we should start investigating there."

John snapped himself out of his thoughts; they would get him nowhere. He got out his computer and checked on the internet. He found that the Alaskan gold rush had been in the 1890s, which fit with the claim's date. After California in the fifties, the sites remarked that the next gold rush area was in the Klondike, located in Northern Canada, close to Alaska's border. The wilderness could get very mingled in those remote regions. At that time, country boundaries in the wilderness were nonexistent.

This claim was for an area near Nome, in Northern Alaska. He learned that this was the third area of gold finds for the prospectors. Most prospectors went to Nome once the Klondike became dried up and money was not forthcoming.

He then Googled the name "Donald Wicker." Nothing came up, so he retried using the name "Don Wicker." Much to his surprise, there were several articles relating to that name. He opened the first. A Don Wicker had been murdered on the second of June 1900. It had been a brutal killing; he'd been stabbed fifteen times from head to toe. The murder had happened in Nome, which fit with the claim.

The article described Don as being six foot three inches tall and thirty-nine years of age. It stated he looked older than his tender years, no doubt due to the cold weather that had to be endured in Alaska in the winter. *Everyone looked older than their age in Alaska in those days*, thought John. *Is this our Don Wicker?* There would not be many people with that name in Nome at the same time. *I bet it is.*

No one had been caught for the dastardly deed. As John closed the page, he decided not to tell Cloe what he had found. It would only upset her. He did print the page for future reference, though. There were several other references on Google, but John would consider those later. As he closed the computer, he realized that while Don had been murdered on the second of June, the note had been written on the first, a day earlier. *Is that significant?*

Later in the day, Cloe said she would go into town for some groceries. "Do you want to come?" she said to John.

"No, dear, I'll leave that to you. You know how much I love shopping; besides, I want to investigate Don Wicker some more."

When Cloe left, John opened his laptop again and Googled "Don Wicker." This time, he read each entry in detail. They all basically said the same thing, except for one newspaper article on the incident. It was an interview with a young lady named Susy Wong, a Chinese worker in the bar tent.

The article said that she cooked food for the drinkers and remembered Don Wicker well. She related how he'd come to the bar each evening and eaten her Chinese food. She told the reporter that they had become friends. The reporter emphasized the word "friends." She said Don had come into some money from gambling but had let her down in his promises; although she wished him no harm, she was not surprised by what had happened.

John found another entry, posted by a Frederick Douglas. It was dated two years ago. John read it through slowly, taking it all in because it was controversial. It referred to the fact that Don Wicker had been murdered in his sleep, but then it went on to say that Frank Douglas, who lived in San Francisco, had been arrested for the crime. He'd stood trial for the murder, but the prosecution had put forward no evidence because Frank had admitted to it. There was nothing in the article to say how Frank Douglas had been arrested in the first place. John took that on board and doubted the authenticity of the article.

The web page said that the jury had gone solely on Frank Douglas's admission, but the writer said that he could categorically say that Frank was not in complete control of his mind. He added it was much more likely that Don's wife had carried out the dastardly murder. John thought a relative of the deceased had obviously written the article. He was biased, but he must keep an open mind, as John did with all his investigations.

John closed his computer, thinking there are always two sides to a story. Maybe Don had been having an affair with a married woman in camp and been killed by a jealous husband. John thought about his readings a lot while Cloe was out, but when she returned, he put them out of his mind for the moment.

After their success at the auction, he looked at himself in the mirror, feeling good. He had four tattoos on his arms and legs. He said to Cloe that evening, "I think it's time I got another tattoo."

She smiled. "And what do you want this time?"

"I want one of you, darling."

"Me?" She laughed. "And what pose would you like?'

"I want one of you in that fishnet body stocking you wore when we first met."

"I don't think I could get that on now. It was two years ago, you know. I'm not even sure where it is."

"Oh, I do." John left the room, only to return five minutes later with the stocking.

"Here it is."

"You want me to put it on now?" she said.

"Yes, please. Then I can take a photograph for the tattoo artist."

'You're just a dirty old man. What have I got myself into?" she said with a broad grin on her face, loving it. "Alright, give it to me, then." She took the stocking and left the room; she didn't want to put it on in front of John in case it didn't look good anymore.

"There's not much point in you leaving to put it on; I have seen it all before, you know."

"Yes, but if I can't get it on, you will only laugh."

John understood. In the other room, Cloe squeezed into her fishnet body stocking. It was challenging, but after much huffing and puffing, she returned to the room.

"Wow, you look as gorgeous as ever," said John, "You know, when you first wore that, I was hooked." The stocking was so tight that her nipples stuck out through the netting.

"You do realize that was why I wore it. But my nipples did not stick out so much then." John got his phone out and took a photo. Then he walked over to her, and they kissed tenderly as he held each nipple.

She said, "It was difficult enough getting it on now. I suppose you want me to take it off now that you have roused my nipples." She obliged, of course; she was now anxious for sex and could feel herself getting wet. They made love for the rest of the day.

Two days later, John went to the tattoo artist and had a tattoo of Cloe put on his arm. When he got home, she said, "I like it, but you didn't have to make my nipples so big; it will embarrass me in front of our friends."

"They will only be jealous," said John.

That afternoon, Gloria edited her program on the auction sale to make an exciting story, as was required by the television company. Channel 5 included Gloria's report on the chest's sale in the six o'clock news.

The next day, many viewers called into the television station to say how much they enjoyed the feature and would like to see a follow-up on the goldmine claim. Gloria Rowbottom received many personal congratulations. Her boss promoted her, saying he would like her to deal with more emotional problems. He was not aware that Gloria only had a week left on her contract. She did not remind him.

Surprisingly, other networks took up the feature, and eventually, it was taken up nationally. The feature was repeated on NBC and other networks.

Edward Isaacs, who lived in Seattle, saw the program, and it gave him some ideas. He had not realized that these gold mine claims still existed. "I wonder…" he said to himself. He then searched on the internet to find out the history.

He had heard of the gold rushes of the late 1800s but did not know details or locations. The internet told him there had been three: California. the Klondike, and Nome. He thought he would contact Gloria Rowbottom. Maybe she had more information. He had recorded the auction's TV program, and he found that Gloria worked for Channel 5 in Nashville.

He dialed the station. "Can I speak with Gloria Rowbottom, please?" he said to the lady who answered the phone.

"Just a minute, please, sir, and I will see if she is available." The line went silent.

When the lady returned, she said, "I am sorry, but Gloria is out reporting at the moment. If you leave your phone number, I will get her to phone you on her return."

"Thank you," said Edward, and he gave the lady his phone number.

Two hours went by, and no phone call. Edward thought Gloria was not going to phone back, and he was just about to call the station again when his phone rang first.

"Hello, sir, this is Gloria Rowbottom from Channel 5. I understand you wanted to speak with me."

"Ah, yes, thank you for calling me back, Miss Rowbottom. It's regarding the mining claim report you made at the recent auction."

"Yes, that went viral, didn't it? I was surprised how many people were interested, but it's all good for business. What can I do for you?"

"I wondered what you knew about these claims, and do they still exist today?"

"My station researched the matter after my interview, and yes, they do exist today. As you might know, there were three gold rushes, but the important ones were the Klondike and Nome. California was much earlier. There are many outstanding claims out there still, like the one you saw on the television screen," Gloria said, adding, "I was personally interested in Don Wicker's claim. Do you remember how the purchaser came to buy the chest at the auction? Well, I was there, and I saw it vibrate and glow. There is definitely something to this situation." Gloria knew she was exaggerating somewhat, but she thought, *So what? I am a reporter.*

"Me, too. Well, thank you for your good work and for coming back to me. It has given me some ideas," Edward said. As he put the phone down, he thought to himself, *who does she think she is, and who did she think she was talking to?*

CHAPTER THREE

In the 1890s, men came from all over the United States of America to the Yukon region of Canada, which is right on the border with Alaska, men who thought they could make their fortunes in gold. There were very few other ways a man could make a fortune and get rich quickly. If one man found gold, that was enough to light the fire of enthusiasm, or was it greed?

Canada is a dominion within the British Commonwealth but is self-governing. However, Alaska was purchased as a territory by the United States of America from Russia in 1867 for a paltry seven point two million dollars. Borders along that section were on paper only in those days. There was nothing on the ground to notify one of a change of countries. All those areas were open for people and animals to roam freely.

The terrain was rough and ready, and in the winter, it was hell on earth. Temperatures hardly ever rose above freezing. The pioneers' living conditions of open tents were unthinkable to John and Cloe today, with their central heating and comforts.

It was just bearable in the summer, and gold in small quantities was initially panned from the Klondike River.

Would-be miners came streaming into the area, expecting to make their fortunes. A few had successes, but not many, and the value was equally small.

The number of claims submitted to the local government was substantial. They covered just about every square foot of the lower area along the river. That rush came about fifty years after the Californian gold rush in the mid-1850s. There were no additional restrictions imposed on the miners, so to speak, other than the land's general laws.

The reality was that only a few people raised enough to make enough money to survive, particularly in the winter, when the weather was so harsh, which made panning impossible as the river froze over. There was a lot of crime, and jealousy amongst the miners was rife. If you were lucky to find any gold, you had to sell it before it mysteriously disappeared.

There were many reports of killings, with prospectors fighting over claims, especially when they were adjacent to each other. Everyone was trying to get an extra inch of land, all of which was barren and wild.

The problem was that the prospectors were humble men who did not know how the gold formed in the first place or where to look for it. If your neighbor found a speck, and that's what we are talking about, then you set up next to him and hoped for the best.

The mining claims lasted forever, mainly because subsequent governments saw no need to cancel them, as there was no gold there at that time. But by the end of the nineteenth century, other areas in the region had found gold, notably around Nome.

Nome is on the coast of Northern Alaska; prospectors only found the gold on the beaches after the flakes had been washed down the river to the sea. That led to the failed prospectors in the Klondike heading up north. Forever optimistic, they hoped their luck would change at the new site. That was what had happened to Don Wicker. *God rest his soul*, thought John as he read through the history on his computer.

The beaches in the Nome area were thoroughly dug up, not that there was anything else to do with them in that godforsaken place at that time. Being further north than Klondike, the weather was colder, and the snow was deeper. Wildlife was scarcer, which meant food had to be transported from the south. That raised the cost, and the miners were living hand to mouth.

The original claims in the Klondike still exist today. No one ever bothered to close them because there wasn't enough gold in those days, let alone 2021. But were they looking in the wrong places? Dawson City and its surroundings originated in the Klondike and were built up after the gold rush. No one cared about the old useless mining claims; most residents did not even know they existed, and the original miners' families never took any interest.

No one turned up to complain that their mining claim had been built over. Of course, by 2021, the original prospectors had long since died. Most of the prospectors had been single, middle-aged men without offspring, and even if they'd had kids, it would have been three generations before now.

However, some family men with wives and children lived in various parts of the United States. People who had gone off to make their fortune or, more likely, get away from their wives, or perhaps both. Most of the descendants of those pioneers had no idea of their ancestors' mining aspirations, let alone actual claim details.

In the year 2021, one person, an Edward Isaacs, came up with a scam after seeing the auction on NBC and speaking with Gloria Rowbottom. As a Jewish child, Edward had been bullied at school and had ended up in fights every day with his schoolmates; children are racist and can be so cruel.

However, after experiencing the bullying and living through it, he was stronger in mind and body, and he became determined never to let that happen in his adult life. Sadly, he chose to become a bully to others, as so often happens in life. The bullied often becomes the bully as history repeats itself throughout the centuries.

Edward saw the mining claim from the chest, and he wondered whether other claims still existed. He researched and found that the old gold mine claims in the Klondike still existed and would be honored. A local Dawson City newspaper ran an article on the subject once the NBC program was seen. Some local residents were horrified at the thought that a mining company could exercise those claims. But they did nothing except complain to each other.

Edward realized that if he were to purchase as many of these claims as he could—notably, the ones that had been built over with substantial properties—the owners would not want their buildings to be pulled down. Then he would be able to make significant money by blackmailing them. His sights were set on Dawson City, so he caught a plane and flew there once he received his Canadian access permit.

Edward had been a criminal ever since he'd left school without any achievements, and his parents could not afford to send him to university. That had been over twenty years ago, and now he was in his mid-thirties. When he first left school, he became a pickpocket, but he soon gave up that idea when he was caught in the act and got his jaw broken.

Since then, he had carried out many scams, mainly involving the internet. It surprised him how gullible people were, especially the elderly, and he decided that being on a computer did not get your jaw broken. He told a friend once how easy it was to get someone to give out their Social Security number; he could steal their identity from that. He dressed like it was the 1920s again, always in a smart suit and shoes with white spats. He looked very dapper, or so he thought.

Edward toured Dawson City in a car he rented at the airport; he chose a four-by-four in case he had to go off-road. His first day there, he concentrated on the suburbs, and after purchasing a street map of the area from a local gas station, he marked the areas that interested him: streets full of shops and other commercial properties. Those owners, he knew, would be easier targets for his scam than residential owners.

Pay up, or I will dig up your property. That was his thought on the current scheme he was working on with Klondike's mining claims. He calculated that he could purchase those claims for a song if he could track down the current owners. The difficulty would be determining who the current owners were. Records held by the local authority would all be out of date; he knew that. The original owners' names would be on the record, but no amendments would have been made, as there had been no mining for over a hundred years. Finding the current owners would be his problem.

After picking out the commercial area he wanted, Edward went to the local council administration's claims registration office. A cute receptionist stood behind the desk, a young blond bombshell, and he wondered whether the hair was her real color. *There's only one way to find out*, he thought, *but not today,* and being a man about town, as he saw it, he straightened out his tie and entered. He thought she might be able to help him in exchange for a meal or two, and that might suit him in another direction.

It was mid-January, the height of the winter. The weather is freezing, and the ground outside was frozen solid and covered with two feet of snow. Large mounds of snow were piled up six feet high on either side of the roadway. Edward thought, *how could anyone have survived in this cold in 1890?* At least he was staying in a centrally heated hotel on Main Street.

When he went into the office, he looked at the large claim map on the wall. It dated back to 1890. He compared the claim map to the one he had marked with the buildings he wanted and wrote down the related claim reference numbers. Then he went over to the cute receptionist at the desk; she had a nametag on her chest that read, "Pat." This made him smile, and he thought,

I'd like to pat your breasts, but no jokes now; he wanted her help. He'd tease her later if the opportunity arose, but he did give her a seductive smile.

He explained he was an archeologist and interested in the gold mining rush. "I am writing a thesis for my degree," he said. That seemed to satisfy her, although anything would have pleased her that day. She was bored with life, and that morning, her live-in boyfriend had announced he was leaving her. At the age of twenty-one, she thought there had to be more to life. What about the big cities of the East, New York, or maybe Chicago?

Edward pulled her out of her thoughts, asking her for the claimants' names and any other information she might have.

The receptionist replied, "Good morning, sir. I am sorry for my delay. I was daydreaming. Please forgive me. Could I ask you to sign our visitor's book, please? I have to ask everyone that." She passed the book to him.

Edward did not want to leave his name on record, so he said, "Gladly, miss," and wrote the first name in the book that he could think of, John Brown, and today's date. Then he handed the book back to her.

"Thank you, Mr. Brown," she said as she read the name, smiling. "We used to sing a song about a John Brown at school, but he was a slave protester who was eventually executed. 'John Brown's body lies a moldering in the grave, but his soul goes marching on,'" she sang.

Edward had learned nothing about John Brown in school; he'd hardly gotten past the six times table, and as for slaves, he had no concerns, but to please her, he said, "Well sung. You have a lovely voice."

He handed her the list of names he had written down. "Back to business. Can you please give me the names and addresses of the owners of the claims for these numbers?"

"I am sorry, Mr. Brown, but I cannot do that for data protection reasons. Do you know I spent three months last year placing all the names and addresses on this computer? It was very boring, I can tell you. Look at how many there are." She opened the program on the computer and scrolled down the list.

Edward was not interested in her problems—he had enough of his own—but he wanted to keep in her good books for the moment. He said, "I am sorry to interrupt you, but do you have a restroom here? I have an urgent call of nature."

"We don't have one for the public, but if there is a problem, you can use our staff restroom. I'm in the office alone now, so there is no one else to worry about."

"Oh, thank you. You are very kind."

She turned around, opened a door behind her, and indicated for Edward to follow her, which he did, admiring the sway of her bottom as she walked.

He followed her through the door into the room behind. The receptionist closed the door from inside, and as she turned around, he threw a punch to her chin, followed by a second to her right eye. The girl screamed in shock and sank to the floor, unconscious. Edward picked her up and placed her on a comfortable armchair in the corner of the room, wishing he had not needed to do that. He had hoped to go out with her on a date, but he realized that was out of the question now.

He opened the door into the reception area and checked to make sure no one else had come in. It was clear, so he went back into the outside office, and the program he needed was still running on the computer. He spent ten minutes transcribing the names and addresses for the claims he needed and then promptly left the office. As he headed out into the cold, he pulled his coat tighter, feeling pleased with himself for having gotten the information he wanted.

Once he had the names logged into his laptop, he decided to change hotels, moving to one outside of town in case the police traced John Brown back to him. In his new hotel, he visited the internet on his laptop. He opened ancestry pages first and then searched anywhere he could to track down the original claimants' descendants.

Finally, he decided to employ a private detective to help him, but in the meantime, he flew back to Seattle, as he knew it would take the detective some time to come up with the information. "You are only looking at a hundred and twenty years, after all. Surely, that can't be so difficult. In most cases, it was only three or four generations," he said to the detective after he had not heard anything for three weeks.

The detective went back to his work with a flea in his ear. Three weeks later, he had obtained a list of fifty people, descendants of those original pioneers of the area where he was interested. The area covered about a square mile of shopping and commercial properties. He reported his findings to Edward, who said, "I told you it was easy if you worked at it."

"Bastard," the detective said under his breath. *I pity the people who are involved with this goon.* "I will send you my account, sir," he said.

"Yes, please do," Edward said, thinking, *you have a fat chance of being paid, my friend!*

He then contacted the current owners of those claims and went to see each by appointment. He would tell them on the phone, "I have some fascinating information for you that will be to your financial advantage. Can we meet, please?"

That sort of approach worked with everyone; people always want something for nothing, and greed was a great help to Edward in his business. Strangely, he did not appreciate that he was the greediest of all. Edward went to see each one individually; that way, he had control of the situation and could get a contract signed then and there. None of the owners knew they were owners of the original miners' claims.

They all knew that Great Uncle John or whoever had been a gold mining prospector in the 1890s, but on the death of the person concerned, that had been it. The claims had long been forgotten. The paperwork had not been transferred on death, and why would it? No one had thought it was of any interest.

Edward approached each owner with a legal contract to transfer their interest in the claim to him, and he offered them five hundred dollars in cash to sell. "No tax is involved," he told them. They were over the moon and immediately took the money. One man said with delight, "That will pay for my upcoming vacation."

Edward would tell them he was a collector of antiquities and relics. He pointed out that there was no gold in the Klondike originally or now, which was probably correct, or at least, no one had found anything of any significance. "All I want are the documents for my collection," he said. They were all happy to sign over the claims. Within six months, he had all the claims that he needed for that square mile.

Edward then approached all the owners of the buildings that had been erected on the sites concerned. He had chosen commercial sites, shops, and offices, as he thought these owners would be easy targets.

His plan was now coming to fruition; there were over fifty owners, and he applied what can only be described as extortion to make them purchase his mining claims at one hundred thousand dollars each. He thought that was a fair profit, but the owners of the properties thought differently. They called it blackmail, and everyone refused his first attempt, but many soon changed their minds.

Several of the victims agreed quickly, and the money was transferred to Edward's bank account. They were the ones who had thriving businesses and for whom money was no object. They did not want the aggravation of dealing with Edward. After several weeks of pressure, their lawyers advised them to settle speedily, not wanting their clients to find out that they had been negligent in not bringing the mining claims up when they'd purchased the property.

Edward told them all quite bluntly that he would mine under their businesses if they did not pay. Their lawyers advised them that although this was clearly a scam, it was a legal one. Edward Isaacs did have the right to mine on their property. The owners were told by their attorneys, "Better to settle now or move. Your business is good where you are, and you can make more money without further hassle. If you move outside the mining claims area, you don't know what will happen. Customers are fickle, you know." They were slow to take any advice, hoping that Isaac would just go away.

However, Edward knew what these owners were being told; he had done his research, and he said to each of them forcefully, "If you do not purchase the claim, I will exercise my rights and start mining. Of course, that would mean demolishing your building. That is not what I want to do, but you would leave me no option."

Edward repeated this on many occasions to different business owners; he knew it was a bluff, and so did the owners, but they could not take the risk. It was all reported in the local newspaper.

Several owners were still holding out because they believed that Edward would eventually go away with the money, he had extorted from those who had given in if they did nothing. Edward thought he needed to take action to prove he meant what he said.

He arranged for demolition vehicles to be delivered to the town's commercial parking area. When the owners saw the trucks arriving, their faces dropped as they realized that Edward meant what he said. Having paid the rental fee for the vehicles, Edward left them where they were. *That should serve the purpose,* he thought. Several more owners gave in after that, but a few still held out.

CHAPTER FOUR

Following the complaint of one property owner, the newspaper agreed to investigate, but all they could come up with was that a receptionist at the claim's office had been beaten up by someone calling himself John Brown. It was felt that John Brown was a part of the scam, but he could not be traced now. Even the receptionist was unable to give the police a definite description.

The paper editor had to admit there was nothing he could do other than expose the fraud. That did not concern Edward; he wanted to make a quick kill and then move on. The more people advised the owners there was nothing they could do, the more it helped his cause.

After three months, negotiations were dragging on with some victims, as Edward had expected. One owner, George Young, was particularly challenging. He refused to pay a cent to someone who was clearly a crook. "This is blackmail," he said.

Edward knew he was doing nothing illegal—unscrupulous, maybe! George threatened Edward when he came to his shop, throwing his fist in the air and saying, "My son is an FBI agent, and I will report the matter to him if you don't back off. You are nothing but a crook who should be behind bars."

In his late fifties, George was a forthright man who ran a small hardware store in town, sadly, in the area where Edward Isaacs had purchased his mining rights. Unfortunately, George had lost his wife five years ago in a car accident on the icy roads just after Christmas. That had made him go gray overnight, and he had never recovered.

His face now had a gray pallor and was traced with worry lines, and now he had the problem with Edward. *Oh, God, why have you forsaken me?* Still, George had a son in the American FBI, a very respected son who had done well in his career. George and his son did not have much contact now that his mother had gone. She had always been the one to phone him at least once a week.

Edward said to George, "This is Canada, not the United States of America; the FBI has no jurisdiction here. What I am doing is not illegal. I own the mining rights to this land. I am merely exercising my right to mine my claims. I believe there is gold under your building, and I'm going to dig for it. The fact that you have built on the site is your problem, not mine. You should have been more careful at the time you purchased the property. Perhaps you should sue the attorney who acted for you if he didn't advise you of the outstanding mining rights."

George knew Edward was right. His lawyer had found the mining claim on his purchase, but everyone had agreed it was historical and of no consequence now. No one had thought that the prospectors, their relatives, or a con artist would turn up a century later. It was common knowledge that no gold existed in the claim area. George was determined to fight this, and he contacted his son, Agent Josh Young, in Washington, DC, to tell him what was happening.

"Dad, it's good to hear from you," Josh said. He did not hear much from his father these days, but he realized that this was his fault as much as his father's.

George told him about Edward Isaacs and his scam.

"I am sorry you are having these problems, Dad, but this is extremely tricky. Edward is correct; we don't have any jurisdiction in Canada. I can report the matter to the Royal Mounties, the police force in Canada. Still, from what you tell me, this Edward Isaacs hasn't committed any crime yet."

Then Josh added, "Leave it to me. I have an idea before we go to the Mounties. I'll send up someone to investigate. Let's see if we can get an angle on this extortioner."

Josh had done well in the FBI since his involvement in stopping a terrorist attack a couple of years before. Two Islamic State soldiers had tried to attack the White House and kill the president after their families had been killed by an American drone attack on their houses in Iraq. It had all ended up satisfactorily, and the president had survived. Sadly, his double, whom Josh had arranged as a stand-in, had died. However, it had been touch and go with all the double-dealing while the terrorists traveled to Washington from Florida.

Two American women had helped them; one of them had gone off to Syria to fight with the Islamic State, while the other had had enough of treachery and moved to San Francisco to try to forget the incident. John had gone to

Iraq to get one of the girls back, at the request of the CIA, as he was the only person who would recognize her in her yashmak. She had married an Islamic State general, which is what the CIA was really interested in. Neither girl was prosecuted. The hierarchy had decided it was best to let things quieten down.

Josh is twenty-five now, still very young for the position he held. The terrorism case and a subsequent drug-smuggling case had scored him his promotions. Josh worked with several informants, and his favorites were John Smith and Jack King.

John had been directly involved in stopping the terrorist attack, though it had been his fault that things had nearly gone wrong. He had been an informant for over fifteen years now. Jack was a newcomer, but they worked well together as a team. Not only were they informers, but they did work the FBI was unable to take on, such as this.

Josh picked up the phone and called John. "Hi, John. We haven't spoken for some time. How would you feel about a trip to Dawson City in Canada to investigate something for me? Why don't you get Jack to fly you up there? It is a personal matter with my father. I have no jurisdiction in Canada, but we'll pay you both, just the same. If necessary, I will pay for it myself, or maybe we can call it a trade-off, for all those times I turned a blind eye for you."

"Wow, you have a father! I thought you arrived in a flying saucer!" John said affectionately, not wanting to deal with the blind eye bit yet.

"Funny," said Josh. "Do you want the job or not?"

"Okay, I'll do it. I'm sure I can talk Jack into coming with me. We can put the cost down to something in the future."

The call was on speakerphone, and Cloe was listening in. Her eyes opened wide when she heard Josh mention Dawson City. "You realize that is the Klondike and the connection to Don Wicker, don't you?" she said to John.

"Yes, I do. Is that coincidence or what?" John said.

"No, as I have told you in the past, there is no such thing as coincidence. These things are meant to happen. For what reason, we do not know as yet, but I am sure the little chest has something to do with it," she said very pensively, looking at the chest sitting o the sideboard.

Jack King is a pilot; he owned a small aircraft freight company operating out of Nashville's airstrip. He was single but always on the lookout for that special person. He was good-looking, with dark hair and blue eyes. John was continually surprised that Jack had not found a girlfriend. They'd met two years ago on a drug and treasure hunt adventure from which they made considerable money, enough for Jack to purchase a new Cessna after the old one crashed into the Caribbean. It was the same adventure in which John had obtained the relics he had sold in the recent auction.

John and Cloe had most of their adventures together, but he thought the Yukon was not the best place for her to go in the winter due to the severe cold. In any event, they had already planned to go to Alaska later in the year to look at Don Wicker's claim, traveling in luxury by cruise ship on the proceeds of their past exploits. So, Cloe was happy for John to go with Jack on their own this time.

John phoned Jack and asked, "How do you fancy a trip to the Yukon on the FBI's dime? I know it is cold up there, but you would be helping me out. We both need to keep in with Josh Young."

"I'm in," said Jack. "Things are very quiet here now, and I miss our little exploits. Is Cloe coming with us? I miss seeing her."

"Not this time; I thought it would be too brutally cold for her, and in any case, we are going to Alaska next summer on a cruise, but I'll tell you about that when we meet. Don't forget to bring warm clothes."

Two days later, they loaded up Jack's Cessna with suitcases and supplies. Because of the Yukon weather, they decided to stay in hotels rather than tents like they normally would. As they were preparing to leave, Cloe came to the airport to wave them off.

She said to them, "Good luck with the investigation. Look, John, about that key we found in the chest, I think you should take it with you. We don't know what happened to Don Wicker, but I guess he would have been to the Klondike before going to Nome. The key might relate to somewhere in the Klondike." She handed John the key.

"Good idea, Cloe. I'll see what I can find out," said John. To Jack, he added, "I will explain all this on the flight to Canada."

Their flight plan was initiated for Vancouver and deposited at flight control in the airport. On the way to Vancouver, John told Jack about all that had happened with the chest and what they had found inside. He also told Jack about what he'd found on the internet about

Don Wicker. Jack was surprised, but he realized that things like that were not unusual for John and Cloe when he thought about it.

After arriving in Vancouver, they drove up to Dawson City in a rental car.

"We should expect trouble," John said on the way.

"There is always trouble with you, my friend. That is why I like our adventures so much. I am intrigued by the key you found, though. I wonder where it fits," said Jack, smiling. They both knew that what he'd said was true.

They booked into a hotel and drove straight to see George Young at his shop. After introducing themselves, John said, "We have heard about your problem. Your son has asked us to come and see what we can do. It's not going to be easy, as Edward Isaacs has purchased these claims and now wants to exercise his rights."

"Thanks so much for coming to my aid. Edward says he has the right to demolish my store, and he has brought in demolition equipment to the commercial parking lot, but it's clearly extortion," said George.

"Yes, but let's see if we can lead him into something illegal. In that case, we can call in the cavalry," said John.

John and Jack went back to the hotel. "We need to make Edward do something illegal. Any suggestions?" said John. They found out that Edward had extorted one hundred thousand dollars from thirty owners already. That left four, including George, in this chunk of claims. They did not doubt that if this scam were a winner for Edward, he would repeat it.

Edward was now growing impatient with the four remaining owners who were holding out. To increase their pressure, he had employed two henchmen, who were actively threatening the owners. One owner, Colin Wayfair, a gentleman's retailer, was paid a visit by Isaac's henchmen, resulting in him getting beaten up as an example.

The henchmen called at his shop as he was closing for the day. They picked him up and took him into his backroom, where they punched him and beat him with a cosh. When he did not come home for dinner, his wife went looking for him, and she found him in the backroom, unconscious. Colin spent the next two days in the hospital. His shop was ransacked, and his stock was scattered all around the shop so that it appeared to be a burglary.

When he came out of the hospital, Colin went to see George. "Look what they did to me," he said as he held his face so George could better see his injuries. "I cannot carry on, George. I am sorry, but I'm going to have to capitulate."

George was horrified at what had been done to Colin; they had spent many an hour at the local pub, enjoying a beer. "I do understand, Colin, but I will fight on. I've asked my son for help. He's with the FBI, you know."

They embraced. "Are you going to start up again in business?" said George.

"I hope so, but I might want some advice. Will you help?"

"You know I will. We buddies must stick together. United we stand, divided we fall. The old sayings are the best, you know," said George, and Colin left.

The incident, which was referred to the Royal Mounted Police, did not get far. Interviews followed, but Edward, of course, denied any involvement or that it had happened. He responded that it was probably the victim's wife. It was his word against the victim's, and there was no corroborating evidence. The police said that they would need more to go on before prosecuting.

Edward thought that this was the starting pistol to apply more pressure; he felt more confident now, believing that the Mounties were ineffective.

"Now we know he's overstepping the mark, but we need to lay a trap because nothing can be proved," John said.

He got on the phone with Josh at the FBI and told him they might have something now that Edward threatened people and used violence. "One man has already been beaten up, and there are three more who will not sell, including your dad," John told Josh that the Mounties were involved with the first beating but could not prove anything.

"Okay," said Josh. "I'll get on to the Mounties. I have a contact there in Calgary, on the other side of the Rockies, and I'll get him to communicate with you. He is a good man; we have acted mutually before. I'll come back to you with details." He disconnected the call.

Josh called back an hour later, saying that Inspector Jones would be contacting John. "That's a good old Welsh name!" said John.

An hour later, Inspector Jones was on the phone. John told him that extortion with violence was happening here.

"I'll be with you tomorrow. I have checked our files. I see that a local officer investigated the beating but could not take any action due to a lack of proof. We need to have a plan, which I will discuss with you tomorrow," said Inspector Jones. The Yukon was right on the extreme of his jurisdiction, as he was based in Calgary. He joked to John, "I'll drive over the Rockies. it's a bit far for the horse!"

"That sounds a good idea, besides riding on the horse would take weeks!" said John.

"I can see we are going to get on fine, I like your sense of humor. See you tomorrow.'

CHAPTER FIVE

The next day, Inspector Jones arrived at John and Jack's hotel room. *He seems an amiable fellow*, thought John.

"The names Albert, by the way," the inspector said as he held out his hand. He was very impressive, dressed in his bright red tunic with gold braiding and dark blue pants and high riding boots. He joked, "I had to leave the horse at home but couldn't come without the boots. In truth, I love my horse much more than my dog." He loved his uniform, too, with all its braids.

They spent the next hour going through the whole story.

"This is tricky on the face of it because it's legal but positively immoral," said Albert. "I can only exercise the law. Beating up the owners is a different matter altogether, though; this is 2021, not 1890. What we need to do is set Edward up. Would Josh's father be willing to be a decoy?"

"I am sure he would. He's had it up to his eyes now with this crook," said John.

They went to see George in his shop. Inspector Jones introduced himself and asked when George expected Edward to contact him again. "Anytime now," George said.

"Are you prepared to be a decoy? We'll have you guarded at all times," said Albert.

"Absolutely," said George. "I will do anything you suggest. I have to beat this crook. I know I must be careful, but I do have a gun in the back office. It's used for hunting, but if necessary, I will use it."

"Well, let's hope it's not," said Albert. "Self-defense is always a good defense. Let me say that you are courageous. I gather this man is very dangerous."

"Thank you, officer, but you know, there are times we all have to stand up and be counted," said George.

"I couldn't agree more," said Albert, and he held out his hand to shake George's.

"These types of people make their point on one individual, as Edward has done, but now he will just apply pressure on all who remain. We need him to do more, though, as he will get overconfident. They always do. Then we have him.

"Here's what we'll do. You call him and say you want to see him. He will think you are going to give in. We will have you wired, and when he comes, annoy him so that he makes more threats against you. If he goes for you, just move backward. We'll be in the back room, listening, and can be with you within seconds."

George contacted Edward as arranged, and an appointment was made for him to come to the shop that evening at eight o'clock. At seven o'clock, George was wired for sound. John, Jack, and Albert went into the back room. When Edward arrived on time with his two henchmen, George shouted so they could hear him in the backroom, "What are they here for, then?"

"I assume you have agreed to my demands," said Edward, not answering the question.

"What are your henchmen here for?" George repeated to make sure they heard in the back room.

"Oh, they are here just in case you pull a gun on me. Are you ready to pay up now?" Edward said with a sickly smile on his face as he gritted his teeth.

"No, I'm not. This has gone on too long. There is no way I am going to pay you the money you want. Here, I'll give you a dollar to go away, and that's it," George said sarcastically as he threw a dollar bill towards Edward.

Edward became enraged, and the blood vessels in his face bulged. He had misjudged George's position, and now George would have to pay. Edward was not used to being beaten, and he knew the only way to get the others to pay up was to get everyone on board. He stepped up to George, grabbed him by his collar, and said, "You saw what happened to Colin Wayfair when he refused to pay. Do you want that to happen to you?"

The henchman did not wait for George's answer. They pushed Edward aside, and one of them grabbed George by his neck, throttling him. The henchman said loud and clear, "If you don't pay, you're a dead man. Obviously, a beating did not work with you."

When a gun was pushed into George's back, he started to panic. *Where the hell are you, Inspector Jones?*

Jones had been listening to the conversation in the back room, and his reaction was immediate. Throwing open the door, he rushed into the shop with his truncheon raised high and said, "You're under arrest, all of you."

Canadian Mounties are not armed, but they do carry a heavy baton. John and Jack had followed the inspector into the room. The henchmen were surprised. Not realizing they had been set up, they were not thinking too clearly, and they made a play for the inspector. One of the henchmen flashed his gun at the Mountie and said, "Back off, or you're dead as well." He knew that Mounties were not armed.

That was all the inspector needed; his baton flicked around and smashed into the henchman's arm. The villain let out a yell of pain as his wrist broke, and the gun fell to the floor. John immediately lunged for the weapon, grabbing it before the henchman could, and handed it to the inspector.

The other henchman was not armed, but he dove at the inspector. John, who was a capable fighter, took the initiative and jumped on the crook. He pulled him off Albert.

"Here, John," said Albert as he threw the gun back to John.

John raised the weapon and brought it down on the man's head, and the henchman went out like a light.

Edward realized this had gone too far. He had already made a small fortune, but now he faced losing it and going to jail. He wished he had stopped on the last occasion and not been so greedy. As the remaining henchman surrendered, Edward ran out the door. The inspector, a very fit man, ran after him.

Edward was caught only yards down the road, brought down with a flying leap by the inspector. They slid twenty yards down the icy road before coming to a stop. The inspector cuffed Edward in seconds. John looked on in amazement at the Mountie's speed and agility, extremely impressed.

Edward Isaacs and his henchmen were led off to jail. Albert said to John, "You will be needed for the trial to give evidence. I appreciate you will be going back to Nashville, but can you come back at the time of the trial?"

"I am sure we can arrange that. I want this criminal behind bars for a long time." Says John.

The outcome proved satisfactory. All the criminals were prosecuted, and John received a phone call a month later from the Crown Attorney for Calgary, "Hello, is this John Smith?" the lady said.

"Yes, this is he,"

"Well, I am pleased to tell you that Edward Isaacs has changed his plea to guilty. Following a plea bargain, he will go to jail for ten years. That means you will not be needed at the trial."

"That s good to hear," says John.

"You are welcome, and thank you for your assistance in this matter, and I know Inspector Jones was very grateful to you and your colleague." The Attorney said.

Edward pleaded guilty on the trial day and was sent to prison for ten years without any formalities. He also received a fine of half a million dollars.

The other affected property owners knew this incident was over. They had, of course, lost their money, but they accepted it as experience. John knew that Josh would be pleased with the outcome; it was one more feather in his cap with the FBI. His father had not lost any money, and he'd managed to transfer the mining rights to himself without cost.

John and Jack had discussions over the gold mine claims, particularly those in Nome and what the men had gone through all those years ago. "What we need to do is speak with Ben," said John. "He's the clever one. It seems to me those guys were looking in the wrong area. Keep in mind that most of the finds were in the river. In the case of Nome, they were on the beach. So, the source of gold must be further upstream."

Ben worked at the airstrip where Jack kept his plane. Ben had shared in various exploits with John and Jack in the past. He was a college graduate and had a scientific brain; he was also the same age as Jack. A good-looking young man, he was looking for the excitement that he could not get at the airstrip.

John said to Jack, "Cloe and I legally acquired a claim in Nome. It was in an auction chest that Cloe was getting vibes about. Anyway, it occurs to me that the small particles of gold these miners found must have come from somewhere else. I need to investigate where gold comes from."

"That key that Cloe gave us," said Jack, "we need to investigate whether it came from here. I guess it could be a railway station or airport locker key, or perhaps a bank deposit key. Do you have any thoughts?"

"I agree with you. I can't think of anywhere else. Let's make some inquiries now that we have finished with the investigation for Josh."

The next day, they went to what used to be the railway station and was now a museum. A male clerk at the counter was selling admission tickets. "I wonder if you can help us, sir," John said to him. "Would you know what this key is? We wondered whether it was a station locker key. We think it might have come from here when this was a railway station."

The clerk took hold of the key and looked at both sides. "Do you, by any chance, have a date? It could be a station locker key, but I don't know about the number on one side. All the lockers were removed when the station closed down to become the museum."

John was disappointed; it looked like a dead end. "The key dates back to 1900 or earlier."

"Ah, in that case, it is definitely not from here. This station did not open until 1905," said the clerk.

John took back the key. "That settles that, then. Would you have any guess where it might have come from?"

"It could have come from a bank; they did have banks here then. Try the one in town. It did not exist then, but its predecessor did."

They thanked the clerk and left the museum. They went into town to the bank and asked the same questions there. The teller told them, "I'm sure this is a bank deposit key. The number gives it away, but it is not for here, and there is no other bank in town. If it came from one of the miners in 1900, I would try Nome in Alaska. All those miners from here moved to Nome."

"Thank you very much. That is extremely helpful. We will try Nome," said John.

Before they left the Klondike, they went to the river and stood at a bend where gold had been discovered. It was pretty eerie, thinking that this had been a mining site all those years ago. Now it was just open countryside; nature always takes back what it loses in the end.

John had always been interested in photography, and he took pictures of the area, the river, and its path upstream. Assuming the gold had been washed downstream, then the place to look for deposits had to be upstream. The countryside there was mountainous, its contours made over millennia.

"Before we leave here, let's go to the claim registry. I have an idea," said John.

They drove to the claim's office. Pat was back at work now after her awful experience, but she always had an assistant with her now. On entering, they saw the map on the wall indicating the claim positions one hundred years ago.

"Can we take two claims now?" said John.

"Yes, sir, you can. There is no charge, as no one has been interested in making a claim for over a hundred years. You can take an acre each," said Pat.

Jack and John looked at each other in surprise. Jack looked at the map on the wall. "How about those two higher up the mountains? It would leave at least two more for the others when they come."

John agreed, and the deal was done. They were now the proud owners of mining rights in the Klondike.

John and Jack drove back to Vancouver to return the car to the rental station. On the way, they phoned Josh Young and told him everything was fine with his father. After that call, John said, "Do you want to fly up to Nome in Alaska? It is where the prospectors went from here.

Although I'm coming back later in the year, it would be good to have a quick look now, and it is not far from here, is it? We could do the same there. Maybe we should start a mining company." He laughed.

"Why not? Besides, we can try the banks up there for that key," said Jack.

At the airport, they got the plane ready to fly and set the flight plan for Nome. John said, "I would like to go to the claims office if they still have one after all these years."

When they arrived, they spoke with the residents, but everyone laughed when they said "claims office."

"Are you serious?" one said. "You're a bit late," He laughed and walked off without answering.

"That wasn't very successful. I think we need to go to the town hall," said Jack.

John agreed, and they found it; residents were happy to impart that information.

There they learned that it had been built in 1920, years after the police inspector had found the dead body of Don Wicker. They went in. Both of them were embarrassed to admit why they were there, but John plucked up courage and went up to the receptionist. "Can you tell me where the mining claim office is, please?"

The young lady smiled, turned to her supervisor, who was a lot older, and said, "It's in the room at the back of this corridor. It's not used much these days, but there might be someone there now."

John thanked her, and they walked down the corridor for about a hundred yards. On the way, he said, "I want to check the claims upstream. That must be where the gold came from on its way to the sea."

They found the office, which had a small sign saying, "Claims Office," next to several other departments. On entering, they found a reception bar with another beautiful young lady standing behind it. According to the nametag pinned to her blouse, over her right breast, her name was Susan. John whispered to Jack, "How come all these ladies are so beautiful? Maybe one would take you in hand?" He laughed.

"Give over, John," said Jack.

"I'm sorry. No more jokes."

"We are looking at registering a claim further upstream to the bulk of those recorded on the map hanging on the wall over there. What do you think?" said Jack. John had told him it was his turn to look silly.

The poor girl had no idea what to say, but she liked Jack's look, so she said, "Very few existed at all in that area, probably because, in the 1890s, it would have been difficult to excavate. Those poor souls had nothing but a shovel, and the area you are talking about is rock. Since those days, no one has taken an interest in mining here. You can still make a claim today if you like. You are allowed an area of one acre per person. That was laid down in 1885, and it has never been altered since. So, if you want to do it together, you can claim two acres between you both."

"Let's do it. That would be fun," said Jack, smiling at Susan. He was smitten with her.

"I am certainly up for that," said John.

They studied the map carefully, looking at the areas where gold had been panned in the river. The prosperous regions were marked on the map. They were working on the basis that the gold had been washed downstream over millions of years. John and Jack chose an area upstream and, in the mountains, where four claims were available, thinking that they would take two now, but Jack could not take his eyes off Susan.

"Are you paying attention?" John said to Jack, who brought himself out of his daydream. "Then Cloe and Ben could take the other two when they all returned later in the summer." John was confident that Ben would join them.

They paid the registration fee for their two claims, received their certificates, and left. Jack gave Susan another smile, which she returned in that knowing way.

"We have one other task before we leave Nome," said John. "We found out there was no railway here in the period we are looking at, so the key must be for a bank deposit. Let's go and find the banks."

Nome was now built up, but John could not help but think what the town must have been like for Don Wicker. In those days, there would have been nothing here.

They discovered that there were two banks in town. One was modern, probably only twenty years old, so they chose the other one, which looked much older.

They went into that bank, and John said to the doorman, who was an elderly gentleman, "Can you help, please, sir? We are looking for the bank deposit box for this key." He handed the doorman the key.

"You know, it's good that you asked me. No one else in this bank is likely to know the key's origin," said the doorman, pleased that he could be useful in his old age.

John became excited, but his chin dropped to the floor when the doorman added, "This key won't fit anything here."

He cheered up again, though, when the doorman said, "But I know where it will."

"Where do we go, then," said John, not wanting to delay.

"I used to work in the other bank in town," said the doorman. "It is the oldest, but when the bank was rebuilt ten years ago, I was made to retire. They said I was too old. Can you believe it? This key is definitely to one of their deposit boxes. The number of the key determines it. All their numbers started at one hundred."

"Thank you so much. I can't tell you how much this means," said John.

"Is the deposit box yours, sir?" said the doorman.

"Well, it's not mine originally. I came into it on the death of the owner, who was murdered in 1900."

"Nineteen hundred? That is interesting. What was the person's name?"

"Don Wicker, a miner."

"Ah, Don Wicker. A terrible business, that was. The town has never quite gotten over the circumstances. A stranger rode into town, asked Don to let him use his tent, and then murdered him brutally. How did you come by his deposit key?"

"My girlfriend brought a chest at an auction, and the key was inside."

"I know about that chest. It was kept all these years by the family of the police officer who originally found Don. The last relative was a close friend of mine. He died last year, and all the belongings were sent to auction. My friend never knew what was inside. It intrigued him, but he did not want to break the box to find out. There never was a key. My friend was superstitious and felt that if he smashed the box open, terrible things would happen to him."

"We managed to find a key that fit the lock," said John.

The doorman perked up considerably, thinking the secret would now be revealed. "What is in it, then?" he said anxiously.

"Don's original mine claim form was in the chest. The claim had a note on the back saying the finder was welcome to the claim. It was written the day before Don was murdered," said John.

"Do you have that note with you?"

"No, but my girlfriend does, and we are coming back later in the year."

"Well, you will need that note to gain access to the box. It might be regarded as Don's will."

"Thank you so much for all that. In that case, we will leave it until we come back later in the year," John said, and he gave the man a tip.

John and Jack headed back to the airport, and then Jack flew them back to Nashville. They were both delighted with the way things had turned out.

Cloe was pleased to see John, who told her about their adventures. She was especially interested in the new mining claims, and she said, "We've now got two gold mine claims."

"No, we actually have three, two in Nome and one in the Klondike."

"The key is exciting," said John. "We found it relates to a bank in Nome, but they will want the note Don left giving the finder the claim. That will be regarded as a will. We can get access to the box when we go later in the year."

"We need to speak with Ben," said John. "We need to bring him in on this. When we go back, you and Ben can make the adjoining claims to the ones we just picked out. I have a feeling about this."

"I'm fine with that," said Cloe. "I like it when we all work together. Anyway, Ben's a charming person."

"Don't get any ideas in that direction?" said John.

"I'm only joking," Cloe said, laughing, "but he always did like that fishnet bodystocking!"

The next day, John and Jack went to see Ben, who was still working on the reception at the terminal building at the airstrip. They told him about their little trip up to the Klondike, Dawson City, and Nome.

"That's interesting," said Ben. "It has always been one of my things, how men could live in such disastrous conditions. They were just hoping for a fortune that never materialized. It is different from the exploration of the South Pole, for instance, because the explorers had a choice. These prospectors did not have to go, but there was no work in those days other than having your own business. These gold rush guys saw it as the only way to make money and live. Their problem, I believe, is they were looking in the wrong place. All the explorations in Alaska and the Klondike were by the river or beach panning. All you can collect that way are fragments if you are lucky, and most were not."

"So, what was their problem, then, Ben?" said Jack.

"They didn't sit down and work out where these fragments originated. In all fairness, they didn't have the scientific knowledge to know how the gold was created."

"That is why we're here, Ben. It is a pity they had no internet in those days. How is it created, then?" John said with a smile.

"Gold was produced in the Earth's creation, not at the beginning but in the relatively early days of its existence. Extreme pressure and heat caused it after the big bang, and I mean extreme. It caused some elements, including gold, to form in layers or strata in the Earth's crust. Subsequent movements in the Earth's plates caused further upheaval and melted particles together, forming the nuggets we all know today. Rather than looking in the rivers for fragments, we should be looking at what is further upstream. It's probably in the mountains there, either as a seam of gold or nuggets."

John and Jack looked at each other and smiled. "Just as we guessed, although we didn't know the reasons. So, how do you feel like becoming a gold prospector?" John said.

Now Ben looked puzzled. John said, "Well, while we were in the Klondike, we flew up to Nome, and we made a claim each on the basis you just mentioned. Much to our surprise, that's still possible. The land is barren and a wasteland, but what's underneath it?" John also added that he and Cloe had acquired another claim at Nome.

"In Nome, we could only claim an acre each, so we took two adjoining ones. We left two more for you and Cloe when we go back, assuming you are coming," said John.

"Well, to tell you the truth, anything would be better than working in this boring job. I was getting ready to move on anyway," said Ben.

CHAPTER SIX

John was glad to be back in Nashville, where the weather was like spring now, and the tulips were showing their colors. He'd had enough of the extreme cold that existed in the Klondike. He knew they would all be going back soon, but hopefully, it would warm up by then. John thought about July, or maybe August.

He was having a few quiet days with Cloe, and they were enjoying being together after weeks apart. As she went out shopping, he relaxed in the lanai at the back of their house. She had complained to him that it was always her job to do the shopping. 'But you know I hate shopping, dear," he had said.

"You think I like it?" Cloe had replied, but she'd let it go at that and gone to the store.

Suddenly John's phone rang.

What has she forgotten now? John thought as he got out of his comfortable chair and went to his phone. When he got to it, he realized it is not his that was ringing. *Damn. Cloe must have forgotten to take her phone*, he thought, and he walked over to where the ringing was coming from.

He answered her phone, saying, "Cloe's phone. Can I help you? She is out at this moment."

"Hello, you must be John. This is Gloria, you know, from Channel 5 TV. I just phoned for a chat with Cloe."

"It's good to hear from you, Gloria. I'll get Cloe to ring you when she gets back from the shops," said John, and he hung up.

When Cloe got home, he told her she'd forgotten to take her phone and that she needed to ring Gloria, the TV interviewer.

Cloe dialed Gloria's number. "How are you doing?"

"I'm OK, thank you," said Gloria. "I like San Francisco a lot. All settled in at the new station. They liked my interview with you so much they have assigned me to deal with similar matters over here, so I wondered how you were getting on with the Don Wicker thing. Did you know he came from San Francisco?"

"Yes, we do know, and we will be looking into that situation shortly. John got called away to Dawson City, but he is back now. It's funny that all these things seem to happen on the West Coast."

"Well, look, if you come over here, please contact me, and let's meet."

"You bet," said Cloe, and they finished the conversation.

Back in Canada. Edward Isaacs was starting his sentence of ten years of imprisonment at the Calgary Correction Center. This is his first time in prison. He'd come very close a few times but had always managed to keep out; however, he was not looking forward to it at the age of nearly forty. Edward enjoyed his comforts too much and was determined to keep away from the bad influences that existed there. He was committed to getting the maximum allowance for good behavior. He was hoping that, as this was his first offense, he might even get early parole. He certainly would not make the same mistakes again.

After a month, he decided he had learned his lesson. *At least do not be greedy*, he told himself. Life went on, and he had to make the best of it. Each day was like the one before. He tried to break the monotony with reading, and after a month, he had read twenty books and got a job in the library, handing out books to inmates.

He liked his job, as it got him around the prison and provided relief from the intense boredom that caused some prisoners to have nervous breakdowns. He could deliver and collect books from prisoners as he moved his way around the prison, getting a little exercise as well. He was something of a loner; there were gangs, but he stayed clear of anyone involved with one, and those criminals were not interested in books, so they left him alone.

He had befriended one fellow inmate, though, a Michael West. They spent a lot of time together, just chatting about nothing in particular. Michael was like Edward in that he kept himself to himself. You are out of touch with the outside world in servitude, but the inevitable question always comes up after a few days.

"What are you in for, Edward?" said Michael.

"Extortion, although I call it good business," replied Edward. "How about you, Michael?"

"I'm in for intimidation. I suppose that is a similar offense." Michael says but then continues. "I will say for your information only that I got away with a bank raid ten years ago. Unfortunately, the other three people involved were caught and received ten-year sentences. They should be out soon with good behavior. I was lucky to get away with it because I was hiding in a closet in the building. I owe those guys something. They did not quell over me. What was your extortion over?"

"You were lucky, you old sod! You need to make it up to the others when you get out of here." Says Edward.

"It's even more complicated than just that; unbeknown to me, one of the others took a gun, and a bank guard was shot. I would never have got involved with something like that if I had known."

"Didn't the police search the building in detail if someone was killed, Michael?"

I am sure they did, but as I said, I was fortunate to get in a closet that had a sewer manhole in it. I was so lucky. When I lifted the lid, it led down to the main sewers ten feet deep. It was very messy, but it enabled me to get out, walking down the sewer until I came to a ladder and climbed up to a distant street." Said Michael.

"I bet that turned a few eyes when you arrived on the sidewalk." Said Edward laughing.

"It certainly did, and a few noses as well, I guess, but I didn't care I was free and walked away. I followed the paper's reports, petrified that I would get a knock on the door from the police, but the other three did not squeal on me. I read that the Police Inspector handling the case didn't believe the crooks, thinking that there was a fourth person. I don't remember his name, and I'm in here for an earlier offense." Michael said, and that incident was dropped.

"Your situation is a lot more complicated than mine, but I purchased several mining claims for the Klondike area; the gold mine claims related to the 1800s. Everyone had forgotten about them now; they were worthless then and still are. There is no gold there; however, the properties' present owners have built on those sites. I tried to sell the claims back to the current property owners or threaten to mine under their buildings if they didn't." Edward laughed, feeling pleased with himself.

"That sounds perfectly legal and like good business sense to me," said Michael, laughing loudly with Edward, "You clever bastard. Why didn't I think of that one?" He slapped Edward on the shoulder, congratulating him.

"Yes, the problem was I got too greedy, and one of the victim's sons is an FBI agent and got involved unofficially. They set a trap for me, and I used a bit too much pressure. My bodyguard attacked a Mountie. My man got a broken arm, and he is in another prison somewhere."

"I see. I always say it's best not to get too greedy. I have found that from experience. Best to take a fair profit and leave a little for someone else," said Michael.

"So, I have now learned from experience," Edward said. "You never stop learning in life, do you?"

Michael spent several days thinking about that scam. He liked the principle and eventually said to Edward, "You know, this gold mine scam sounds interesting. I didn't realize those claims still hold good today. How on earth did you come up with it?"

"Oh, they do," said Edward, "not that anyone wants one. I must admit I heard about the idea from a colleague. It sounded good, so I found out that the claims still hold good today, although there never was any real amount of gold there. I did hear that the two informants the FBI sent up to the Klondike went to the Mining Registry afterward. They took out two new claims further up the valley.".

"Now that is interesting; they either knew something or had a hunch, at least," said Michael.

"Hmm, you must be right. I had thought about that. By the way, how long have you got to do in this place?" said Edward.

"Just a month now. I've done my three years and can't wait to get out of here. I want to talk to you again about your gold mining scam. I need to think about it more."

The next few weeks went by quickly for Michael, but not so for Edward. Before Michael left for the outside world, he said to his friend, "It's been great having you to talk to in this godforsaken hole. Before I go, will you tell me the names of these FBI informants? I'd like to look into this gold business further. If there's anything in it for me, I'll cut you in, you can trust me on that."

Edward was not so sure he could trust Michael, he is a crook after all, but he decided he had nothing to lose. "Sure, their names are John Smith and Jack King. I don't know much else about them except that they come from Nashville in Tennessee. Oh, and the Mountie is here in Calgary, Inspector Albert Jones."

"Thanks for that. If anything comes of it, I know where you are, and you're not going anywhere fast," said Michael, smiling.

"Not for the next ten years, anyway! But once I'm out, I'm away for good," said Edward.

Two days later, Michael finished his jail sentence. He went back to his home in Calgary and spent two days unwinding from his ordeal. He had been in jail for three years, with time off for good behavior; this was his third offense. He calculated that he'd spent a quarter of his life in prison, but he knew no other life. While he rested, his mind wandered back to the gold mines in Alaska.

Why did these two jokers take mining rights today? They must know something. He picked up the phone and called the Royal Mounties Office in Calgary. He asked to speak to Inspector Jones, and he was put through by the telephone operator.

"Good morning, Inspector. My name is Cornelius Constantine," said Michael, giving a false name. "I work for the *Calgary News*. We are reporting on the scam that took place in the Klondike earlier this year. I believe you were involved in that incident."

"Hello, Cornelius. I know most of the reporters at the *News*, but I don't think we have met. Nice to talk to you. Yes, I was the officer who dealt with this, and the offender is in prison now," Albert said, but he was concerned that he did not know this reporter. He knew them all at the paper.

"Yes, I know. I have only worked for the *News* for a week. In fact, this is my first assignment; I have most of the facts. I'm keen to speak with the FBI informants who were involved. I understand it was a John Smith and Jack King." Michael thought his introduction would soften Albert up a little, and he was right.

"That's correct; it was John Smith and Jack King," said Albert.

"Do you have a contact for either of them?" Michael asked quickly, hoping that the inspector would answer before thinking about it.

Before realizing that he shouldn't, the inspector gave Michael John Smith's telephone number.

"Thank you, Inspector. You have a good day." Michael put the phone down, thinking, *that was easier than I expected.*

As the line was disconnected, Albert recanted what had just happened. *I was stupid just then. Cornelius was only fishing then, and I should not have given John's phone number.*

He picked up his phone again and rang the office of the Calgary News. "This is Inspector Jones of the RCM. Do you have a reporter named Cornelius Constantine on your staff?" Albert said to the operator.

There was silence for a minute until the young gentleman came back and said, "No sir, I'm afraid we don't."

"Thank you." Said Albert putting the phone down and kicking himself for his stupidity.

CHAPTER SEVEN

It was now April. Winter was turning into spring, and the flowers were just coming out into bloom in Nashville. After a week of being back, John received an unknown call on his phone, but he answered it as usual.

"Hello, my name's Cornelius Constantine. I'm a reporter with the *Calgary News*. I've been trying to get you for weeks, so I'm glad to speak with you now," Michael said in his best speaking voice, using his alias again.

"Well, I'm here now. What can I do for you?" John said apprehensively.

"I'm writing a story about the criminal you were involved in apprehending in Dawson City and the scam on the gold mine claims. Edward Isaacs is his name. I believe I have most of the details, but I heard that you took out two claims of your own while you were there. After so many years since gold mining was done in the area, it seemed strange to my editor. Can I ask why you did that? Do you know something my readers would be interested in?"

John was immediately suspicious of this approach, but it was a matter of public record, so he knew there was no point in denying it.

"We did as you say, and now you're going to push for a reason, so I'll answer it first and say we saw it as a bit of fun, just owning a little part of Alaska, and no, we don't think there is any gold there. Does that answer your questions?"

"It does, thank you, but I am sorry if I have caused you offense." Michael sensed from John's tone that he had.

With that, John put the phone down, immediately looked up the number for the *Calgary News* on his laptop, and then dialed it. A lady receptionist answered the phone on this occasion and said, "Can I help you, sir? My name is Andrea. Who do I have the pleasure of speaking to?"

"Thank you, Andrea. My name's John. I have a simple inquiry. Can you tell me whether you have a Cornelius Constantine on your reporting team?"

"Thank you, John, if I may call you that. Can I put you on hold for a moment while I check it out?" The line played patriotic music while John waited.

Five minutes later, Andrea returned and said, "Sorry to keep you are waiting so long John, but I have been checking it out. No, sir, we don't have anyone of that name here. Would you like me to put you through to the reporting office?"

"That will not be necessary but thank you very much for helping me, and I am sorry to have troubled you," said John.

Michael West drove from his apartment in Calgary to the Klondike. It was a long way over the Rockies, and he spread the journey over two days. He was not usually a tourist, but he enjoyed the drive, thinking that the scenery was splendid. He even saw two black bears, which he hadn't seen in the wild before. He passed the Rocky Mountaineer train on three occasions as it wound its way around the mountains.

When he got to Dawson City, he went straight to the Mine Registry Office. An attractive lady stood behind the counter: "Susan," he read from the label on her breast. Although she only worked every other day, by chance, she was on duty that day as well. She was a well-made girl of twenty-five, with short blonde hair and blue eyes, just how Michael liked his women.

She was wearing a low-cut blouse that day, and Michael couldn't stop staring at her breasts. Her skin tone was perfect, and he hadn't seen a naked woman for years. Susan began to feel uncomfortable. Pulling up her blouse, she said, "Can I help you, sir?" which yanked him out of his trance.

"Oh, sorry. Can I see the mine registry map, please, Susan," Michael said.

"Certainly, sir. There's one on the wall behind you. Over there." Susan smiled and pointed.

Michael West is thirty-nine years of age and short at five foot six inches tall. At that height, he had to watch his weight; it's effortless to put it on when you are shorter than most people. He had been driving for two days, so he was stiff, and he had not bothered to change clothes today. His white shirt was getting dirty, but he did not care; he was that type of man.

He went over to the map and noticed the recent entry showing John Smith's and Jack King's claims. He could see the claims to the north of them were free, so he went back to the receptionist and said, "I would like to register a claim, please."

"Will you please fill in this form, sir? The number refers to the number on the map; you can only register one claim," said Susan, handing him the application form. She thought it was strange that, after a hundred years, people were registering claims in this area again.

Michael filled out the form and entered the number of the claim to the north of Jack King's. He gave the form back to the receptionist, who said. "Oh, that's north of Jack King's claim. He made it a few weeks ago." Privately she thought she would like to be on top of Jack King; she was the leading type, but she had to admit that being underneath would be very acceptable. She snapped herself out of that one.

"Very well, sir. I will have the paperwork set up." She left the room and returned five minutes later with the claim certificate. "This was a surprise to my supervisor. Until a short while ago, we had not had a claim filed here for over a hundred years, and now we've had three."

Michael did not reply; he just smiled.

With that, he left the office and drove over to the area of the claim. He stopped there and looked around, thinking, *where are these guys coming from? Do they really believe there is gold here? It's just a wilderness. At least the registration only costs a few bucks.*

John had been back with Cleo for a month now, during which time they had been planning their summer experience. They had two gold mine claims in hand, and after checking on the internet, they found that there had also been a gold rush in California in the 1840s, just inland of San Francisco.

"It's amazing to me how little we know about our own country, isn't it, darling?" John said to Cloe.

"Yes, but that's because it is such a big country, and the real history of the people is not taught in schools. That's what we need Ben for; he seems to know everything," said Cloe. This made John feel a little humble, but she was right, he thought.

"Let's plan our cruise to Alaska. This is a special trip for us, so we need to have a luxury suite," said John. Neither of them had cruised before. Although both were good sailors, they wondered how they would do on a ship for a week without stepping on land. They had heard the scenery was spectacular on the way to Seward. John was particularly keen to see whales, and he had heard there was a good chance of seeing them on this trip.

It was April now, and they did not want to go to Alaska before the summer because of the weather. The travel agent had advised John that from June on is the best time to go. They chose July, and John booked a grand suite on the *Argonaut*, the luxury cruise ship of Oceanic Highway Cruises.

It was leaving Vancouver on July fifteenth and would take them up the inner waterway to Seward in Alaska. The brochure told them that the scenery would be spectacular, and it almost guaranteed them that they would see whales.

That gave them four months to plan the trip to Alaska and research their claims. The two claims were a long way apart. While Nome was on the west coast of Alaska, the Klondike was in Canada, near the border with Alaska.

"Let's meet Jack and Ben at Tootsie's bar in Nashville, on Main Street," said John. "I love that place, with its country music. It will be an excellent place to work out the details, and we can enjoy the evening out with the music at the same time."

"That's the best idea you have had lately," said Cloe. "We might even make it your lucky night after hearing my favorite music."

They arranged to go to Tootsie's with Jack and Ben to make their plans. On entering, they were shown to a table on the second floor, in front of the group of country singers. The first thing they agreed on was that Jack and Ben would also travel on the cruise, although they only went for a suite with a balcony to keep the cost down. They decided that they would each do their own thing in the daytime, but it would be nice to eat together in the evening.

As the cruise ship headed to the north of Alaska, they decided to extend the journey with a rail trip to Denali National Park to see the wildlife. Then they would drive up to Nome and investigate that claim. They agreed to divide whatever money they made from the trip four ways.

From Nome, they would drive down to the Klondike to investigate the claims there. After taking the two claims planned for Cloe and Ben, they would again split everything.

"That's a plan, then," said John. "Ben, in the meantime, can you investigate on the internet to see what you can find for both areas?"

"Will do, boss," Ben said in a friendly manner.

John also wanted to do further research on Don Wicker. Having found a quiet afternoon when Cloe was out shopping, John sat down at his computer. He had still not told Cloe of the circumstances of Don's death, as he knew she would be upset. He typed "Don Wicker" into Google again and came up with the account of Don's murder and several other entries related to California's gold rush. That rush had been fifty years earlier than the one in Alaska. Indeed, it had been before Don was born. John read that Don had acquired an interest in a Sacramental Valley claim, gifted to him by his uncle.

One article suggested that he might have been murdered because of the earlier gold mine. He'd never made any money from his Nome claim. It said that the San Francisco claim had not been very profitable and had been sold for a considerable sum for the land it occupied rather than the small amount of gold under it.

Another entry recorded that Don was a family man. He'd had two children, who had died under mysterious circumstances just two years before his death. It also said that after Don's death, his wife moved into one of what was now known as the painted lady Victorian houses near Alamo Square.

Those houses were now treasures and were the focus of the tourist trade for San Francisco. While he appreciated that the houses had not been so desirable in the late 1800s, they'd still been well above Don Wicker's means.

John's mind was now whirling. Don's two children had died two years before him. He had also owned an interest in a California gold mine. Maybe that was what had given him his interest in mining. John searched "Mrs. Sophie Wicker" and found only three small entries. When he finished reading them, being an investigator for the FBI, he knew this needed further investigation. His suspicious mind thought, *Did Don's wife murder him?* If he'd had to put money on it, he would have said yes. *We must look into this.*

He had always known Cloe was somewhat physic, and that little chest had been calling to her at the auction. Was this the reason why? Was Don reaching out to her? And how had it gotten into the auction? John knew now was the time to tell all this to Cloe. That evening, after an excellent homemade meal and a bottle of wine, he started the long tale.

He told her that Don Wicker had been murdered on June 2, 1900. He had been butchered, and his two children had died mysteriously two years earlier. He'd owned a share of a gold mine in the California gold rush, which he'd acquired at birth from his uncle. His wife, Sophie, had gone on to move into one of those Victorian mansions in San Fransisco, the ones now worth millions.

Cloe listened intently to what John had found on the internet. She was speechless for several minutes. John said, "What do you think?"

"She murdered him, no doubt about it," said Cloe.

"What should we do?"

"We have to investigate. It's right up our street, isn't it? And the chest drew me to it. I am sure Don Wicker is calling us or wants something." Cloe hesitated. "Or maybe it was Sophie."

"I agree," said John. "We have three months before we go on the cruise. Let's do it now."

He went back to his computer and searched for the region involved in the California gold rush of forty-nine. It turned out to be the Sacramento Valley. "Let's make a start there," he said to Cloe, who stood beside him.

"There is one more coincidence, you know," Cloe said, looking at John to see whether he would realize it. He didn't and looked at her blankly.

"Gloria Rowbottom, the television interviewer who was also drawn to the chest, has moved to the San Francisco TV station. Is that coincidence or what?" she said.

"Hmm, I wonder. Well, we must make contact when we get there," said John.

As they would be going for several weeks, they decided to rent a small car. The Harley couldn't carry the luggage for such a long trip. Three days later, they loaded up the car and headed out on their expedition to Sacramento, California.

They took their time, enjoying the countryside and calling in at Las Vegas again. They'd loved it the last time they'd visited, so they stayed an extra two days at the Mirage Hotel. Neither of them gambled, agreeing it was a waste of money, but they enjoyed watching others lose theirs.

The drive across the Nevada desert was hot and dry. On the way, they stopped off at an old mining town. It was now just a ruin, but they wanted to see what such a town had been like in the old days. It might give them ideas for what was to follow. What they noticed most of all was the heat. The sun beat down, and the rocks seemed to make it worse, reflecting the intense heat inwards.

They moved on, and upon arriving in Sacramento, they booked into a cheap motel. It was now so late in the day that they decided to leave their investigation until tomorrow.

"Why don't you phone Gloria Rowbottom? She may be able to help us in this venture," John said to Cloe.

"Good idea. I'll ring her now." Cloe took her phone from her bag and called the number, and she put it on speakerphone so John could hear.

"Hello, Gloria, this is Cloe. Remember, from Nashville?"

"I do indeed remember you. How could I forget that experience? I often think about what really happened to Don Wicker," said Gloria. "What are you doing now?"

"We are investigating just that. What did happen to him? We have found out a lot more information since we last met with you, how the wife came into a lot of money, moved to a new house in the affluent area of San Francisco, and other things. So, we are coming to the area to see what we can find out. As you know, I was drawn to the chest for some reason."

"Do you think the wife did it, either personally or through someone else? It's usually the wife," said Gloria. "This is exciting. Look, can you give me a few minutes? I will make inquiries here to see if I can become involved professionally again."

"Sure, we are not going anywhere tonight," said Cloe, and she hung up.

Gloria did not call back that evening.

The following day, after an excellent cooked breakfast, they headed for the county offices of Sacramento. *A typical government building* thought John. "These government buildings must all have the same architect," he remarked. They went inside and saw that the mining offices were on the third floor.

After taking the elevator up, they knocked on the office door and entered. John studied the lady behind the desk. She must have been about twenty-eight, with long, dark hair, a beautiful girl by anyone's judgment. *I know those eyes. I've seen her somewhere before, but where?* Cloe immediately picked up on the recognition, as women so often do.

The receptionist became concerned, and her face tightened up. Even John recognized the wrinkles on her forehead: she was in panic mode. *Will he recognize me?* She thought. *Has he come to arrest me? I know he worked for the FBI.*

John wondered what was happening. *This girl looks petrified, but of what?* He gave Cloe a look of surprise.

Cloe's intuition was telling her that something was happening. "Do you two know each other?" she asked loudly in frustration.

"Well, yes, I think we do, but I have no idea where from," John said honestly.

"Let me refresh you, then," said the girl behind the desk. "I'm Alexandra. We met during that terrorist business a couple of years ago with Mohammed and Khan Ali. We were all supposed to be on the same side, but I think you forgot that" she said sarcastically. "Your girlfriend was Carrie at the time, but she has moved on."

"Oh my God," said John. "You don't know how much of a coincidence this is."

Alex realized that John truly had not recognized her and, therefore, had not come to arrest her.

"Do you have a break, Alex? We'd like to talk with you," said John. Cloe was a little put out by all this but said nothing.

"I do in ten minutes. There's a coffee bar next door. I'll see you there."

John and Cloe left the office and went to the café next door and ordered coffees. They did not mention what had just happened, but John sensed that Cloe was upset. After fifteen minutes, in walked Alex. John stood up and properly introduced the two women.

He said to Cloe, "You might be interested in all this. It happened before your time with me."

"I would," said Cloe, still a little put out.

So, for Cloe's benefit, he related the story of the terrorists Mohammed and Kahn Ali. He explained to Alex that the FBI had employed him to locate their hideout. He had not been successful, and with the help of Alex and another girl, the terrorists had gotten away. The other girl involved was his old girlfriend, Carrie.

Cloe became annoyed with herself; she realized that she had been jealous for no reason. She thought it would be better if she excused herself and left the conversation. "John, dear, I will go and get that map that we need of San Fransico while you carry on with Alex, and I'll meet you back in her office shortly." As she got up to leave, John was surprised, but he said nothing.

"Tell me more about Carrie. Although we only knew each other for a matter of months, we became very close," said Alex.

"Well, when she left you after a few months, she was indoctrinated into the Islamic State. She told me much later that it was her love of Khan that caused it. She saw an advertisement calling for women to go to Syria to help the army as cooks, cleaners, etc. She applied to be a cook."

"Carrie was not a good cook," said Alex, "but then I suppose the food would be stews or something of that type."

"Probably. Anyway, the group she applied to sent her to Syria and paid for the airfare. When she arrived in Syria, No one spoke English, and a rifle was pressed into her hand. She was sent with the other troops into the war zone and ordered to kill anyone who moved."

"Oh my God, she was not like that. It's a wonder she didn't shoot herself," interrupted Alex.

"Carrie was befriended by a general who took pity on her, and eventually they got married, but she had to take up Islam. They moved to Iraq, but she had to wear dark clothes from head to toe, including her face. The United States government wanted to arrest this general, and they sent me to Iraq with army assistance to get him to the US. The way to do this was via Carrie."

"So, if she was covered up, how did you recognize her?"

"That was the problem. Basically, she recognized me, but it was a long story, which resulted in both her and the husband being airlifted to Washington. In truth, all our government wanted was to get the general out, but Carrie was the means to get to him, and she came back as well, much to her delight. She was given immunity by Uncle Sam when she got back as a reward."

Alex was amazed; she knew that Carrie had been taken with Islam, but she was still surprised that her friend had gone to such extremes and even more shocked to hear John had gotten her back. She then became concerned. John had confirmed that he worked for the FBI. That meant she might be in danger, as the government presumably would still be interested in her regarding the president. She frowned.

"Thanks for bringing Carrie back," she said. "I feared for her, you know when I left for California two years ago. I just wanted to get away and start a new life. I bear no bad feelings towards you. You were doing your job. I was not involved in the actual terrorism, only transporting the Alis to Washington. I have a new life on this side of the continent now. I got married last year and put the past behind me. I have to say, I brought so much disgrace on my father. I don't forgive myself for that."

After a pause, she asked, "So, what brings you to California, John."

"Well, I, too, moved on after our last encounter," said John. "By the way, you need not worry about me; I will not report that I have seen you. To be honest, I think the government wants to forget the whole incident."

"Thank you for that. What can I can do for you, then?"

CHAPTER EIGHT

"The reason we came to your office was to look into a mining claim from 1849," said John.

"Really? What interest would that be to you or the FBI?" said Alex, still shocked. She did not know whether she could trust John after their last dealings. "Tell me about the claim, and I'll see what I can find out."

"I can assure you that I am not here for the FBI. You need not worry; the past is the past and better left there," said John, as he could sense Alex's apprehension.

He told her how Cloe had purchased the chest at an auction. "Inside the chest was a mining claim form for Nome, Alaska. The name on the claim form was 'Don Wicker,' and a Don Wicker was brutally murdered in Nome shortly afterward. We found that Wicker also had a claim registered in Sacramento, which an uncle gave him at his birth. There was a wife involved, and this was all well over a hundred years ago."

Alex thought about this for a minute. "It's interesting about the chest. Was there anything else inside?"

"Actually, yes, there was a small pebble and a key."

"A key? That's fascinating. Was there no explanation?" asked Alex. Before John could reply, she said, "You believe the wife murdered this Don Wicker, don't you?"

"Yes, it's very likely, and I want to see what we can find out. There is also the gold mine here in California in which Don Wicker had an interest. There must be some records, which is the sole reason we are here today."

"Indeed, there will be. Let's go back to the office, and I'll see what paperwork I can find."

They left and returned to the office just as Cloe came back from her shopping expedition. Cloe had thought about Alex while she was shopping; she knew Alex was the type of woman John would go for, but then she realized that she was being jealous for no reason and put it all at the back of her mind. Accepting the situation, she walked into the office and held John's hand. He smiled at her.

Alex told them to sit in one of the comfortable chairs reserved for visitors. "Wait here a minute, and I'll see what I can find." She disappeared into another room at the back. After fifteen minutes, she returned. "Sorry for the delay. These papers go back so far it was difficult to trace, but I have found some interesting facts. All our modern records are on the computer, but the old ones going back to 1850 are on these cards."

She held up the cards she had brought out with her and showed John the card he needed. "This is what you need, I think." The card said that Joshua Wicker had transferred a forty percent interest in the Wicker and Docker mining company to Don Wicker on March 10, 1850. The other shareholder was George Docker, with twenty percent. That left the other forty percent with Joshua Wicker, the uncle.

"That's just what we need to know. Thank you, Alex," said John. He turned to Cloe. "We need to research George Docker and the mining company."

Then he reiterated to Alex that her secret was safe with him. "I am delighted you got over the business with the Alis, and I hope it did not leave you too traumatized."

"Thank you, John. My husband and I are truly happy, and I've put the incident behind me. I am sorry Carrie did not, but once again, thank you for bringing her back home. All the best in your investigations, and thank you for explaining about Carrie. I can put that matter to bed now."

John and Cloe left the office, and John found a quiet corner in the reception area and Googled "Wicker and Docker Mining Co" on his laptop. He confirmed that it had the three shareholders, as Alex had told them.

The company was incorporated on October 1, 1849, in the California gold rush's early days. A small amount of gold had turned up in the Sacramental Valley near Jackson. Several prospectors started it. John discovered that this was one of the first companies to operate in this way.

The workers were pleased in that they were paid a basic wage even if they didn't find gold; those that did received a bonus. That way, at least everyone earned something. The company registered its claim over a large area.

Over the years, the company mined only small quantities of gold; there were never any dividends. John thought this was nothing to write home about, but then he came to the interesting part. Towards the end of the 1800s, the company came under pressure to sell the land for redevelopment now that this part of California was expanding its businesses.

The claim was located in Jackson, a town that was up and coming at the time. Many developers wanted to get in on the action and build skyscrapers at the end of the century now that the gold rush was entirely over. Most of the other mine claimants were happy to sell; there was little gold coming in then. Only the Wicker and Docker Mining Company held out, thinking the price would rise even higher if they did.

John read on. Joshua, who had a controlling interest in the company, didn't want to sell. He'd always thought the company would hit gold in a big way soon. At least, that was the excuse he gave to the other shareholders. John thought that it must have been Joshua's genes coming out in Don Wicker. *That's interesting.*

The article said that the company finally sold out in September 1899 for the sum of one million dollars. It said the price was not justified, being far above market value, but the prospective developer wanted the property, as it was holding up his other developments.

Once the property was sold, the company, which had no other assets, was liquidated. John read all this out to Cloe.

"That meant that Don Wicker had four hundred thousand dollars," he said, "reason enough for the murder. But it is unlikely, due to lack of communication in those days, that Don would have known about it."

"We need to check on the wife. She has to be the main suspect," said Cloe.

"Hmm," said John. He liked to check things out rather than just guess, but he had to admit that Cloe's intuition usually paid off. "We need to go to the personal records office. As we walked in, I saw that it is somewhere in this building."

They went downstairs to the board at the entrance, which told them that the Births, Marriages, and Death Office was room 2150. They went up to that office and asked to see the entries for births in the 1800s.

The clerk looked at John painfully and said, "Hold on a minute, sir. I will try to find the record book."

He was not happy and didn't return for ten minutes, but he was carrying a large black leather book when he did. "I found it at last. Thank goodness all these documents are kept on computers these days," he said, agitated at the inquiry.

John sensed the man's frustration and said, "Well, thank you for your perseverance."

The clerk placed the ancient book on the table, and John looked up the records for Don Wicker and Sophie Wicker. He found that Don was born on March 1, 1850, married Sophie on September 24, 1875, and died on June 2, 1900.

The search on Sophie Wicker confirmed her death on December 12, 1901. The cause: suffocation. The record also stated the address where Sophie lived. On seeing that, Cloe looked intently at John. "What do you think now? That places a completely different light on the matter. Sophie died only a year after Don and under suspicious circumstances. Does suffocation mean she was also murdered or was it an accident?"

John nodded. "I believe we need to find out more about Sophie and what happened to all that money. Let's go to that address we just found on Steiner Street. Maybe the present owners will know something about the history. You never know with your luck; some of the family might living there now." He laughed.

"Don't make fun of me, darling," Cloe said with a smile. She loved John's quips, and she kissed him to acknowledge that.

They drove over to the address, which they had written down. Cloe's phone rang on the way. "It's Gloria," she said, and she answered it, putting it on speakerphone.

"Hello, Cloe. This is Gloria. Sorry, I couldn't get back to you the other day, but my boss was not available. I have since spoken to him and related our experiences in Nashville regarding Don Wicker. He saw my original broadcast and wants the television company to get involved. Is that alright with you? All you need to do is tell me what is happening in your searches. There will be some money in it for you, but I do not have a figure now."

After hearing what was said, John said, "That is fine with us, Gloria. We are going to the house on Steiner Street where Sophie Wicker, Don's wife, lived. We will let you know how we get on. You might like to get there yourself with a camera crew." He gave her the address. "On second thought, let us go there first and see how the land lies. We will come to you if the present occupier will have TV cameras at the house."

Gloria agreed that was best. "Steiner Street. I know that street. It's very exclusive. I did an article on a family that lives there. Hmm." She didn't comment further, but John knew where she was coming from.

Sophie's house was, indeed, one of those beautiful Victorian houses affectionately known as the 'Painted ladies of San Francisco' that the tourists flock to see when visiting the town. The house was on a steep incline and had a stucco exterior; all the houses formed one long terrace and were painted in different colors. These were the only properties to survive the great fire and earthquake of 1906.

The house had curtains at the windows, and it appeared occupied, although the exterior needed redecoration. They went up the steps to the front door and rang the doorbell. No one answered at first, and John thought no one was home.

"Don't be so impatient, John. The owner might be old and infirm," said Cloe.

After waiting several minutes, Cloe heard someone approaching the door. "See, I told you," she said to John.

An elegant elderly woman slowly opened the door. She looked very Victorian herself, with her blue-rinse hair and immaculate full-length gown. She must have been in her late eighties, at least, thought John. But she had a beaming smile, and he could see she was glad to have company. She looked as though she might be lonely.

"We are very sorry to trouble you, ma'am, but we are investigating a Sophie Wicker, who lived here in early 1900. We wondered whether you might know anything about her," said John.

"Well, you have come to the right place, young man. Do come in," she said. She showed them into the lounge, a very Victorian room with Tiffany shades and long drapes at the windows, which were closed to stop the tourists from peering in, or maybe she didn't use this room much. The furniture was of the art deco period and covered with white sheets. *A lady's room*, thought John, definitely not his style at all. The lady pulled the sheets off the chairs, and John promptly moved to help her. They all sat down in the comfortable armchairs.

"Let me introduce myself," she said proudly. "I am also named Sophie Wicker. I am the granddaughter of the lady who interests you. This house has been in my family ever since the original Sophie lived here. I don't see many people here these days, so it is nice to see you. Old age can be very lonely, you know, young man."

John couldn't believe his luck, and he smiled at Cloe. "I told you, didn't I?" he whispered to her with a smile.

He turned to Sophie and said, "That's amazing, Sophie. I am John Smith. I work with the FBI, although I have to say I am not here today at their instigation, and this is my wife, Cloe." John thought a lady of this generation would prefer for them to be married. "I hoped you could fill us in on events that took place at that time. We are particularly interested in Sophie's husband, Don, who was murdered in Nome, Alaska."

"Ah, that. Well, that part is very sordid, but I suppose it was a long while ago now. It really doesn't matter anymore, and I'm the last in the line of the family. The story will die with me; I have not written it down anywhere. Initially, I wanted to forget it all, as it was not good for the family.

But times move on, and who cares anymore? Anything goes now; the finer points of life have gone now." A tear formed in Sophie's eye.

"I am well into my eighties now, so it's good that you've come to see me. I don't think I have long left in this world; you get tired of life at the end, young man."

Cloe felt sorry for the old lady, who was shedding some more tears now, so she went over to Sophie and put her arm around her.

"Thank you, my dear. I must pull myself together. I have had a good life," Sophie said.

She started to say something else, but John said, "Sorry to interrupt, but do you think it is possible that we could bring in Gloria Rowbottom from ABC 7? She has been following us on this adventure and would like to be included in your story."

"Oh, I'm not so sure about that, young man. I don't know that I would be a good subject for television, although I have seen Gloria, and she seems a fair lady. She was the interviewer who was present when someone purchased Don's chest." Sophie suddenly realized that Cloe might be that purchaser, and she touched her hair in that feminine way.

"I can assure you it will not put you out, and it might help us clear up a few points," said Cloe. "You see, we purchased a chest that was Don's, and we think either he or Sophie is contacting us to look into what happened in 1900."

"Ah, I was just wondering that," said Sophie. "You know, I have always thought similar things myself. Although I have some information, I believe there is more." She looked deeply at Cloe. After a brief pause, she continued. "Very well, I suppose I have an obligation to my ancestors to make this known publicly. Perhaps Don and Sophie can then rest in peace."

"Thank you, Sophie. Let me ring Gloria; I know she will be here in a flash."

Cloe phoned Gloria, who had been waiting for a call from her. "Can you come now? Sophie's granddaughter lives in the house and will allow you to interview her."

"Wow, what luck," said Gloria. "We'll be with you in twenty minutes."

"While we are waiting," said Sophie, "let me get you both a drink of something. Tea or coffee?"

They settled on tea, and Sophie left the room to put the kettle on; she was an old-fashioned lady who used a copper teapot on her gas stove from the sixties. Cloe had followed her, and they chatted while the kettle boiled.

The tea took about fifteen minutes to brew, and when the women returned to the lounge, John thought Sophie looked a lot younger.

As they were enjoying their tea, there was a knock at the door. Sophie went to the door and let Gloria and her cameraman in.

"Madam, I am Gloria Rowbottom from ABC 7, and I am very grateful to you for allowing us to film this interview."

To Cloe, Gloria said, "It's good to see you again, dear."

CHAPTER NINE

"Let me begin," said Sophie as she settled into her armchair, enjoying the attention. The cameraman had turned on the camera and was recording what was said.

"The original Sophie lived in a poor part of town; that whole area consisted of small wooden cottages hemmed in together. It should have been demolished much earlier, but the landlords were greedy and did not care how their tenants lived.

"Fate took over in that sense, and the district was completely burned down in the fire of 1906, which was caused by gas burning following the earthquake. Perhaps God stepped in when the landlords would not do their job. Anyway, Sophie had moved into this house by then. She was married to Don, as you mentioned, and they had three children. Two of them died in a yellow fever outbreak. No doubt, that was caused by the mosquitoes living in the squalor of the district.

"Sophie was devastated, but after Don's death, there were suggestions that the girl's deaths were suspicious, but that was rubbish. The third child was a boy named Matthew; he was my father.

"Don had this gold rush thing in his blood; his uncle was involved in the gold rush of 1849 here. Don was given shares in the mine here by his uncle at his birth. As he grew up, he became interested in the mining company and followed what it was doing. I think it gave him the impetus to get into the mining business to get rich quickly.

"Not satisfied with just following his company, he went to the Klondike in 1895, along with so many other folks who thought they could make their fortunes there. He had no luck there and moved to Nome, Alaska, in 1899. The family thought Don might have made a small amount in Nome, but they had no real reason to believe that.

She paused for a moment. "I need to rest. All this talking wears me out."

The camera stopped.

"Don't worry if you want to rest, Sophie. We will edit that out later on," Gloria said.

Sophie returned her story. "Sophie had been on her own for several years by now, and she missed a man's company. She was, after all, still a young woman with the urges. You know what I mean. Even I had them when I was young."

Sophie paused and said to Gloria, "You had better edit that remark out. I don't want people to get the wrong impression,"

"Don't worry, Sophie. We will sort it all out later," Gloria said sympathetically, though she was thinking, *That's what the viewers would love to hear.*

Sophie continued. "Sophie always made it clear to everyone at the time that Don was the love of her life."

"Excuse me for interrupting," said John. "Did you say the family thought Don found some gold in Nome?"

"Yes, Don did send a letter, but Sophie never received it. She was dead when it arrived. I'll show you the letter later. It's upstairs in Sophie's bedroom, which is still in its original condition."

John made a mental note to see that letter.

"In her loneliness, Sophie met a man named Frank Douglas. From what I have heard, she did not really love him, but he was convenient and filled in a gap until Don returned to her, as she believed he always would. I have to admit the story gets a little sordid from here onwards."

John and Cloe's ears pricked up a little more now, as they both thought maybe something new would come out.

"Sophie was destitute. She did manage to get some occasional cleaning work, but not enough to pay all her bills. The rent, in particular, was difficult. The landlord's agent was always calling on her to extract a few dollars to reduce her arrears, which were slowly building up. Don had shares in the mining company given to him on his birth by his uncle; I can't remember the name of the company now. Oh, what was it called?"

"It was called Wicker and Docker Mining Company," said John. We found that out from the claims office at the town hall."

"Yes, that was it. Anyway, the shares never produced an income, but in 1899, the company was sold for a fortune. I think it was for property development. However, by that time, Sophie had moved in with this Frank Douglas. She had told neighbors that the landlord was going to evict her due to the arrears, and she had no other option. They had heard about the sale of the mine; it was common knowledge locally. Of course, Don, in Alaska, would not have known this. His uncle had trusteeship of Don's shares, which was a condition of the original grant.

"Sophie and Frank talked about arranging Don's murder. That way, Sophie would inherit the money. The rumor was that my grandmother was pushed into the decision, but in all honesty, who knows? I like to think that it's true."

Sophie paused. "I'm embarrassed to tell you all this. It doesn't put my family in a good light, but they were different times, the wild west and all that."

"We understand," said Cloe. "We just want to get to the bottom of it all. You see, I purchased a chest at an auction recently, and it contained Don's mining claim in Nome. On the back is a note saying the finder is welcome to the claim and the hope that they have more luck than he did. The note was written the day before he died, and we think he intended to go home to Sophie."

"Oh, that is interesting. I do hope that was the case. It would put my mind at rest. You know, I don't want to leave this world with bad thoughts of my grandmother." Sophie was quiet for a minute, trying to work out whether that would change her opinion of what had happened.

Cloe smiled at her, thinking, *I hope you leave contented.*

"I'll carry on, then," Sophie said as though she understood what Cloe was thinking. "Actually, I'm glad to get it off my chest before I die.

"Well, the story goes that Frank and Sophie discussed killing Don. Neighbors of my father told him that many years ago. If that happened, then Sophie would inherit the money. My father thought it was only a passing thought, but who knows? Maybe he said it for my benefit.

"Anyway, Frank took it upon himself to go to Nome and kill Don in 1900. My family never understood why it was so brutal, though. If Frank wanted to kill Don, why not stab him while he was sleeping or use poison. But to mutilate the body is unthinkable. After Frank killed Don, he returned as though nothing had happened, telling Sophie he'd had to visit a sick family member.

"He was away a year, and I believe Sophie guessed what he was doing. Although there was nothing she could do during that time, she started to have a guilty conscience, thinking she had encouraged Frank. By the time he came home, she hated him. She started going to church every week to make confessions. She had not been a regular churchgoer before that time.

"Sophie eventually inherited the money from the sale of the mining company, and she purchased this house, moving out of Frank's place without telling him."

Sophie stopped and looked around. "I need a break for a moment. Can I get you more tea or coffee?"

"That sounds good. Tea for both of us, please," said Cloe.

Gloria added, "That will be good for us, too."

When Sophie left the room, John and Cloe looked at each other. Gloria had turned off the camera.

"What a story," said John. "We're so lucky she is still alive. Otherwise, it would all be lost forever."

"I am so pleased you bought me in on this. It will make a good story," said Gloria.

"Yes, and that must be the reason Don reached out to me with the chest. By the way, did we bring the chest with us?" Cloe asked John.

"Yes, it's in the car outside," said John. "I think we should bring it in to show Sophie, but we should keep hold of it."

Five minutes later, Sophie returned with five cups of tea. As they drank, she continued her story, and the cameraman switched on the camera again.

"Now, how far did I get? Oh, yes, Sophie moved in here. I can show you her bedroom if you like. It's just as it was all those years ago. Remind me before you go. Anyway, Frank was not happy with the situation. He thought they had an understanding, and he'd kept his side of the bargain. So, he broke into the house one night and murdered Sophie, strangling her while she was in bed.

"I don't know how they caught Frank, but they did, and he was hung a year later. Sophie, as I said, had had three children. Two died of yellow fever, and the third, Matthew, my father, inherited this house, which passed to me on his death. I'm the last of the line, having no children, so I've left it to the state in trust. That way, the house will be open to the public. It is the only house in the neighborhood that is still in its original Victorian condition."

Sophie looked at everyone. " I hope this has explained everything."

John said, "Thank you for that. It must have been difficult for you. Can I make a suggestion? From what you have said, I think that Sophie did love Don. Why don't you have a plaque erected outside referring to both Sophie and Don? I know he never lived here, but he came across to Cloe recently and wanted us to investigate, so I think he would like that, too."

Cloe added, "I think Don loved Sophie as well; in fact, I'm sure of it. It's all to do with the chest we purchased at auction. I know there is something there. We have the chest in the car, and I'll go out and get it."

"Thank you, both of you. I'm nearly ninety now, so I will do what you say. I always wanted to think they loved each other," said Sophie, "and the letter I will show you will establish that."

Cloe went out to the car and collected the chest, but she removed the key and the stone. She took the chest back inside and showed it to Sophie, who took it in her hands. "This is amazing; this chest belonged to my grandfather. I am so pleased you have come to see me. Let's take the chest upstairs to my grandmother's bedroom."

They went upstairs to see Sophie's bedroom, which, like the present Sophie had said, was just like it had been in 1900. The wallpaper was brown with age, and parts were peeling off. "I suppose I should have had the room decorated, but I didn't want to touch it. I do clean it every week, though," said Sophie.

As they walked into the room, John and Cloe immediately noticed a stone on the old oak dressing table. It was identical to the one they'd found in the chest. Cloe went straight to it and stared at it. "Can I touch the stone, please?" she said to Sophie.

"Certainly, my dear. I don't know why it is there, but it always has been, so I just leave it. Silly, really, I suppose."

Cloe picked up the stone and moved it around in her hand. She closed her eyes. The stone felt like it was warming up.

"Do you know anything about the stone?" Cloe asked, although Sophie had already said she didn't.

"No," said Sophie. "As I said, it's always been there. I've never touched it. It must have had a significance to my grandmother, though, as she clearly kept it in a special place. Look, it's right in the center of the dresser."

"I think it is special, Sophie," said Cloe. "You see, we found the exact pair of this stone in Don's chest. That means Don kept one stone and Sophie another. If only we knew why. We need to look into that as well, John."

"That is incredible," said Sophie. "That may put a different aspect on the whole story. Perhaps the stones were some form of connection for Don and Sophie. I would die happy if that were the case."

"I think there was more of a connection than you think," said Cloe. "I know it's an odd request, but could we take the stone and put it with the one we have to see what happens? We will, of course, return both stones to you when we have completed our exploits."

Sophie thought about it. She didn't, after all, know these people at all, but she liked them, and the stones should be together, so she agreed. "You promise you will bring them both back to me, won't you?"

John said, "You know, Cloe here is psychic about these matters, so I think you can rest happy."

"I mentioned downstairs that there was a letter from Don, but it didn't arrive until after Sophie had died. It must have been hanging around in some mail office somewhere. Here it is." Sophie opened a drawer and took out an ancient letter. "Please be careful when you read it; the paper is very fragile. As you can see, it was written the day before he died." She handed it to Cloe, thinking that, as the lady, she would look after it more than John.

"Thank you, Sophie. This is incredible," Cloe said, and then she read the letter aloud.

Dearest Sophie,

I am sorry that this is the first letter I have written. I have been away for a total of five years now, and I miss you passionately. I had very little success in the Klondike, but I managed to find a few gold flakes in Nome, though not enough for me to make my fortune. Conditions are terribly cruel up here. I don't think I have been warm since I arrived.

You were right all those years ago, my darling, but I had to try; it would have given you a better life, and you deserved it for marrying me. I know that I have let you down, but I have decided to come home in a few weeks. I do hope and pray every night that you have waited for me, although I don't deserve it. There are a few things I need to tidy up here first, and I will head out after that is done.

As I said, I did have a small amount of success here in Nome and made a special purchase. I will explain when I get home. Keep watch for me down the road.

If anything happens to me before I get home, you should come here and collect the little chest, the one you gave me on our first date. It contains a key to a safe deposit box at the bank. There is only one in town.

I love you with all my heart, dear, and will soon be home with you, maybe even before you get this letter.

The letter was signed by Don, followed by six x's

"How sad that Sophie never saw it," Cloe said as tears ran down her face.

Old Sophie, feeling very emotional, took a seat. "I'm like this every time the letter is read, and you read it with such feeling, Cloe. It was as though Don was reading it to us. Thank you for that. I have just realized that the letter mentioned a key in the chest. I never noticed that before. It is strange how you can read something time and time again but never see the crucial point. Do you have the key?"

Once Cloe had dried her eyes, she said, "Yes, we have the key. We will go to Nome and find what this is all about. We will be back with the stone and fill you in on what we find afterward."

"I would love to come with you, but I can't do that anymore. Old age is not good, you know," said Sophie.

John had picked up on the special surprise, and he wondered what it could be. *Maybe the key will tell us*, he thought. "Do you know anything about the surprise, Sophie?"

"No," she said. "My father tried to work it out; he even went to Nome when he was old enough, but it was long after Don was murdered, and most people had forgotten about the incident by then. That left him sad, and he returned home without any information."

John made no further comment but privately thought there was something to investigate there.

John and Cloe said their goodbyes, as did Gloria and her cameraman.

Gloria said, "Don't worry, Sophie. We will only present this in the best light for your family."

"Thank you," Sophie said.

John and Cloe left the house, thanking Sophie for all her input and taking the stone with them.

John said to Cloe, "I don't know why the internet referred to the mysterious deaths of two children if they died of yellow fever. I think we have done our task here. Don will be remembered at the house with Sophie, so let's hope he is happy, too."

Cloe said, "I believe people have gotten the situation all wrong. I think Don and Sophie were very much in love. The stones are love talismans. Each had one on the basis that they could put them together when Don came back from Alaska. We must wait till we get back to Nashville before putting them together."

Outside, Cloe spent a few minutes with Gloria; they had formed a bond now. Gloria said, "You will keep in touch. I need to hear the outcome, and I will see that a donation is given to the trust that Sophie is setting up."

"We will be in touch. Fear not," said Cloe.

John had no idea why they had to wait to put the stones together, but he went along with it. The next day, they headed back to Nashville.

CHAPTER TEN

1889

It had been a particularly severe winter in San Francisco this year; the newspapers talked about the planet going into another ice age, but Don said to Sophie, "It's all rubbish. They have no idea what they are talking about. They just want to sell papers. They would say a man has walked on the moon to sell papers."

They both laughed about that. Sophie said, "Man walking on the moon. Now you are talking rubbish."

The snow had been falling for some days now, and it was heaped up six feet on the sidewalk. Sophie Wicker sat in her small hovel in the center of town and froze; they could not afford to buy coal to heat the house. Her house had one room downstairs, a living area, and a kitchen. Upstairs was one bedroom, which they shared with their three children. There was an outhouse in the backyard. At least they had mains drainage, but somehow the back entrance to the terrace always stank. On many occasions, Sophis had complained to the landlord's agent, but he'd merely shrugged, and nothing had happened. The agent knew the drains needed to be fixed, but the stringent landlord would not pay for it.

That was the sum of their house, and they had to pay one dollar a week for rent. The home was timber-built, with shingles on the roof. The building must have been at least fifty years old, and rain always leaked in. Even in good weather, there was plenty of rain in San Francisco.

Sophie did have a cleaning job at the moment, but those residents were in similar financial situations, and often she did not get paid. There was not much work available in San Francisco. Don often said, "It will be alright in the new century." That was his attitude. He believed in the American dream, where everyone had the opportunity to make a fortune, but how? The grass would be greener on the other side, which was another of his favorite sayings.

Sophie never understood why Don had that attitude; his parents were no better off than them. His father had been a coal miner, and sadly, he'd died in a mining accident when Don was twenty. There were many of them in those days. The mining companies were more interested in dividends than worker appreciation. In those days, the American dream meant anything goes!

When Don and Sophie had me, she'd been an attractive girl in her late teens; her dark hair had been in a bob style, ahead of her time. It was easy for her mother to cut, but Don liked it that way. She was now thirty-five, and the hardships of their lifestyle were showing. Wrinkles had replaced that soft complexion and her hair was turning to gray, but Don still loved her. She tried her best to look nice for him, but it wasn't easy without any money. Her blue eyes from her Irish origins always sparkled when she was excited, and they still attracted the men.

The cold was horrendous that winter, and coal was so expensive that Don would steal a few lumps at a time from the railway yard. Coal was used for cooking and heating the house and as a dietary additive to aid digestion. There were no luxuries in those days in the cities derelict districts and no help for the lowly paid. Labor was cheap, so she couldn't earn much, either, and she had not been paid for three weeks by her employer. She had been looking for odd jobs when she could. Each one made her a few pennies, just enough to keep the wolves at bay, but no more.

She and Don had been married for ten years now. When they'd first met, she'd been over the moon, swept off her feet. He'd been a very smart man of twenty-five then, good-looking and bold. She liked a man who was forceful and knew what he wanted. In turn, he knew what she wanted, and she had said to him many times that sex with him was like a mountain erupting inside her.

For this period in history, Don was a tall man. People tended to be smaller back then. He had wild red hair. Sophie always thought he had some Indian blood in his veins, or it might have been Viking. His excellent temperament pleased her; she knew he would do anything for her.

Their problem became apparent after a few years, as Don wanted to make his fortune mining gold. Like his uncle, he always said, "I'm only going to do this for you, darling."

The trouble was, and Sophie knew it, life was not that lucky for everyone. For every wealthy gold miner, there were several thousand who were broke. But she did love him, no matter what everyone said, and all her friends said she was mad to stay with him.

Her life was no different than anyone else's in that area; in reality, some poor souls were worse off, living on the street. At least she and Don had a house, she told her friends. Life just goes on, she thought, from one day to the next. Lately, Don had managed to get a job at the local shipyard, repairing boats as a carpenter. The word "carpenter" was taken quite loosely, but that also raised a few dollars each week, which he gave straight to Sophie. She looked after the household's money; she knew Don would drink it away.

She remarked to her close friend once, "Why is it that men always turn to drink to bury their sorrows?" She did not get an answer, and neither did she expect one.

Early in 1890, Don heard about the gold rush in the Klondike area of Canada. "I have to go there," he said to Sophie. "I have this feeling in my gut that I will make a fortune for us, and we can get out of this dump." Sophie didn't think that was realistic and told him so.

He spent many days pondering whether he should leave Sophie to bring up the children while he went off to the gold mines. He knew that if he was successful, he could give Sophie a much better life. She wouldn't have to work then, but he was no fool. He knew not everyone made money from mining. Don had been putting a few pennies aside from his wages for a few weeks now in case he decided to go; he knew he would need a horse and some clothing. Anything else, he would have to earn once he arrived.

The more he thought about it, the more he realized that his mind was becoming made up. His uncle had been very fortunate in the California gold rush, but the gold had been scarce, although the developers were pushing him to sell. The more Don thought about it, the more he was coming around to deciding to go to the Klondike.

Their house was near the railway line, and Don spent many days watching the trains coming and going from the depot, which was the main hub for that part of California. Large rows of freight carriages were lined up each day to head north. He talked to the railwaymen, who were constantly working, and he found out that one train went to Vancouver on alternate days, leaving at seven o'clock at night.

"I could do with a trip on the train to Vancouver," Don said to one worker, who looked at him suspiciously. Don thought he would be reported.

On the contrary, the man looked around to make sure no one was listening and then said, "It is easier than you think, chum. There is always one empty carriage at the end of each train. They keep it that way in case some goods come in late. Transients often ride the trains that way, and some even use them as a home! Make sure you are here early and get in the last carriage. The doors are always open until the train is leaving the depot. Keep your head down when the guard comes to close the doors. You might even have company."

"As easy as that, is it? Thanks, mate. I appreciate it," said Don, and he bid the man farewell. He'd made up his mind; he would go.

The next day, he took a walk on the beach. As he thought, he looked at the pebbles. He didn't know why, but it just concentrated his mind. He saw two stones side by side; they were the most unusual stones he had ever seen. Each was perfectly round, light brown, and with identical flecks of color running through them, just like the glass marbles that children played with. *It's a sign from God,* he thought. That made up his mind.

He picked the stones up and put them in his pocket. When he got home that evening, he said to Sophie, "I need to give this gold mining a go. If I can make even a small fortune, that will be enough for both of us to have a real life. I was down at the beach today, and I found these two identical stones. They are a sign from God that I must go."

He showed them to her. "This one is for you, and I will have the other; they are a token of our love. Keep them safe, and we will put them together when I return with my fortune."

Sophie took the stone but protested that he should not go and leave them. However, one day that summer, he packed his bags, said goodbye to Sophie and the children, and left for the Klondike. Sophie didn't hear any more from him. She still loved him, but then she thought, *How can you love someone who deserted you?*

Don arrived at the train depot at three in the afternoon. He knew today was the day for the train to Vancouver, and he had a bag with him containing some clothing, his Bowie knife, and a small amount of food for the journey. He would have liked a gun, but he couldn't afford one. He had now collected fifty dollars in cash, which he kept on his person. He knew any travelers with him would be after any money he had.

The depot was alive with movement now, and carriages were being shunted around to form the Vancouver train. The carriages were in two lines, each about a quarter of a mile long, on different tracks. Don walked along the lines to find what would be the last carriage. At the end of the second line, he found what he wanted, the only carriage with the doors open.

No one was around, so he looked inside the carriage and confirmed that it was empty. He threw his bag inside, climbed up, and walked down to the end, where there was a small pile of straw. He concluded that the truck must have been used to carry bales of hay. The truck had been swept, and all the loose straw was at the end, but Don thought he could use the pile to take cover when the guard came by.

Don settled down in the corner furthest from the door, with the straw in front of him. He was not completely hidden, but he thought that he would get away with it with any luck. He uses his time waiting for the train to move to look around at his home for the next few days. No luxury here, not that Don would know what luxury was. The wood timbers seemed tight, though, so it should not be too drafty.

On one side, the carriage was burned black in the center, and Don guessed there had been a coal boiler there and hot coals had fallen out and started a fire. There was an escape hatch in the roof, but it did not seem to have been used for a long time; it was padlocked closed.

After what seemed to be a couple of hours, Don could hear two people outside, talking and coming towards his carriage.

He heard, "I'll just have a look in here, Jack, and we can close the door."

Don was now worried they might come in, but he made himself as small as possible, close to the wood floor, in the shadowy area of the carriage. He heard the squeak as the man leaned against the doorway, and he held his breath. The door slid closed, and he released it.

"They need to oil these doors," Don heard the guard complain.

The line of carriages started to move as they were shunted back to the end of the other line. For the next fifteen minutes, Don fell over at least three times. Finally, the operation was complete., and Don waited patiently for the train to leave the depot. He knew that these freight trains moved very slowly, and he had no idea when he would arrive in Vancouver.

The train squeaked and thumped as it slowly moved forward. Each carriage bumped into its neighbor until the train settled down, but it was still moving at less than a walking pace.

Suddenly Don heard a thump on the side of the carriage, followed by the sound of a man calling out, "Open the door, please, mate." Don was a little shocked; why would anyone wait this long to get in the carriage? He became suspicious. When the man repeated his request, Don moved to the door and slid it open with great force.

He agreed silently with the original guard: the doors needed oiling!

Don stepped back from the doors as the man ran alongside the train, which had now sped up to a fast walking pace. The man threw his bag into the carriage and hauled himself up. Don watched him the whole time. He is a young man, about twenty-five years old, with dark hair. He was roughly dressed but appeared to be friendly. He was puffing and panting after his exertion.

"Phew, I think I must be getting too old for this travel," he said. "By the way, my name is Bill."

"Well, I suppose it is good to meet you, Bill, although unexpected. My name's Don."

Bill was starting to get his breath back now, and he closed the door. "That's better. It will keep the wind out. It will get icy as we get nearer our destination. Sometimes these carriages have a stove in them, but I can see this one doesn't."

"You've traveled this way before, then, Bill?" said Don.

"Regularly, Don. You could say that this is my residence," Bill said, laughing.

"This is my first and last trip, I hope. I'm off to the gold mines in the Klondike."

"We shouldn't have too much trouble on this trip; the railway company employees will not be coming into the carriage until we reach Vancouver, and we will have gotten off the train by then."

"But you do expect some trouble, then?"

"Well, there is a group of highwaymen who operate around the Seattle area; they have been known to attack the train, but since this is a freight and not a passenger train, I think we will be alright. However, I do have a weapon." Bill pulled out a Colt .44 pistol from his bag.

"Well, I have a knife, but that's about it. How long is the journey to Vancouver?"

"It's about four days, and we'll be fine," Bill said, trying to pacify Don, as he could sense his apprehension.

Four days, thought Don. He had bought a loaf of bread with him, which would undoubtedly last three days at a push, and he had cans of meat. *Should be enough food.* He noticed that Bill had prepared food, being experienced at this type of travel.

The next day, the train sped up to its maximum speed of about twenty-five miles per hour. The weather was warmer today, and they opened the doors to get some fresh air into the van. Don saw that Bill was constantly peering out the door, scanning the horizon. *Is he watching for bandits?*

Two more days went by without incident, and they opened the door as often as they could. They had passed through many towns on the way, but the train did not stop. It only stopped when it was taken onto a sidetrack so a fast train could pass them. The next day would be the last full day before they reached Vancouver. They were approaching Seattle, and the weather has chilled off considerably. Don didn't want to open the door, but Bill insisted on it.

"We need to open the door today to keep watch. This is the area where any attack might happen, and we need to see it before we are taken by surprise," Bill said.

Don knew now that Bill expected an attack. The landscape had also changed. Gone were the rolling hills and flat ground of the farms, replaced by mountains, which meant that the train would crawl along uphill before running fast down the other side.

On one of the slow climbs, Don saw a dozen men in the distance, riding horses and coming towards the train. He immediately turned to Bill. "Are they what you meant?"

"Yes, that's them. We need to close the door now and keep quiet," Bill said, and they closed it.

"Why would they attack this carriage? There is nothing in here but us," said Don.

Bill shrugged. "No idea."

"I think it's unlikely they want freight from the train. What would they do with it? That leaves just two passengers, you and me." Don stared directly into Bill's eyes. "They wouldn't want me. I'm of no value. So that only leaves you. Who are you?" Don waited for a response.

"Okay, they want me. I am Bill Clinger, the son of a wealthy businessman in Las Vegas, and they want to hold me for ransom. They have been chasing me for months now. I ran away from home because I was not happy, but it's out of the frying pan and into the fire."

"In that case, you should get off the train as soon as possible. We are slowing down to climb the hill, so it will be easy to slip off rather than shoot your way out with the gun, and we would probably both be killed."

Bill looked at Don, and then, without saying anything, he opened the doors and threw his bag out. The bandits were not in sight. They must have been behind the mountain. "Quick, go now," said Don. Bill looked at him and then jumped out and rolled away from the train, which was moving slowly now. Don watched with relief as Bill scurried off down the hillside. After throwing out any evidence that Bill had been there, he closed the door and sat at the end of the carriage.

After a while, he heard gunshots, and the train slowed down even more. Finally, it came to a complete standstill. Don could hear voices outside. "There are no passengers on the train." He listened as the bandits led the driver and guard along the train.

"Just open the carriage, or I'll shoot that wig off your head," a bandit said. The guard slid the doors open.

"What do we have here?" said the bandit as he looked inside.

"Must be a stowaway," the guard said.

The bandit climbed in and saw Don sitting at the far end. "You don't look like Bill Clinger," he said, annoyed. He rushed over to Don, grabbed him, and lifted him up.

"I'm not anyone called Bill Clinger, I can assure you," Don said, "I'm Don Wicker, and I don't think I would be worth any money to you."

The bandit knew Don was not the man he wanted, and he looked all around the carriage, kicking the straw aside. Then he saw there was a sliding door in the roof. "Ah," he said. Another bandit climbed into the carriage, and the first bandit got on his back and tugged at the door. It didn't budge. "This isn't going to open. It's padlocked. Bill has evaded us again."

He climbed down and looked at Don, thinking. Finally, he said, "Have you been here on your own all the time?"

"Yes, sir," Don said, thinking politeness might help him.

The bandit muttered something under his breath, and then he and his partner left the carriage. Don could hear through the carriage wall, "He's lying to us. Bill Clinger was on this train. Our informant would not dare to lie to us. He undoubtedly jumped off before the train stopped. It's so long he could be miles away by now. Let's ride back down the tracks. We might find him." As they moved off, their voices grew fainter, and Don sighed with relief.

Ten minutes later, Don heard the bandits ride away in disgust at their failure, and the train started to move again on its final leg to Vancouver.

Just outside the depot at Vancouver, the driver stopped the train. He knew that Don was in the last carriage, and he allowed him to get off without being caught by the station staff. As Don stood beside the track, he waved in the direction of the engine. He thought he could see the driver waving back, but it was a long way, and he was not sure. The train pulled forward, and eventually, it was a dot on the horizon.

CHAPTER ELEVEN

Once Don left the train, he walked along the track, heading to the town center, a distance of a mile. He left the tracks before the terminal, and in front of the building, he saw a stable with dozens of horses in the corral. He went into the office. "I need a horse to take me to the Klondike, but I am limited financially," he said to the owner.

"Don't worry, sir. We have plenty of reasonably priced animals. Let's go to the corral. You choose a horse, and we can agree on a price."

Don chose a chestnut stallion. When he heard the price, he told the owner it was more than he had.

"If you give me a week's work in the stable, you can have that horse. I need help this week, and my stablegirl is off sick," the owner said.

Don was delighted and gladly agreed. He spent the next week clearing out the stables, washing down the horses, and feeding them. It was very energetic work, but by the end, he felt fitter. He was given a bunk in the stable to sleep in, and the owner's wife provided food, so he was happy.

When his week's labor was finished, Don rode off on his new chestnut horse. The stable owner had given him a rough map of the route to Dawson City, and the man's wife had made him a basket of food for his journey.

The ride through Canada was challenging, and for the horse's sake, he traveled at a slow pace. The terrain was very mountainous, but after a week, he could see the Klondike River ahead. As he got nearer, he saw the miners panning for gold along the riverbank. He could feel himself getting excited. *This is it. Now I can make my millions,* he thought. He reflected on Sophie, wondering what she was doing. "I'll make this work for you, my darling!" he shouted as he rode on to the mining site.

Sophie was working as a cleaner in one of the large houses in San Fransisco, situated on the high ground, where all the finest houses were. She had been fortunate to get that job, as they were few and far between. At one of the smaller homes that she cleaned, the owner had been sympathetic when Don had left. She had said to Sophie, "What's wrong with these men? I'll keep an eye out and see if we cannot find you better work."

Sophie thanked her but did not expect anything to come of it. The following week, though, the woman said to Sophie, "Mrs. Ling from the Heights is looking for a cleaner and general housekeeper. I know people don't like working for the Chinese, but she is very nice. She is a member of our club."

"I would be delighted to work for the Chinese, for any nationality, to be honest. When can I see her?" Sophie said.

"Leave it to me; I will come to your house and tell you."

Three days later, there was a note on Sophie's front door. On it was an address and a message that said, "Go to the Heights tomorrow at nine."

Sophie attended her interview, which was over in minutes. She and Mrs. Ling got on well, and Sophie was to start the job immediately. The work was daily, and the money was significant now that Don was not around.

There was a horse groom on the staff by the name of Frank Douglas, a single Irishman at heart. As the months went by, he and Sophie became friends, two lonely souls, you could say. Frank lived in a better house than Sophie, on the other side of the railway track. It was larger and in a more central location.

On many occasions, Frank said to Sophie, "My house would be more convenient for you to live for your jobs. We can be good company together. We are both lonely. Let's share our loneliness, and hopefully, it will go away."

But Sophie always resisted, saying, "I can't leave Don's house. He will be back one day soon, I know."

They went out for a drink at the local bar when they could afford it. After about a year, Frank said to Sophie, "Look, your husband has deserted you. He's not coming back."

"You don't know that. You don't know him as I do," said Sophie, who was trying to be loyal, but it was true. She had not heard a word from him since he'd left.

"I don't think so. When did you last hear from him? Why don't you move in with me? You know my house would be more convenient for you and the children."

"I don't know, but I promise to think about it," said Sophie, not wanting to jump out of the frying pan and into the fire. She knew she must consider the children, though. What life did they have? And they did, indeed, need a father figure who lived with them.

Sophie and Don had three children. Susan, aged six, was a pretty young thing who, one day, would be a beauty. The other daughter was Wendy; she was a little plain, more of a tomboy, which made no difference to Sophie. Then there was Matthew, the boy; he was nine now and growing fast. Sophie had to admit that the four of them sleeping in one room was not good for any of them.

After six months of pressure from Frank, Sophie relented and agreed to move into his house with him. She still did her cleaning jobs, but there were now two wage earners in the family arrangement, and they got on well together, although the sex was nothing like she remembered with Don. It became more of a house-sharing understanding for Sophie, but she did what was necessary to keep Frank happy. He liked sex every night, and sometimes in the morning, but it was speedy, so much so that she often wondered what he needed her for.

The months turned into years; there was still no news of Don. Although she had no way of telling him that she had moved, she stopped at the old house every week to see if there was a letter, but there never was. She didn't pay any rent there anymore, but no one had moved in, and the place was now uninhabitable. She realized she still had fond memories of Don sitting in his armchair, which was falling to pieces. She hoped that Don would write to her, but alas, no.

In 1895, there has been an outbreak of yellow fever in the Los Angeles region. It quickly spread up the coast to

San Fransisco; the mosquitos were dangerous at this time of year. It was a hot summer that year, and both girls came down with a fever. Sophie and Frank couldn't afford a doctor, so they treated the girls with poultices to get their temperatures down. Their efforts had little effect. The fevers got worse and much too late, they called in a doctor. He told them that there was nothing he could do now; the disease had taken too great a hold. Two days later, both girls died within an hour of each other. No one else in the household caught yellow fever, which was a blessing, but Sophie was devastated. The girls were buried at the local cemetery for the poor without any ceremony.

Sophie went into protection mode with Matthew, her only offspring left. She did not let him out of her sight. The yellow fever epidemic eventually passed, but she still protected him in the same way, and he became very introverted.

Months went by without hearing anything from Don, and Sophie and Frank settled back into their routine. Frank continually pressured Sophie to divorce Don for desertion and marry him. But she always carried a spark for Don; she knew he would return one day. Besides, why would she want to marry Frank? She did not love him in that way.

She thought it was time to be honest with him, and one day, at dinner, she said, " Frank, I can't marry you, and I never will. I am married to Don in my heart, and I always will be, no matter what he has done to me."

Frank was upset but did not even bother to respond. He already knew in his heart that this was the case, and the matter was not raised again.

After another year, the word had spread in the news about the Wicker and Docker Mining Company's potential sale of redevelopment interests. Sophie knew all about Don's interest of forty percent. The holding had never produced any income—another pipe dream, Sophie had thought. Now with the possible sale of the company complete, the figures being talked about were staggering. However, Sophie was a realist and thought everything was exaggerated, which, of course, it was.

She mentioned it to Frank in a weak moment, showing off about her love for Don, saying, "I could do with a share of that money when the mine is sold."

As soon as she'd said it, she realized she should have kept her mouth shut because Frank wouldn't let the subject drop before he had found out all about it. She had never told him about Don's gold mine shares—there had been no need, and it was none of his business—but now she had to tell him.

At first, he was very quiet, thinking about what he had heard, but then he said, "This completely changes things." Sophie could see dollar signs in his eyes; they reminded her of Don's eyes before he had left for the Klondike. *What is it with men?* she thought.

"Why does it make a difference? The money is not mine," Sophie said casually, hoping Frank would drop the subject.

"Well, we don't know that, do we? It may be Don is already dead; the money would come to you then," said Frank. He paused and then said, "In any event, it would now be worth your while to divorce him. The money will be beneficial for us."

Sophie didn't like the way the conversation was going. She noted that he'd said "will" rather than "would." She changed the subject, but Frank didn't forget it. Over the next few months, he kept bringing up the possibility of Don's death. Once, he even mentioned to Sophie, "If he hasn't died, maybe we should help things along."

Sophie was stunned, and she made it clear that this was not an option. The deal was finalized two months later at the mining company, the sale was closed, and the money was paid into an escrow account. The attorney acting for the mining company sent a letter to Don at the only address they had for him, explaining what had happened. They held his share of the proceeds, four hundred thousand dollars, and waited for his instructions.

CHAPTER TWELVE

All this time, Don had been panning for gold in the Klondike. When he'd arrived, having ridden from Vancouver, he'd been full of enthusiasm. He knew he would succeed in his efforts. He still had some food left over from that given to him by the stable owner's wife, but he knew he had to establish a home amongst all these tents lining the river and spreading far back as well.

He rode into the makeshift town, not knowing what to expect. There were many shops, hardly more than sheds, selling everything needed in day-to-day life. The roads were dirt tracks. It was a wet day when he arrived, and the tracks had turned to mud. The horse was having difficulty walking in the thick mud, but Don managed to find a side road that was not used much to get to the corral. The owner told Don there would be no charge if he provided the horse feed. Don readily agreed and left his horse there.

He checked in his pocket and found that he had very little money left, so he needed to find work before he started anything. He went from shop to shop and managed to get an hour's work here and there.

Don had managed to earn a few dollars on the journey doing odd jobs for people, and he had just enough to purchase a small tent for himself, which he erected on the only space he could find that day. He collected his mining equipment for the next few days, mainly from items left behind when other miners had given up and gone home. Sometimes he was paid for his work in the shops; other times, he took goods and food.

Don built up his home, and by the end of the week, he had enough equipment to start work. Spaces on the river were very territorial. Each miner had what he regarded as his own territory, and if anyone moved in on it, there would be a fight, often resulting in death when someone had a gun. Don found a space between two other tents, and he set up his camp.

For five days, he worked alone. His neighbors were not friendly, so he kept to himself. He hears lots of arguments around town, but he ignored them, thinking it was safer that way. He just wanted to make enough money to get back to Sophie, whom he had been missing a lot lately.

He panned for gold in the daytime and drank at night in the bar tent, spending the small amount of gold flakes he had on drinks and food. Like all taverns in history, women gravitated to bars, looking for men to give them a few cents for the use of their bodies. Initially, Don was not tempted in that direction, but like most men, he eventually succumbed.

It is only sex, he told himself, but the girl was one of the prettier ones. She said she was only twenty years old, but Don thought she was older. He said to a miner later that the feel of her skin was older than that of a twenty-year-old girl, but he didn't mind; she only filled a need at that time. He loved his Sophie, and she would forever be the only love of his life. It worked for the girl as well; she also had other men, although she always said that Don was her beau.

Gold was very scarce in the area, so he had little to spend on luxuries, but one evening, a newcomer walked into the bar. He appeared to have more money than most, but Don kept to himself at his favorite corner table. The other drinkers left him alone, and though he was getting lonely, he didn't want to be played for the little money he had. There was always gambling in such places, mainly poker, and some people were experts; they were professional gamblers, not miners.

The newcomer recognized that Don was a loner, but the tent was getting full, so he walked over to him and said in a broad Welsh accent, "The tent is busy tonight. Is it always like this? Perhaps I could join you at your table.'

"Gladly," said Don, who felt like company. "My name is Don."

"I'm Taffy. Sorry about the accent, but I come from Wales."

"You are a long way from home, then, Taffy," said Don, who was having difficulty understanding the strange accent.

"I know, but I had to leave Wales, you know," Taffy said. "I was on the run, and it seemed a good idea for me to join the gold rush. I was involved in the gold mine industry, if you can call it that, in Wales. When my problems started, I took a job on an Atlantic steamship heading for America, and here I am."

"I don't know Wales, but it joins England, doesn't it?"

"That's right, but we like to say England joins us; it's a matter of pride, you know." Taffy grinned and then added, "Have you been lucky with your mining?"

"Not really, just a few flakes every day, but I will say it isn't mining as such; it's merely panning for gold in the river. A few flakes if you are lucky. What type of mining is it in Wales?"

"It's not like that; it is drilling into a mountain and hacking it out of the rocks, but you are working for the mining company, not for yourself."

"Isn't there a temptation for you to run off with some of the odd flakes that get left behind at the end of the day?"

Taffy laughed. "Yes, that's why I had to leave in a hurry. The company has stringent rules and police to enforce them, brutally if necessary. If you are caught stealing, it's prison for life; that is, if they don't kill you during the arrest. They just throw away the key. I was concerned about coming into this country, you know, what with this new radio communication. I thought the authorities might be waiting for me at the dock in New York. So, I jumped ship outside of the harbor."

Don smiled. "I doubt whether they would have known, but the swim probably did you good."

"It was bloody cold, and I know that." And now Taffy had to laugh.

They spent the evening drinking, and they got on well together, laughing at each other's jokes. Towards the end of the evening, Taffy said, "I have this large tent that would hold two people easily, and it is so bloody cold out here that two people sharing a tent would make it warmer, wouldn't it?"

"I suppose it would. Do you want me to share with you?" said Don, who liked his evening with Taffy and thought it might work. In any case, what did he have to lose?

"Why not? We seem to get on well together, even if I can't understand some of your words. The problem is, I speak the Queen's English," Taffy said with a snigger.

They left the bar tent, and Taffy showed Don where his tent was, stuck behind many others at the back of the tented area. Don said, "Why don't we move your tent down to where mine is on the riverfront? It would be more convenient, and we will have access to the river frontage, which we can claim as ours, and share the proceeds."

"Sounds good to me," Taffy said as he slapped Don on the back in friendship. They took Don's small tent and replaced it with Taffy's larger one. After an hour, it was all done, and Taffy agreed that Don's position was much better. It was freezing outside, but Taffy was correct: two people sharing the tent seemed to warm it somewhat. The heat was mainly supplied by either expensive candles or an oil lamp. Taffy agreed that a candle might cause fire, so they traded Don's tent for an oil lamp and oil.

"I noticed some girls in the bar tent, parading their wares, with lowcut blouses that bearly cover the dark nipples. I have to admit I haven't had a woman for weeks," said Taffy.

"Yes, there are several girls who will satisfy your needs for a few cents. I visit one when I can afford it, or when the need is great," said Don.

"I'll try it out tomorrow. Perhaps you can show me the best. I have always found that many of these women are more interested in other women than men, but occasionally you find one that really enjoys it."

"Tomorrow, then. I'll treat myself as well. Talking about it turns me on," said Don, and they both laughed.

The next night, they took their pleasures. Taffy was pleased with his new girl, Annie, who had dark hair and large breasts and nipples that delighted him. She enjoyed their time together, too, so much so that she only charged him half her usual fee.

Over the weeks that followed, Don and Taffy became very close. They shared everything, including the gold flakes they panned, but that only paid for the essentials and occasionally an evening with the girls.

One overcast and chilly day, Don told Taffy that he would not be panning. He still had chilblains on his hands from weeks of work and he did not want to get them wet. Taffy said he understood, "What are you planning to do?" he asked.

"I just need a quiet day to get rid of these bloody chilblains. I'll have a walk around town. When we work every day, we don't see anything other than the river!" Don said.

"Do you want any company, my friend?"

"No thanks, Taffy. It will be good for me to have a quiet day."

"I understand, buddy. Enjoy." Taffy went off to his usual panning site.

Don was pleased that Taffy understood. *He's a good man*, thought Don. He put on in his heavy overcoat, which he had recently purchased, and felt good with himself and warm inside. He hadn't felt like that for a long time. Although he enjoyed Taffy's company immensely, he missed Sophie tremendously. He thought about her every minute he was awake and would dream of her at night.

Today he planned to relax. He went to several stores to see what was new and decided that there was nothing; he has seen all the goods for weeks now. The town was relatively quiet, as most of the men were out at the river, panning. A few women were shopping for essentials.

The ground was reasonably dry, as it had not rained heavily for some time, although it looked as though it might. Thick black clouds were gathering above, masking the sun.

Don knew most of the men by sight, even if he didn't know their names, and he would raise his hat to them as he passed. Nearly all the men were dressed in blue jeans and a thick cotton shirt. Everyone wore a hat to keep their head warm. That was where most heat was lost.

After walking down three streets of stores and the back line of tents for prospectors who could not get near the river, Don noticed someone, a man who looked out of place. He wasn't sure why he noticed him. The man was dressed like the other men in town, but he had on a full-length leather coat and a hat to match, which stood out from the miners' cloth outfits. There was something else about him as well, but Don couldn't put his finger on it. The man looked around all the time as though searching for someone. Don thought he would follow him. He had nothing else to do, and it would pass the time.

Don could still not figure out why the man looked different, and then it dawned on him. The man did not look like a miner. First, he was dressed in better-quality clothing, and second, his hands looked like he had never done any physical work. He definitely did not have a miner's hands, scratched and full of chilblains, so who was he?

Don thought he would find out, and he caught up with the man from behind. The man could hear Don coming from the sloshing of his boots in the mud. He turned and said, "Good morning, sir. Are you one of the miners?"

"I am, indeed, sir. My name is Don Wicker." Don noticed that the man's speech was very well polished, much too good for a miner. He also saw that when the man turned, his coat opened, revealing a gun holster.

Don was apprehensive. No one in town wore guns, and it was frowned upon by the police officer of the Northwest Mounted Police, who had told the miners earlier in the year, "If you wear guns, then eventually someone is going to get shot, and I don't want that on my patch."

This stranger was secretive in that he did not say what he was doing in the Klondike, but he did say his name was Robert Dogood. And as he said it, he doffed his hat. Don asked him precisely what he was doing in town. "You do not look like a miner."

Robert was slow to respond, and when he did, he did not answer the question directly, saying that he was on a touring vacation and wanted to see how the miners lived. Don did not believe him. Robert had allowed his coat to close over his holster, and Don was relieved by that.

Robert looked about him as though he was concerned someone might be watching. He then said, "Actually, I am a private detective with the New York Investigations Agency."

"Very impressive. Have you met our police officer here? He is an accommodating man." Don said.

"I have not as yet. We investigators tend to work on our own. I am looking for three people who are of interest to the agency. Maybe you could help me identify them. I assume they are miners. There is no other reason anyone would be here, is there?"

"Who are you looking for?" Don inquired, beginning to dislike the stranger.

Robert studied Don's eye reactions as he said, "I'm looking for John Doe, Chuck Evans, and Taffy Jones."

Now, Don knew that John Doe was a term used by the police for unidentified bodies, which meant it must be a lie. He had no idea who Chuck Evans was, but he knew he'd looked surprised at the mention of Taffy's name. Robert picked up on it straight away but said nothing. Don realized he had to do something to protect Taffy.

"John Doe is a common name. I'm sure there must be several in town. Taffy Jones sounds very Welsh to me. I would recognize anyone with that strong accent, although there are a couple of Welshmen around town. I had a friend in San Fransisco once who was Welsh. I could never understand a word he said. Chuck Evans, no, I don't know him." Don guessed the detective didn't believe him about Taffy. "What have they all done? You are a long way from home. These people must be significant."

"Various forms of theft, mainly, and my agency will chase our men to the ends of the earth if necessary."

'Well, I wish you luck."

"Thanks, Don. I certainly do not want to hang around this godforsaken hole longer than is necessary," Robert said, and he walked off.

Don stood there for a few minutes, thinking, as Robert squelched through the mud in his riding boots. When Robert got to the end of the block, he turned and saw Don still standing where he'd left him. That made him think, *Don knows more than he's admitting.*

Don knew he had to warn Taffy, but he knew Robert would follow if he went to see Taffy now. He went to their tent and wrote a note to Taffy to meet him at the clothing shop when he could, but he added, "Be careful. There is a detective here looking for you."

Don spent the rest of the day walking around. He noticed Robert was following him, so he took him on a wild goose chase. By the end of the day, as he suspected, Robert had had enough of that exercise, and it was almost time for Taffy to finish his day's work. The clothing shop was on the edge of town, not far from their tent, and Don thought he could head there and still see if Robert was following him.

Robert had given up for the time being, and as Don arrived at the shop, Taffy walked up, too. They went around the corner, where they could not be seen. Don said, "This chap Robert from the New York Investigations Agency is in town, and he is looking for you. I think he suspects that I know you. Sorry about that, but I was surprised when he said your name, and I am sure he picked up on it."

"Damn," said Taffy. "It's not your fault; it's probably about me jumping ship outside of New York." Taffy was quiet for a moment, and then he said, "Look, I think I need to move out of the tent until this is resolved. I'll see if I can stay with that pretty wench we have spent time with. What does this detective look like?"

"Well, just like anyone else, to tell you the truth, but he does wear a leather coat and hat," said Don.

"I'll slip off now. It is getting dark. You know where Annie lives, don't you?"

"Yes, and I'll come around to you every evening until we can work out how to get rid of this detective. Do you have a gun? The detective is wearing a gun holster."

Taffy nodded.

CHAPTER THIRTEEN

Taffy went the back way to Annie's shack, and she was delighted that he was moving in. He impressed upon her that she must not mention he was with her. "Look, for the time being, I will use the name Joseph, and I will have to stay inside until this detective is dealt with."

The next day, Don went about his business like usual, panning in the river. He had a good day and managed to collect half an inch of flakes in the jar he kept for his gold. He noticed Robert Dogood pass nearby several times during the day, obviously searching for Taffy and the other guy if he existed. Don wondered how he would know what Taffy looked like. Don had not given him a description, nor had the inspector asked for one. *How strange*, he thought.

During the day, Taffy had plenty of time to think. Annie had gone to the bar tent to get things ready for the evening's entertainment. He paced the room. It was small, but it was better than a tent. He knew he had to deal with the inspector situation. In his first encounter with the inspector in New York, Taffy had been lucky to get away, and he knew he could not rely on luck all the time. *I have to have a plan*, he thought. *I need Don's help.*

Don stopped work early, collected his gold jar, went to the gold assay office, and cashed in his day's collections. He was pleased with the day's result. He stopped at the gun shop next door and bought a rifle, handgun, and ammunition for each. He covered the rifle with a blanket in case he bumped into the inspector on the way out.

After checking that the road was clear, he walked briskly to Annie's room. Taffy saw him coming and held the door open for him.

"Good to see you, friend," Taffy said. "I have been thinking all day that I need to do something about this inspector. He will not go away."

"I agree," said Don as he uncovered his new rifle.

Taffy looked at him. "I'm afraid it's the only way, but I don't want you getting into trouble over me."

"We'll have to be very careful, then."

"Do you have a plan? I see you are well armed."

"I have been watching this inspector. I am sure he is here alone. He wears a gun holster, but I have not seen him carry a rifle. He claims to be looking for two people, Chuck Evans and you. We don't want to have a gunfight in town. The police would get involved, and things would escalate. So, why don't we encourage him out of town somehow to meet you or this Chuck and then ambush him on the way?"

Taffy quietly took this all in. "It might work, but how are we to convince the inspector to venture out of town? He will be suspicious."

"Ah, that is the problem that needs working on. I need to spend tomorrow riding in the hills and choosing a suitable place."

They spent the rest of the evening discussing a plan, and they agreed that Don would have to do the reconnoitering, as Taffy could not be seen outside for now.

The next day, as Don left his tent, he noticed that Robert was watching from a distance. He got his horse from the corral and rode out of town, towards the hills upriver. He was surprised that the inspector did not follow, although he had anticipated that.

He rode along the river as it went through a gorge in the hillside. There was a severe drop down to the water, about two hundred feet. He stopped and looked over the top, stepping back quickly as he realized he did not like the height.

Behind him, he saw a copse of large Maple and pine trees. He rode along the narrow track and shortly found a small hamlet of six houses. He rode down to the hamlet, where a lady from one of the houses was in her garden, tending the plants. Don stopped his horse and went over to her. He doffed his cap and said, "Good morning, madam. You have a beautiful garden. This is an attractive little village. What is it called?"

"Thank you, young man," she said politely. "The village is called Miners Creek. We only named it a month ago. I take it you're from the mining site at Dawson," she added, wanting to chat to break her loneliness.

"I am, indeed, and I thought I would take a rest day today and explore the countryside."

"You know, my husband says you are all wasting your time down there, panning in the river. The gold comes from up here in the mountains, so wouldn't it be more sensible to mine up here? The gorge you just rode through would be the place where the flakes you pan for probably originate."

"That makes sense," Don said, and he doffed his cap and left her to ride back over the gorge to Dawson. He passed the wooded area again and stopped his horse. Selecting a large pine tree just off the track, he climbed up to a limb twenty feet above the ground. The height thing kicked in, but he persevered, and after ten minutes, he felt comfortable. *This will do*, he thought, and then he climbed down. As he did, he saw a cave entrance through the trees.

He could not see the cave from the ground, but he found it after walking through the pine trees. He went to the entrance and peered in; it was pitch black inside. Taking a few steps in, he called out, and the echo reverberated down what he decided was a long cave. He smiled, thinking, *This could be useful.* Then he jumped back as a native Indian walked out from the depths of the cave. The Indian was dressed in casual clothes, not dissimilar to what Don was wearing, but he did have a feather in his headband.

The Indian held up his hand as though to stop Don from going any further and said in English, "This is a burial site for my tribe. You are not allowed here."

"I am sorry," said Don, and he bowed slightly. They both backed out of the cave, and the Indian left, taking a path up the mountain.

Don was relieved, and remembering what the lady had said to him about the mountain's gold, he walked back to his horse and headed home. When he returned to town, he did not see the inspector. That evening, after making sure no one was watching him, Don went to Annie's home. Taffy was getting bored with being stuck inside, and he was glad to see Don.

"I think I have a plan," said Don. "There is a small hamlet of six houses on the other side of a gorge up the river. On top of the gorge is a copse of oak trees that would make a good place for me to hide in with my rifle. By the way, I am a good shot. We need to get the inspector up there. How about if I go to him and say I have heard you are staying in one of those houses. I could ask for money to make it more convincing."

"Yes, but how are we to get him there at a particular time?" said Taffy. "No, wait. I don't want you committing murder. It's bad enough that I am a felon, but I don't want to make you one, my friend. How about I be in the tree with the rifle, and you can escort the inspector on the pretext of showing him the hideout."

"That should work," said Don. He was pleased; he did not want to be a felon either.

They spent the rest of the evening working on their plan, allowing for things that might go wrong. By the end of the evening, they had it all arranged, and Don went back to his tent after first making sure the inspector did not see him leaving Taffy's hideout.

The next day, Don saw the inspector patrolling Main Street, as he continually did, and he went up to him and said, "Any luck finding the people you are looking for?"

"Not yet. But I don't give up. I will make it worth your while if you tell me where Taffy Jones is. Several people have said you know him."

"I don't know him personally, but I might know where he is hiding. I met someone yesterday who implied as much. There are not that many Welshmen in this area. What's in it for me?"

"A hundred dollars when we go and another hundred if we get him."

"Right. I heard he is in a village nearby. Meet me at five o'clock here, on a horse, and bring the money."

"I'll be here."

During the day, Don called in on Annie at the bar tent and gave her a note for Taffy telling him to be in the tree as arranged at five o'clock. He added at the bottom, "Don't forget the rifle."

Annie delivered the note, and Taffy asked her to bring his horse to the back of the room she rented in a small guest house. After an hour, the horse was in place, and Taffy waited, watching for the inspector. At three o'clock, he decided to leave for the prearranged ambush site, and he slipped out to the rear of the building. He put the rifle in its pouch on the saddle, and then he climbed on and rode out toward the hills Don had indicated. He found the wooded area and hitched his horse well back from the track, behind a clump of trees.

He found a suitable tree, probably the one Don had climbed because it was in the best position for their action, and climbed up with the rifle. Heights did not bother him, so he settled comfortably on the large branch twenty feet off the ground. He aimed the rifle along the track to see where his best shot would be. Finally, he decided on a place close enough not to miss, and if he did, a second shot could be fired while the inspector was still in shock.

If that happened, then Don would fire from close range with his pistol.

Taffy was happy with his arrangements, and although the wait concerned him, it was not long before he could see two horses coming along the track towards him. He had to make sure that these were the two men he was waiting for. It was still light, but the sun is beginning to set below the horizon. Soon he could clearly see the leather coat of the inspector as they got nearer.

Don had dropped back slightly to give Taffy a better shot. *Now is the time,* he thought as he felt for the pistol in his pocket.

The inspector saw that Don had dropped back, and he stopped and turned toward him. "Hurry up. It will be dark soon," he said.

At that moment, a shot rang out. Taffy was grateful the inspector had stopped; it gave him the perfect shot. The bullet hit the back of the inspector's head, killing him instantly, and he fell off the horse, which bolted at the sound of the gunshot.

Don got down from his horse, comforted it, and checked to make sure the inspector was dead. By this time, Taffy had climbed down from the tree, and he came running over to Don.

They went through the inspector's pockets. In one was an envelope with a hundred dollars, and in the other was his detective badge. Don kept both items, saying to Taffy, "That is beer money for some time. Now, what are we to do with the body?"

At one side of the track was a ravine going straight down to the Klondike River. "We could drop him into the river. The trouble is, the body will be discovered in town within a few hours, and many people know he was looking for me," said Taffy.

"I agree. That is not a good idea. I know. There is a cave at the back of the trees. We should take him there. It is an Indian burial site, so that would be appropriate," Don said with a wry smile.

"That sounds more like it. It's unlikely anyone will be exploring that, and if we lodge a claim up here, that will give us extra protection."

The inspector was wearing his leather coat, which made it easier for them to drag him to the trees, where they found the inspector's horse. They tied up the horse, which was calmer now, and pulled the inspector's body to the cave behind the trees.

Outside, they saw a pile of stones three feet high, and on top was an old human skull. "What is that, Don?" said Taffy, disturbed by the sight.

"No idea, Taffy, but maybe that is where the Indian is buried," Don said.

Higher up the mountain behind an overhanging rock is a Native Indian, he is smoking one of his roll-up cigarettes. He makes them very thin so that his tobacco lasts longer. His duty today for the tribe is to watch over the burial site of the tribe. It is a tiresome task, and hence the cigarette. No one ever comes near here, but today there are three people in the vicinity.

He lays down his cigarette on the side of the rock, not wanting to put it out, but he needed both hands to hold the telescope that the tribe chief had loaned him to watch in detail what is happening.

Don and Taffy drag the body into the cave until it was out of sight from the entrance.

Taffy is relieved the inspector was dead. He had been following Taffy all across America. They sat by the trees to catch their breath. "Thanks, Don. I certainly owe you, my friend."

"That's what real friends are for," Don said, but he was thinking of Sophie as he said it.

All of this was watched by the Indian from his vantage point. When the intruders had gone, he finished his cigarette, rode back to his tribal village, and reported what he had seen to the chief.

The chief immediately called for a council meeting, which declared that the burial site must be abandoned as it had been desecrated by the addition of a dead white man.

Meanwhile, Don and Taffy took the Inspector's horse back to town, making sure that nothing on it could be traced back to the inspector. Taffy moved back into the tent with Don, and life returned to normal for a couple of months.

Don thought about what the lady from the village had said about the gold being in the mountains, and he called into the claims office one day and submitted a claim on the area where the cave was. *Maybe the woman's husband is right.*

They had two hundred dollars for beer money, which lasted several months. Winter set in, and the cold was severe. Taffy, in particular, was feeling it. He remarked several times, "This cold is getting into my bones. I don't think my body was made for this. I'm not working tomorrow, and I'll spend the day resting if that is possible in this godforsaken hole."

Neither of them could get off the sleep that night, and Don wondered if he had too much to drink, or perhaps he had not had enough. He spoke to Taffy, saying, 'Are you asleep yet, Taffy?"

"No, my body aches all over. It's keeping me awake."

'Sorry to hear that, Taff, but as we are both awake, tell me, have you ever been in love? Don says.

Taffy manages a laugh, thinking I'm glad I can still laugh. "Well, since you ask, I was in love once with a girl from my village in Wales, the trouble was that I was twenty-two and she was seventeen. Her mother was horrified when I said we wanted to get married. Her family was pretty wealthy, and they shipped her away within days to an aunt in London. I had no money so that I couldn't follow her. She was a pretty thing, though, and I often wonder what happened to her in later life. The other problem was she came from a Catholic family, and I was brought up protestant. It's terrible that religion rules our lives, isn't it?"

"I agree. Fortunately, I did not have those problems over here, although religion is taken seriously. Catholic and protestant religions don't matter. After all, both are Christain. Even the Jewish religion is the old testament in the bible, so what the hell?" said Don.

"My Sophie has been the only girl for me. We met young and fell in love straight away. Our problem has always been money or its lack, which is the only reason I am here today. I promised her a better life when I married her. I just need to make a sizeable find. I won't be greedy, just a little. I lay awake here often and think of her. If I concentrate hard enough, I can visualize her on the roof of the tent. Her picture is very bold, isn't that funny?" says Don.

'I don't think it's funny. In fact, I think it's beautiful, and secretly I will admit, I wish I had someone that I could visualize on that roof." Says Taffy.

"I can see my Sophie now, and she is smiling down at me," Don says.

Taffy did not reply, and Don could hear from Taffy's gentle snore that he is asleep. It was not long after that don drifted off to sleep as well. The next day Taffy did not work, which was just as well as it rained all day. Taffy slept it off and felt better for that by the evening. Don is concerned that Taffy might have the flu or something.

A few days later, Taffy started to cough; he always apologized to Don at night for keeping him awake, but Don told him not to worry. After a few drinks, Don slept like a log once he got off. They spent all day panning for gold and had limited success, but nothing like the fortune that Don had promised Sophie. Taffy's cough did not improve; sadly, it seemed to get worse. There was no doctor in the makeshift town, so all aches and pains had to be self-treated.

"I'll be fine," Taffy would reply when Don urged him to leave town and find a doctor, but the coughing grew worse.

For weeks, Don's fears about the illness were confirmed when Taffy coughed up blood. Don had seen something like this in San Francisco when a pal had died from consumption. The doctor had told Don there was no cure.

Taffy deteriorated quickly, no doubt due to the harsh conditions they were living in. Annie often came to see him and comforted him through his illness. Taffy was coughing up blood regularly now and choking it.

One morning, he knew the end was nigh. He could only speak quietly, and he beckoned Don to come near. Although they shared the tent, they each had their own cupboard to store personal belongings.

Don leaned over Taffy so his friend could speak more easily. "I know the end is coming now," Taffy whispered while coughing up blood, "and I wanted to thank you for looking after me at the end. Your friendship has been a godsend. Please take anything you want of mine when I am gone, and open that drawer in the cupboard there."

Don went to the drawer and opened it. Inside was a jar full of flakes of what appeared to be gold. He took it to Taffy, who said, "I want you to have this. I can't take it with me, can I, you bugger? This is what that inspector was after all that time ago." He tried to laugh, but it did not come out.

Don took the jar and squeezed Taffy's hand. He could feel his eyes watering. Taffy opened his eyes once more and whispered, "Goodbye, old friend." And his eyes close for the last time.

Taffy was buried in the town cemetery. There are only two people at the funeral, Don, and Annie. The priest said a few words and comforted Annie, holding her close to him. Don was devastated at the loss of Taffy; although they had only known each other for a few months, they had become very close.

Don said to the priest, "I don't think I can stay here any longer. There is no gold to speak of, and the loss of Taffy has really affected me, although I only knew him a year or so. I need to move on. I hear there is a new gold rush happening at Nome in Alaska. I think I will move on there."

The priest said, "It is often a good thing to move on in these circumstances. Make a new life. God bless you, my son." He left Annie and Don at the graveside to share their personal losses.

"Did you see how the priest held me just then? I thought he was going to grab my tits," said Annie, forcing a smile.

This made Don laugh, the first time he had done so in days. Annie added, "I wouldn't have minded if he had asked, but he wouldn't have wanted to pay for it. He would think I owed it to him for his religious services. The dirty bugger." She began laughing loudly, too.

Don said, "Taffy would have been happy that we could laugh like this at his funeral. He was a really good man. I will miss him tremendously."

Annie embraced Don, and he could feel her tits and hard nipples against his chest. She whispered, "I think we should go back to bed and have one last one for Taffy on the house." They did just that and parted company afterward.

Wasting no time, Don left the Klondike the next day. He took all of Taffy's possessions, some of which he traded for an additional horse to carry his extra belongings. He had managed to provide food for his original horse all this time, so the hostler was happy. He set off early that morning and rode up to Nome with his pair of horses, including the extra one from the inspector.

CHAPTER FOURTEEN

Sophie opened the letter from the Wicker and Docker Mining company's attorney, addressed to Don when she went on one of her excursions to the old house. She read it with excitement and took it back to her new home with Frank. She had always known she must have a place to hide things if necessary, and she placed the letter in the secret drawer of her dresser.

Unbeknownst to Sophie, Frank had seen her going to that drawer in the past, and he checked it at least once a week. When she was at work one day, he did his usual inspection of the drawer and found the letter. Reading it carefully, he decided to take matters into his own hands. If Don were dead, the money would automatically go to his wife. If he was not dead already, then Frank needed to speed things along.

The trouble was, and he realized it, if the money went to Sophie, she might dump him. She had always said she would not marry him. Frank knew he needed a plan to keep her attached to him. He decided to work on that.

He set about planning a trip up north to the Klondike. He didn't know where Don was precisely, nor did he know where the Klondike was, except that it was in Canada. But the Klondike would be a good start. Someone there must know of Don's whereabouts; he'd certainly gone there all those years ago.

Frank knew the area he needed to go to was in the wilds of northern Canada. He had to come up with a good excuse for Sophie. He knew he could not tell her the truth or even part of it; she would never forgive him. They had discussed the possibility, but she had ruled it out.

He knew he had to do this on his own, so that evening, he said to Sophie over their meal, "I have heard in the mail that my great aunt who lives in Seattle is dying. She is not expected to last longer than a month. I was always her favorite nephew, and I think she will leave me some money when she goes, so I have to see her before she dies. I plan to leave tomorrow if that is alright with you."

"Oh, I am so sorry to hear that, Frank. I know you have mentioned your aunt in the past. Of course, you must go to her. I hope you get to her in time. How are you getting there? I think the new railway line extension is open now, which will cut the journey down considerably. Please give her my wishes, and I am sorry I never got to meet her."

"Yes, I'll go by rail, but I expect to be away for several months. I will stay until she goes."

The following day, Frank set off, but not for Seattle; he was going up the coast to the Klondike. He sailed from San Francisco to Vancouver. He thought the ticket's investment would pay off in the long run. At Vancouver, like Don, he purchased a horse for the long ride to the Klondike; that trip took him four weeks. He was glad to arrive at Dawson City, which was beginning to grow. Frank had a sore bum from riding on the horse every day.

He'd remarked to a fellow traveler, a prospector, that he met along the way, "How do these cowboys stay in the saddle for weeks on end?" He'd passed many cowboys en route but had never stopped to ask them.

"No idea," the traveler had said, but he'd walked away with a limp, which had said it all.

Frank spent the next four days making inquiries with the miners about Don Wicker. It was a big task due to the size of the town. Several people knew of Don by name but had no idea where he was. Some sent Frank in one direction, saying try so and so, while others sent him in another.

He was beginning to wonder whether this trip would fail. Then he found one miner who had been in the tent next to Don; he said that Don had been staying with a Welshman called Taffy a couple of years ago, but no one knew where he was now. He'd heard that Taffy had died, and Don had become disillusioned.

"I know the feeling," Frank said with a grin. He had now established that Don must still be alive somewhere, or at least, he had been a couple of years ago.

At the end of the seventh day in town, he found someone else who had been panning for gold at the site next to Don's. The miner stated that Don had become disillusioned with the Klondike after his good friend Taffy's death and had heard of new gold discoveries at Nome in Alaska so he'd moved on to there.

Frank decided that he must go up to Nome; he spent the next two weeks traveling by horseback. It was an arduous journey across Alaska; he had to go up and down mountains to get to the coast. Once again, his butt was sore.

Don had made the same journey some months ago and was now established in Nome. After a week or so of doing the same things he'd done in the Klondike, Don concluded that he was wasting his time and life. He'd only managed to collect a few gold flakes, no more than he needed for everyday living, and this time, he had no company, having lost Taffy.

The evenings were again spent in the bar tent, where the girls offered the same services as in the Klondike. Don enjoyed sitting at a table and watching them as they lifted their blouses to show off their tits, hoping to earn some money. He ate in the tent every night; they served Chinese food, which he adored. The cook was a young Chinese lady named Susy Wong. She was a pretty young thing, very slender. Her mother worked in the kitchen as well, but she was fat. Don couldn't help but think that the daughter would turn out like her mom one day.

Susy clearly fancied Don. She would come out from the kitchen, which was just a compartment at the back of the tent, and come over to him with dished she had made especially for him, and she did not charge him. Don knew no one did anything for nothing out there, and she had ulterior motives, but he wasn't having any of it. She wasn't his type; he liked his women a little meatier.

He had his favorite girl to watch, though, and at times, he wanted to hold her breasts, but money was tight, and he was getting disillusioned with being a miner. It was not what he'd expected.

One night, the only table available in the bar tent was one next to the wheel of fortune gambling table. The owner of the machine and his lady tried to entice Don into having a go.

"It's only twenty cents," the girl said as she pushed out her chest, revealing her large nipples through her tight-fitting blouse. At first, Don refused, but then she came and sat on his lap. She could see that Don was interested in her body, and she whispered in his ear, "I'm a free woman. He's just my fancy man at the moment, but I'm tiring of him." She pushed her breasts against his chest.

He was aroused, and when no one was looking, he touched her breasts. She moaned with pleasure, saying, "I can feel your hardness on my leg." As she wiggled around more to enhance the feelings for them both.

Don knew it was a put-on, but it was enough for him to say, "Alright, I'll spin the wheel," and he gave her his last twenty cents. She got off his lap and looked down at his bulging jeans. He stood and spun the wheel as fast as he could. The ratchet made considerable noise as the wheel turned.

The man called out to the crowd, "I think we have a winner here. Come on, folks. Let's see you all try." The wheel seemed to rotate forever, but eventually, it slowed down, and the pointer spun nearer the word "Jackpot." Just three spaces away now, and the pointer slowed even more. Two spaces now, and then it stopped on "Jackpot." A loud bell rang out, and the girl said, "You've won," almost as though it was an impossibility. She had a big smile on her face as she went to Don and kissed him.

The machine owner was pissed off at having to give out the jackpot, but he went around to the back of the machine and returned with a wad of money. "Here we are, sir, the jackpot." He handed the cash to Don. Then he said loudly, "Anyone else now? We have one winner; let's make it two." Needless to say, he didn't want any more winners.

Don took the roll of money and left the tent. The girl followed him out. "Hold on. It's Don, isn't it?" she said.

"Yes, that's my name," Don said. As she caught up to him, he clutched his winnings tightly in his pocket, fearing that she was coming to rob him.

She said, " I can help you spend that money, you know. It will be worth your while."

Don looked down at her blouse and saw the top buttons were now undone, and her cleavage was showing so much that the tops of her nipples were exposed, but he knew the temptation would be too much and he would lose all the money, and he had other ideas for what do with it. Now he could get back to his beloved Sophie.

"Sorry, love," he said, "but I have other plans." He left her standing there and went back to his tent. After making sure no one was watching, he buried the money in back of it.

The next day, Don went shopping for a surprise for Sophie. He went to the bank and put in a deposit box the balance of the money and his other belongings. He was becoming disillusioned with Nome; he realized that mining was not what he'd expected, and he missed his Sophie.

The weather was dreadful. Although it was summer, it rained every day and was so cold that snow blanketed the mountains. Eventually, Frank arrived in Nome. His first impression was that one mining site looked like another, filthy and muddy.

Tents had been haphazardly erected all over the town; most miners wanted to be near their claim, so they pitched their tent on top of it. In Nome, most of the gold was found on the beach, which was completely dug up, and most miners' tents were erected there.

Frank thought the easiest way to find Don would be to go to the mine registration office, so that's where he went. "Hello, my name is Chuck Smith," he said, thinking it better not to use his real name, "and I'm looking for Don Wicker. He's about my age. Can you help me, please?"

The clerk was about twenty-five, rough and ready. No one wanted his job, including him, but he did his best. He went through his cards, looking for the name. "Ah, here it is. He is on lot AH2."

"Where on earth is that?" said Frank.

The clerk smiled. "I take your point. Here, let me show you," He took Frank out of the office and pointed in the direction of the beach.

"Thank you," said Frank, and he gave the clerk a dollar tip, one that he had stolen that morning. The clerk was very pleased. No one ever tipped him.

Frank went down to the beach. A few men were panning for gold as the tide came in and out. He guessed one of them was Don, but which one? He had never met Don.

In the meantime, back in San Francisco, Sophie had become worried about Frank. She had expected him to return within three months or so, but now he'd been gone for a year. She searched the house high and low for the letter about his aunt dying. She could not find it, but she did locate another letter, written two months ago, saying that his aunt was in good health for her age.

Sophie became concerned that Frank had tricked her. Why would he do that? She thought of what Frank had said about Don. There was nothing she could do.

Frank went up to one of the miners and said, "Do you know a Don Wicker?"

"I do. That's me. What can I do for you?" said Don.

"Good to meet you. I am taking up mining here, and someone mentioned your name. They said that you and I come from San Fransisco, so I wanted to say hello," said Frank.

Don was glad to stop and chat for a while with an old "neighbor," though he had never met Frank before. He told Frank that he could sleep in his tent until Frank got his own setup. Frank said he was grateful; this was just what he needed for his deed.

Don had not been lucky mining gold in the Klondike, and he'd had only had some minor luck in Nome. He decided to call it a day and head back to San Fransisco.

He'd written a letter to Sophie a few days before telling her that he would be heading home in a few days; he needed to sort a few things out with his bank deposit. Don put the letter in the mail. Two days later, Frank suggested he would treat Don to a drink session that night; Don jumped at the offer, as he had been saving his money for his trip home.

The mining community had few things to offer in the way of entertainment. There were two merchant shops, the bar and, of course, the brothel. Don didn't visit the latter for fear of disease. There were always women plying their wares. In these situations, rates were low, just a few cents to buy food and drink.

That evening, Frank took Don to the makeshift bar set up in one of the tents, and they had a skinful. Frank was secretly drinking apple juice but making sure Don had plenty of beer. They left at midnight and swaggered back to their tent. Frank was acting somewhat drunk, but he was sober enough for what he planned.

Don flopped onto his camp bed; it had been a warm, sunny day, usual for Alaska in June. His mind wandered. *I've had enough of this mining.* A day ago, he had written a note on the back of his mining claim in frustration, saying the finder was welcome to it. He had put that in his little chest, which housed his personal items, the claim, and, of course, Sophie's stone, together with the key to his bank deposit box.

Frank took his opportunity with a nine-inch knife. He had not done this before, but he crept over to Don to stab him. He was not in a good position for murder, and much to his surprise, Don immediately woke up; he hadn't been completely asleep. Don didn't sleep well after drinking, but Frank didn't know that.

Don was able to push Frank off. Frank was shocked, but he recovered and stabbed Don many times to make sure he was dead. Once the deed was done, Frank left the tent in the middle of the night and collected his horse from the corral. He headed south, back to Vancouver.

In the morning, they discovered Don's body, and the local constable made various inquiries. He found out that Don had been drinking with a stranger at the bar and they'd had a skinful. No one knew who the stranger was, but the clerk in the office said he thought a man had come in the other day asking for Don; he'd said his name was Chuck Smith. They buried Don in the pauper's graveyard, and that was the end of the matter, except that the constable made a report of Don's murder to his supervisor in Anchorage.

The constable collected Don's belongings, his clothes, and the little chest. The chest was stored on the constable's mantel. The clothes were thrown away after a year, but the chest remained where it was, as no relative had come to collect things. The incident got into the newspapers, and it went national because the murder was so brutal and seemingly without motive.

Once Frank arrived in Vancouver, he managed to get work on a cargo ship going south down the coast. He terminated his employment in San Francisco, where he jumped ship and headed back to Sophie.

On his arrival, she was suspicious of where he had been. Well over a year had passed since he'd left. "Did your aunt die?" she asked.

"No, she made a full recovery," he said.

"That's good to hear, then," said Sophie, but she didn't believe a word he said now.

She couldn't read very well, so she never read any newspapers. The cost would not have been in her budget anyway. Don's attorney read the newspapers daily without fail, and he read the article about Don's murder. He was shocked and horrified by the details and wrote a general letter of condolences to Sophie at the old house, offering his services to handle Don's estate.

Sophie always called at the old house once a week. She had become friendly now with the new occupants, who had moved in recently, and they waited for her visits. There was always a pot of tea on the stove. She picked up the letter from the attorney, thinking, *This looks formal.* She opened it on the way home, and when she saw what it was about, she burst out crying. The attorney had included a cutting from the newspaper, which was not very sensitive of him, she thought.

Sophie asked a friend who could read to read the newspaper article to her. The dates from the paper and Frank being away coincided; she knew that Frank had killed Don. She called on the attorney the next morning and instructed him to do what was necessary with Don's estate. The attorney said there was no problem. "You will have the money within days. Our fees will be charged to the estate."

She went back home to Frank; she did not want to confront him at the moment for fear of what he might do. She knew now that she was rich. *I have to leave him*, she said to herself. She decided that Frank had done this for the money, which meant that he would confront her at some point.

In the meantime, she started to look for another house. Dressing in her best clothes, she went to a realtor and obtained his services. She soon found a house just off Alamo Square; it was relatively new and just what she wanted. She made an offer to purchase, and it was accepted.

The sellers learned of the situation and were prepared to wait for the money to come through. She arranged to buy some of the house furniture from them, as she had none of her own.

The transaction happened in a week, and the purchase was finalized. Now she needed to make a move, and she was not going to tell Frank where she was going or that she was leaving him. The new house was a long way from Frank's home, and if she could find an excuse to get him out of the house, she would be off.

Frank had not said anything about Don, but he did say to Sophie, "Why don't you go to Don's attorney and see if they have heard from him? It's been five years or more now."

"I'll do that," said Sophie to string him along, for she knew what had happened. She couldn't prove it, of course; no one could. Matthew, her boy, was ten years old now, and she needed to protect him; once she left the house, who knew what Frank would do.

When Frank was at work one morning, she left the house with Matthew and never returned. They moved to their new home. On her dressing table in the new house, she placed the stone Don had given to her in a prominent place. She kissed it before setting it there.

She and Matthew settled in the house very quickly; they were now financially well off. Sophie had never known money, so she still acted frugally, but the first thing he did was hire a housekeeper to help her in the home. The house was substantially larger than what she was used to. She also needed help with Matthew; he was a growing lad, now approaching adolescence. He needed a father, Sophie knew, but it was not to be, so the live-in housekeeper would be a great help. It was a large house, and the housekeeper had a small apartment on the top floor.

Frank was mad when he came home from work to find Sophie gone. He rushed around the house, looking for her and Matthew's clothes, but they were gone. He sat down in his chair and realized that Sophie had duped him; it came to him now that she had discovered that Don was dead. How had she done that?

He realized she must have been contacted by the attorney, but how had he known where she was? He said to no one, "She's run off with the money I earned." He set about trying to find her. He didn't have a clue where to begin. He didn't know her attorney, so there was no contact there. Sophie had always kept that side of her life away from Frank.

Frank spent two weeks walking the streets of San Francisco, hoping to bump into Sophie. He asked every friend that he knew she had, all to no avail. No one knew where she was; Sophie had made sure of that, and she was keeping away from crowds. She had not even been back to her old house. Frank tried there, but the young couple said they had not seen her for weeks.

Sophie felt guilty for not going back to her old house; she had become good friends with the new tenants. But she did not want to put them at risk by telling them where she now lived. She realized that Frank was dangerous.

Matthew was eleven years old now, and Sophie knew you could not keep a young boy indoors all the time. He would play with his friends on the green opposite their house.

Frank happened to be walking that area one day by chance; he had divided the town up in his mind to form a grid, and he inspected one area every day. This day, he saw young Matthew on the green. Although it had been more than a year now since Frank had seen Matthew, he recognized the boy straight away. "So, this is where she moved to. Got her now, the bitch," Frank whispered to himself. He had become very bitter in recent months and was obsessed with finding her.

Frank went to the other end of the green, far enough away that he was not visible from any of the houses and well out of range of Matthew. He could see Matthew in the distance, and he waited there, watching to see where Matthew went after he finished his game. After about two hours, the boy finally got tired. Frank had been about to doze off, but he came to when he saw Matthew leave and go into his house. *That is it, then*, Frank thought. *She must have spent quite a penny on that property—my money.*

When it was dark, Frank returned to the house. He was determined to make Sophie pay for what he believed she had done to him. He decided the easiest way to break in would be through a window at the house's back. All the rooms downstairs were dark; he went all around the house trying windows, searching for one that was not locked. They were all locked tight; Sophie made sure of that each night.

The small kitchen window at the rear looked to be the best place for entry. It had not been overlooked by anyone but was shut tight as well. Frank took off his coat and wrapped it around his elbow. Then he smashed his elbow into the pane of glass, which broke on contact. He thought he had not made too much noise, but he waited to see whether there was any reaction from within the house. After five minutes of not seeing any lights go on, he decided it was safe to go in.

He squeezed in through the small window. It was a tight fit—he had put on weight lately—and it took him five minutes to get in. After puffing and panting, he found himself in the dark kitchen. He took a chance and turned on the light, thinking, *She's even got electricity.*

On the top floor, the housekeeper had heard the faint sound of glass breaking. "Was that glass?" she whispered to herself; she had been warned that Frank might try to break in one day, and she was always alert at night.

Sophie thought she had heard something, too, on the floor below, but she wasn't sure. The housekeeper came downstairs. Matthew was still asleep in his room, next to the main bedroom, and the two women left him there. Sophie didn't think Frank would hurt Matthew—he had liked the kid—but then it might not be Frank in any event; they might just be panicking.

Sophie said to the housekeeper, "I believe that it's Frank. Somehow he has found us. I don't know how. I have been so careful. He's only after me, and I don't want you to take any chances and get hurt because of me. If it is Frank, you must go back up to your room and lock the door. Do you understand? Don't open it for anyone. You are not to take any risks for me. I have caused enough death and destruction." Sophie was annoyed with herself for what she had caused; she knew she should have been more faithful to Don.

Sophie sidled out onto the landing; she could hear someone walking around downstairs. She said to the housekeeper, "It's time for you to go back upstairs. There is definitely someone down there." The housekeeper didn't want to go. With tears in her eyes, she hugged Sophie and did as she was instructed, but she waited at the top of the stairs, looking over the banister to watch what happened.

The housekeeper saw Frank walking up the stairs. He looked brutal; his face was red and contorted with rage. She also knew there was nothing she could do; she was a very slight lady. She made sure she would recognize him again if it became necessary.

There was no way to get help. Sophie has ordered this new device called a telephone. Still, it has not arrived as yet, and the housekeeper thought she would not know how to use it anyway. She had been bewildered went she'd gone to the telephone company with Sophie to place the order and seen a demonstration. She watched as Frank went into Sophie's bedroom. She could hear raised voices, and she walked a few steps down.

Frank said, " I killed your husband for you. You owe me, you bitch."

"You are evil personified; I realize that now. I didn't see it in your eyes before. You can always tell an evil person by their eyes. I did not want you to kill Don. I loved him; it was you who wanted the money, you bastard. I hate you for what you did," Sophie said with daggers in her eyes. She stared him down until he finally had to avert his gaze.

Frank wasn't going to argue the point. He'd only come for one purpose: to kill Sophie. It was too late for any reconciliation. His face had now turned bright red with rage. He took out his shiny knife, which he had polished up this afternoon. It was the same one he had killed Don with; he thought that was poetic.

He stabbed Sophie through the heart. He was surprised that she did not fight him; it was as though she wanted to die. She fell to the floor in a heap and died within seconds. She did not even scream. Frank was concerned that Matthew might have woken up. He didn't want to hurt the kid; he liked him.

He did not move, but after a couple of minutes, he left Sophie's room and looked up and down the stairs when no one came. The housekeeper had moved out of sight. Once he was sure that no one was around, he rushed downstairs and out the front door, which he unlocked on the way.

Hearing the door close, the housekeeper came rushing downstairs. She guessed what had happened, but she hoped Sophie was still alive. As soon as she entered the room, she saw that Sophie was dead, lying in a pool of blood. All the noise had woken Matthew, and when he discovered what had happened, he screamed for his mommy. The housekeeper called on a neighbor, who went to the police. A doctor arrived within a few minutes and gave young Matthew a sedative to get him to sleep.

In the morning, a constable came to the house and was told what had happened. The housekeeper said, "I am sure it was Frank, Sophie's old boyfriend. I would recognize him again; he looks evil."

Joshua Wicker, Don's uncle, came to the house as soon as he heard what had happened. He arranged to bring up Matthew with the housekeeper's aid, whom he took into his employment. The uncle thought that was best; Matthew knew and liked the housekeeper well, but he hardly knew his great-uncle at all. The police track Frank down, and he was arrested for murder. He never denied it—in fact, having come to terms with his actions, he admitted it—and the housekeeper identified him as the killer. The trial was short, and the jury convicted him after half an hour. "There is only one punishment for such a heinous act," said the judge.

On a bright, sunny morning three days later, Frank left this world when he was hung from the gallows at the jail. There was no audience or formalities other than the priest who administered the last rights. Frank was not religious—how could he have been with his lifestyle—and he did not confess to the priest.

Matthew inherited the house and was brought up by the housekeeper. He married and had a daughter, whom he named Sophie, after his mother. He lived in the house until he died in 1960.

CHAPTER FIFTEEN

2021

Micheal West is considering what he should do. He wanted to be at the Klondike when John and Jack were there to find out what they were up to; he knew they were up to something, but what? He certainly didn't want to get there before them; he didn't like the idea of living there for any length of time. Having already spoken with John Smith and getting the brush off, he didn't want to contact him again, but this reinforced the idea that something is going on.

His best option, he decided, was to try the other guy. *What was his name? Jack King? That's it.* He didn't want to contact that Canadian Mountie again, either; twice would be more than coincidence. He booked an appointment to see Edward Isaacs at the jail. Maybe he knew more than he was letting on.

Edward agreed to meet; he thought maybe Michael had some good news for him. They met in the visitor's room of the jail. Edward was behind glass, and they spoke through a telephone. Michael relayed how he had gotten a claim next to John Smith's and Jack King's at Dawson City. "I've already talked with Smith, and I didn't get very far. I know he was suspicious. I need to know when they are going back up north. Do you have any ideas? I need help here."

"Be careful what you say. These phone conversations might be recorded," said Edward. Michael nodded, and Edward continued. "Well, I do know that Jack King is a pilot with a plane. I think he has a cargo business near Nashville, Tennessee. That came out at my trial. I expect they will fly up during the summer. No one goes to that region in winter. It's unbearable. I should know that."

"That's great. Hopefully, I can get the information from Jack King. Don't forget, I'm cutting you in on this." After half an hour of exchanging pleasantries, Michael said goodbye and left.

He went back to his flat, opened up his computer, and Googled "Jack King," coupled with "pilot Nashville." He came up trumps, finding Jack's freight business and phone number. He picked up his phone and dialed the number. Jack answered, and Michael reverted to his alias, saying, "Good afternoon. My name is Cornelius Constantine. I'm thinking of using your company to transfer cargo this summer."

"Thank you, Mr. Constantine," said Jack. "I can certainly help you with that. It's what I do. What is your cargo? I only transport legal goods. When and where is the cargo to go to?"

"Well, there is no problem with the cargo. It's just stationery; I have an office supply company with outlets all over the States. The shipment is not to go for a few weeks, but it's to go from Memphis, Tennessee, to New York City, and there will be other shipments to follow. Maybe, if it works well, we can make it a regular business," said Michael, hoping to keep Jack's interest up.

"Ah, the timing might be a problem for me. I can do a flight for you anytime in the next four weeks, but after that, I will be away for the rest of the summer at least," said Jack.

Michael jumped on that, saying, "Oh, are you going anywhere nice? I wish I had the time for a vacation, but work is so demanding."

"Well, actually, yes. I'm going on a cruise to Alaska, but after that, it will be work."

Michael thought about that. "Oh, I love cruising. Which ship are you sailing on?"

"The *Argonaut*, out of Vancouver."

"Oh, I hear that is a nice ship, not that I have ever been on it. Vancouver is quite near where I am in Canada. You know, maybe I'll think about doing that cruise. Maysee you onboard."

Michael had gotten what he wanted, so he said to Jack, "I'm afraid the timing does not suit my needs. All the best, and do enjoy the cruise." He put the phone down and then looked online for the details of the cruise Jack had referred to. He needed to get on that ship, too, but he had to work out a plan first.

After hanging up, Jack wondered about what had just happened. "What did he say his name was? Cornelius

Constantine, yes, that was it," he whispered. There was something that stuck in Jack's throat about the call. "I think he was fishing," he whispered before he got out his laptop and Googled "Cornelius Constantine" and "office supplies." He found nothing but a long list of office suppliers. There was no mention of Cornelious Constantine, which was what he suspected.

Jack met with John, Cloe, and Ben, and they confirmed that everything was booked and passports were in order. All they needed now was to pack. They were planning to fly up to Vancouver in Jack's plane, but John said, "Why don't we take a commercial flight with all our luggage?" After a long conversation, they decided to do that.

That phone call from Constantine still bothered Jack. He didn't know why, but he mentioned it to the others. John said, "Well, that is just business, isn't it?"

"I don't know," said Jack. "You know when you get one of those feelings that you're not sure of? The conversation was strange and did not seem real; the time issue was the big thing. Why would that be a problem if it was genuine?"

"I know about those feelings," said Cloe. "Did you get the name of the client?"

"He said his name was Cornelius Constantine," said Jack.

John jumped into the conversation. "Did he, now? Cornelius Constantine was the name given to me by the reporter who phoned the other week, but they had not heard of him when I checked with the paper. Maybe you are right to be suspicious, Jack."

"I did give him the name of the ship we are cruising on, so maybe we'll have company. I wonder what he wants. Even we don't know what to expect when we reach Alaska," said Jack.

"Then we should keep an eye out for him. It's not likely he'll use the same name, though. Cornelius Constantine is clearly false. He may have a connection to Edward Isaacs."

"I think that may be it as well."

The next few weeks passed quickly. John phoned agent Josh Young at the FBI to tell him that he wouldn't be available for a few weeks. He made a point of telling Josh their plans in case they needed help.

John also took the opportunity to confirm that the tracking chip was still working, saying, "That tracking clip you had placed in my neck the other year when we did the drug-smuggling case, it's still working, isn't it? Just in case we need your help, at least while we are in Alaska. Hopefully, if we need help in Dawson City, your Mountie friend will oblige."

Josh had a quick look at his monitor. He always kept it on his desk. He knew John often got into trouble, but he was a valuable asset that Josh could not do without. He said, "Yes, John, I can see you are at home. Does that mean you anticipate trouble? Perhaps we should charge you rent for the transponder." He laughed.

Changing the subject, John said, "Frankly, I don't know if there will be trouble, but someone is following us. Not sure why, but when you're in the gold rush country, anything is possible."

"If you run into trouble, just ring, and if you find gold, I want a commission."

"Will do, and thanks, boss."

Michael West had been contemplating his next move; he knew there were three men and one woman in John Smith's party. What did they have planned for this gold mine that they had registered? At least they wouldn't know until they arrived at the Klondike that he had the adjoining claim. He planned to keep that secret until the last minute.

He realized he needed some female company on the ship to loosen tongues and make things look proper; he did not want to attract the wrong people. Michael was a confirmed bachelor; he liked women but only for what they could give him. In the past, he had turned to Judy Wantage. She was an attractive young lady, twenty-five. *She'll be ideal,* he thought. *She'll do anything for a vacation.*

Michael picked up his phone and dialed Judy's number. She answered straight away. "Hello, Judy. It's Michael West."

"Well, hello, stranger. To what do I owe the pleasure?" she said sarcastically. "You only come to me when you want something, usually sex."

"I need your help, and I thought you might like a cruise to Alaska. Can I come around and see you?"

"I suppose so. I'm in right now, but you take me as you find me," said Judy, thinking, *What does he want me to do for a cruise? Usually, I only charge him a hundred.*

"I'll be with you in fifteen," said Michael.

He freshened himself up and went around to Judy's apartment. When seeing a woman, he always tried to look nice. He knew Judy was no more than a prostitute, but that did not matter. *With any luck*, he thought, *I might get some, especially for a cruise. Maybe I should ask for more.*

Michael knocked on her apartment door, situated on the top floor of one of those Victorian buildings in Calgary. When Judy opened the door, she looked as though she had just gotten out of bed. She wore a tight leather skirt and a very loose white blouse, so free that when she bent forward to hold the door handle, Michael could see her breasts as they hung away from her body. He liked those breasts; he suddenly remembered the last time he had seen them, before he had gone to prison. It excited him more than he thought it would.

Once inside, they embraced as friends, and Judy said, "You are pleased to see me, aren't you?" as she felt his body against hers. "It's going to be one of those mornings, is it?"

Michael held her tighter, squeezing his pelvis against her "If you want it."

"Oh, I always want it. I haven't had it for ages now. Well, at least two days." She smiled and kissed him tenderly on the lips. She did not know why she liked Michael, but she did, and he always gave her great sex. He could go on and on, not like her other customers, who wanted a quick fuck and then were gone.

Although Judy had said, "Take me as you find me," she looked good, with her long black hair and dark complexion. She was part Colombian, and she had that Latin come-and-get-me look.

"I can't resist your tits," Michael said as he felt them.

"Don't resist, then. Take them."

She pulled her blouse over her head, and her tits bounced up and down. Her nipples were growing firm, sticking out from her breasts. Michael got to his knees—he was much taller than Judy—and his mouth settled on the left breast. He knew that one was more sensitive for her, and he sucked hard. The nipple grew in his mouth; he played with it with his tongue. She called out for more as she felt down her skirt to her pussy, and soon she was moaning loudly.

"It's a good thing the neighbors are away. I saw them drive out as I came in," said Michael.

"Oh, that's good. I like it noisy," she said. "I like to make a lot of noise when I come as well."

"You are going to come big-time today, babe. Remember, I've been in prison for several years. I haven't had it for all that time. I was surprised you didn't come to see me."

"We couldn't have had sex in any case, could we?"

'Probably not, but a visit would have been nice."

"Just get on with it, Michael. I want to feel your dick." She kissed him.

As Michael undressed, Judy watched with her finger in her mouth, sucking. She said, "I love to watch you grow." She was not disappointed as she slipped her skirt to the floor. She had shaved before Michael arrived, and her pussy was like a baby's bottom. She moved her hips so the slit opened to reveal her tunnel of love.

They made love for the next two hours, and even Judy had to admit she was exhausted at the end of it.

"So, what's this visit all about, then, besides the sex?"

"While I was in prison…" Michael stopped; he'd been about to say something about her not visiting again, but then he had second thoughts.

"Anyway, I met this inmate named Edward Isaacs. The name doesn't matter; he was in for a gold mine scam in Alaska. He was caught by these FBI informants named John Smith and Jack King. Those names are important, so remember them because they took out two claims in the Klondike."

Now, Judy was not an intelligent girl, but she knew the Klondike gold rush hadn't been successful, and she said, "Why on earth would they do that? Are they mad?"

"I don't know. That's where you come in."

"Me? You want me to go gold mining," said Judy, astonished. "What can I do?"

"Stop interrupting, Judy, and let me finish the story. I don't know what their plan is, but they must have one. You are right. There was never much gold discovered in the gold rush. They are going back to Alaska by cruise ship. John will take his ladyfriend, named Cloe, and a young man named Ben is going with them, too. The cruise takes seven days, and during that time, I want you to get to know either Jack or Ben to find out what they are doing. They are up to something, and there should be some money in it."

"Hmm, you mean you want me to use my body on them to spy," said Judy.

"That's about it."

"Well, it will cost you."

"Money always raises its ugly head, doesn't it?" said Michael. "How much?"

"A good suite on the ship plus a thousand dollars, and I'll throw in the sample you just had."

Michael thought about negotiating but decided against it. "Okay," he said.

After a rest, he said, "The ship, the *Argonaut*, leaves Vancouver on the fifteenth of July, so we'll leave Calgary on the fourteenth and spend the night in Vancouver. Don't forget to bring your Sunday best for the formal nights on board. We have to dress up when we stay in a luxury suite."

"Well, that will cost you a bit more, say a thousand for clothes," she said.

"You drive a hard bargain. I'll bring the cash around later."

"You need not worry. You will get your money's worth," she said with a sexy smile on her lips.

Michael left the apartment and went straight to his bank, where he had an account that he used for his criminal activities. He withdrew one thousand dollars; he thought the other thousand could wait until she produced the goods. He put the money in an envelope, returned to Judy's apartment, and knocked on the door.

"Who is it?" she called.

"It's me with the money," Michael replied.

"Thanks. Leave it on the doorstep. I'll get it in a minute. I'm in the shower right now," Judy called back.

Michael did as instructed and then left.

They had three weeks to get ready and pack. Michael booked a junior suite on the ship. *That should please her*, he thought. *Might help her to spread her legs a bit more.* On the fourteenth of July, Michael drove to Judy's apartment to pick her up. She had two large suitcases, and when he loaded them into the car, he said, "I know I said to bring your Sunday best, but I didn't mean the kitchen sink!"

She laughed. "You can't please some people, can you."

They drove over the Rocky Mountains to Vancouver and booked into a cheap hotel overnight. "I hope this doesn't reflect the standard of the week's accommodations," Judy said.

"This is just an overnight; you will be pleased with the suite on the ship," said Michael.

The following day, they arranged for a taxi to take them the short distance down to the dock where the *Argonaut* was berthed. The ship was the largest cruise liner in the world. Judy looked up at it and remarked, "It's massive. I've never been this close to a liner before. It's awe-inspiring."

At the embarkation area, thousands of people were lining up to get on board. Michael and Judy left their suitcases on the docks, where they were picked up immediately by the porters from the ship. They all held out their hands for a tip, but Michael said, "Fuck off."

Judy said, "That might not have been a good idea. I wonder if our cases will get to the suite now."

The *Argonaut* carried over six thousand passengers and had a crew of three thousand. Today there was a complete changeover of passengers. It took a long time to get through all the lines. The staff did what they could to speed up things; they were used to this procedure. Different staff members checked passports and travel documents before the passengers arrived at the check-in office.

Michael and Judy had left early to get to the ship, so they were relatively near the front of the line. About one hundred people behind them stood John, Cloe, Jack, and Ben, going through the same procedures.

Everyone was on the ship by four o'clock in the afternoon. The staff on the dock reported to the ship's captain that everyone was on board.

"Excellent. Make sure all the staff gets back on board quickly. We will leave on the hour," said the captain. The timing was crucial, as the ship needed to catch the high tide.

CHAPTER SIXTEEN

On the first morning of the cruise, our four intrepid explorers had set off early on a commercial flight from Nashville to Vancouver. On arrival, they got a taxi down to the port; hundreds of taxis are lined up to get to the ship dock, but eventually, they were there. As anticipated, the lines of passengers waiting to board the ship were colossal. John tipped the porters to take their luggage.

Jack couldn't help but wonder whether Cornelius Constantine or whatever his real name was, was in the same line. He was convinced now that he was there somewhere.

Eventually, they were all on board; John and Cloe had a suite, a large room with a king-size bed and plenty of dressing area, together with a large balcony. They were very impressed with their suite on the ship's starboard side, which would give them a view of the glaciers on the way to Alaska.

Jack and Ben shared a smaller room with twin beds and no balcony, but they did not plan to spend much time in the room. Michael and Judy had a suite similar to John and Cloe's; they, too, were on the starboard side.

At five o'clock in the afternoon, the captain came over the public address system and said they were now ready to set sail. "All passengers are invited to a sail-away party on the open deck." The decks were crowded with vacationers enjoying drinks and dancing to live bands playing Caribbean music. *Caribbean music on the Alaskan run, that's strange*, thought John, but everyone liked Caribbean music. The weather was kind, a bright, sunny afternoon.

John said to the other three, "Let's have a wonderful cruise and hope the weather stays like it is now." They all said cheers as they raised their glasses in a toast.

Michael had previously looked down the passenger list and found John and Jack's room numbers. That didn't help him for the time being, as he had no idea what either of them looked like, although he couldn't help playing the guessing game, and Judy was keen to dance her native dances.

After an hour, the party came to a close, and the ship sailed off under its own steam. Michael went downstairs in the area of John's suite and stood back out of sight. He saw John, Cloe, Jack, and Ben enter their suites. "Now I know what you look like," he whispered to himself, feeling pleased with his deception.

That evening, Judy dressed in a formal, tight-fitting purple dress of silk. "Do you like this dress?" she said to Michael, who had to admit he did, and he said so. He realized he had better put on a suit to compliment her.

They then went down to the dining room for dinner. Michael and Judy were shown to their table by one of the waiters. Then they checked the very extensive menu and decided what they would eat. They gave their order to the waiter, who brought water and rolls. Micheal ordered a bottle of the cheapest wine on the list, but when it arrived, even he had to remark, "It's quite good."

Michael was constantly looking around to see whether he could locate John and his company. Most of the tables were still unoccupied. Then he saw John come through the dining-room door, and his group was heading their way, led by another waiter. They were shown to a table three away from Michael and Judy's.

"That's handy," said Michael. "Don't look now, but the group I want you to watch are three tables away from us. I'll tell you when to look and do it discretely." Once everyone was seated, Michael said, "Why don't you go to the restroom? On the way back, you will pass their table. They are all seated at the third table in front of me. Remember them."

Judy got up and, without turning, walked to the restroom. When she returned, she strolled back to her table and could see the table Michael had referred to. She put pictures of each of them in her mind. As she walked past Jack, he admired her in her dress. She did not know why, but her nipples poked out.

She sat down at her table. "They make a nice group," she remarked.

"Never mind that. Can you remember them?" said Michael.

"Absolutely. No problem."

"I want you to take every opportunity you can to get to know them. Then you can introduce me. Pretend we are a devoted couple. By the way, that dress is a bit revealing."

She acknowledged that. "What do you want to do after dinner?"

"There is a comedy show in the theater. We should go. After that, I don't know whether any of them are gamblers, but the casino might be a chance to meet them."

They all went to the show. Michael saw John in the theater.

"That was a good show," Judy said afterward. Michael had not been able to get into it as he was still trying to work out what John was doing in Alaska and the Klondike.

Cloe had enjoyed the show as well. She said, "I'm tired now, John. Let's go to bed. I think the wine is getting to me." John was happy with that, but the youngsters wanted to go to the casino. They parted, with John and Cloe going back to their suite to enjoy the gentle rocking of the ship in the water.

Jack and Ben went to the casino; neither of them had cruised before, and they did not realize how large the casino would be. Half of it was filled with slot machines and the other with serious gambling, roulette, poker, and blackjack.

They were standing by the poker tables, watching the players, when Ben noticed Judy at the top of the three steps leading down to the casino.

Ben nudged Jack. "See her at the top of the stairs? Like she is the Queen of Sheba."

"Yes, but she is beautiful. Perhaps she will give us the royal wave," joked Jack, but secretly, he thought she was lovely. He remembered when she'd brushed past him in the dining room.

Judy gracefully walked down the stairs and came over to where Jack and Ben were standing. She said, "That was a good show, wasn't it? By the way, the name is Judy."

Jack said, "Hello, Judy. It's good to meet you. I'm Jack, and this is Ben."

"Do you play cards, Jack?"

"No, I don't play. No one wins against the banker. I prefer more certainties." There was a sparkle as Jack's eyes Judy's.

She said, "I'll try my luck," and she sat down and played a round of poker.

Ben turned to Jack and whispered, "She was flirting with you." Jack nodded.

Judy lost the hand and stood up just as Michael walked over to her.

"This is, er, my husband, Michael," Judy said. The three men shook hands as Jack and Ben introduced themselves.

"Good to meet you both," said Michael. "Have you cruised before?"

"No, this is our first time. We are here with two friends," said Jack.

"I love cruising," lied Michael. "I'm going to get us some drinks, dear. We might as well make good use of the drinks package." He walked off to the bar.

Judy leaned slightly toward Jack and whispered, "He's not my husband, really."

Jack smiled, thinking, *I've made a hit.*

Michael returned with four beers on a tray. The drinks went down well within minutes, and he signaled to a waitress that they wanted four more. "What are you doing after we reach Seward?" he said.

Ben replied, "We are going to Denali for a few days before heading back to Nome."

Jack thought Ben had said too much, but it was too late now.

"Nome!" said Michael, thinking, *I thought their claims were in the Klondike.* "That's interesting. What do you intend to do there?"

Now Ben realized he had said too much. Jack helped him out, saying, "John, the guy we are with, has some relatives there, and he wants to see them since we are up this way."

Michael nodded but said nothing.

For the next few days, Jack did not see Michael or Judy. All the passengers on the ship enjoyed the facilities and spent as much time as possible looking at the fantastic glaciers on the shoreline.

On the third day, the captain announced, "We have located a pod of whales on the port side of the ship. They are moving the same way as us, so they should be visible for some time."

Jack, John, and Ben rushed to the side of the ship. In the distance, they could see the massive animals rising and falling at the sea's surface. As they came out of the water, great spouts of water rose from their holes. It was a spectacular sight, and they were in sight for an hour, as the captain slowed the ship down. Finally, they headed off in a different direction.

The ship came into port at Juno. John and Cloe said they would stay on the ship and rest, but Jack and Ben decided to go on an excursion into the area's interior. They headed off the ship and onto the dock. In front of them, heading the same way as them, were Michael and Judy. Jack said to Ben, "Damn, those two are going the same way as us. I bet they are on our excursion. Look, we must be cautious about what we say. I have a feeling that Michael is the person who phoned John and me for information. However, I have to admit that Judy is exciting. They are definitely not a couple."

Ben acknowledged the rebuke. "I said too much the other evening, didn't I? I'll be careful."

They got into the waiting bus and took seats at the front. Michael and Judy walked past them, saying, "Hello," but then they moved down the bus's back. The bus drove for three hours through the glacier region, and everyone was goggle-eyed at the views. The bus eventually stopped at a restroom, and most passengers, including Ben, took advantage of the opportunity.

Jack stayed on the bus and turned around; the only other person with him was Judy. He could feel his heart pumping faster. He got up and walked over to her. When she saw him coming, she smiled and said, "I've been thinking a lot about you. Let me explain before everyone gets back. I am here with Michael just as a friend. He has some plan in mind, but I do not know what it is. It's probably illegal; he has only just gotten out of prison. To be honest, I think it has something to do with you and your party, but I want you to know that I am not part of it."

Jack sat down next to her in the empty seat, and Judy turned to him and kissed him on the mouth. Jack's heart was thumping so loudly he thought she would hear it." Thank you for telling me that. I was suspicious," he said, but he didn't want to tell Judy anything more. The fewer people who knew, the better. People were returning to the bus at that time, so Jack got up, smiled at Judy, and walked back to his seat.

Michael got on the bus, walked past Jack, and smiled. When he got back to his seat, he said to Judy, "Was that Jack I saw through the window sitting next to you?"

"No, I've been sitting here alone," she said. Michael knew she was lying but said no more.

They completed the remainder of the excursion and returned to the ship. When they got back onboard, Jack went to John and told him all that had happened, although he left out Judy's kiss. He did relate what Judy had said about Michael.

"I am sure he is Corelious Constantine, and I wouldn't mind betting that he is also the stationary dealer who phoned you," said John.

"I agree. In fact, the more I think about his voice, the more I am convinced about it," said Jack.

They did not see Michael again until the last night of the cruise when they had a drink at the bar. John wanted to find out what Michael would be doing next, so he casually said to him., "This has been a wonderful cruise.

We are heading off to Denali. Are you flying straight back to Vancouver?"

"I don't think we will. It is not very often that you get to see these wild places on the American continent, so I think we will go on tour. We might even go to Nome, where the gold rush took place," said Michael.

I bet you will, thought John. "We may see you there, then. That is one of our ports of call as well. There was a murder carried out in 1900 that I am looking into. I work with the FBI, and it is one of their unsolved cases," he said, stretching the truth, but Michael's reaction when the FBI was mentioned said it all.

Later that evening, Judy made a point of ditching Michael and finding Jack at his usual evening activity in the casino. She went up to him without saying anything; she just took his hand in hers. This surprised him at first, but when he realized who it was, he was pleased. Judy pulled him by the hand to the empty corridor outside the casino. Most of the passengers were now in their suites, packing, getting ready to leave the ship tomorrow.

They embraced and kissed deeply. "It has been wonderful to meet you, Jack," she said as she pressed her address and phone number in Calgary into his hand. "Please come and see me some time. It's no distance for you to fly in your plane. I have a feeling we will meet again fairly soon, though. I know Michael is planning something. He is very secretive at the moment."

"I will. I will also text you my details," Jack said.

"I must go now. I just slipped out. I don't want Michael to know about us. See you in the morning at the port to wave goodbye," Judy said, and she left to go back to her suite.

In the morning, they were woken up early at five o'clock by the ship's alarms. All their luggage had been left outside their doors last night, and now the suitcases were gone. When they got downstairs, they were told their cases were in the dock facility.

As they walked off the ship, the rain started; it was the first time they had seen rain on the cruise. John made sure all their luggage was put on trolleys, and then porters pushed them outside; the rain was slowing down by now.

Jack turned in circles, searching for Judy, but she was not in sight. On the dock was a car rental office, and John went in and arranged for an SUV to rent to take them to Denali National Park. The car was brought around to the front, and they loaded in the suitcases. There was still no sign of Judy. John noticed that Jack was preoccupied, but he said nothing.

The rain had completely stopped now, and the sun was coming out. It was still early morning as they headed out to the park on a three-hour ride through beautiful countryside. The trees were colossal, and birds flew from tree to tree. Jack wished that Judy were with them to enjoy these sights together.

After two stops, they arrived at the lodge where John had booked two rooms for three nights. That gave them two whole days to sightsee in the park. They all wanted to see grizzly bears.

The next morning, they drove into the park, searching for the bears and other wildlife, but they saw nothing. The scenery was beautiful, but it was the animals they wanted to see. At first, they kept to the main roads through the park, but then John saw a side road that was no more than a trail. He said, "Why don't we park here and walk down that trail? Perhaps if we get off the main roads, we might see something."

Cloe was apprehensive. "We are safe in the car. I'm not so sure how safe we'll be outside it."

They took a vote and decided to walk down the trail. Leaving the car on the road, they walked down the track. Still, they saw nothing. Then they turned a corner, and there, in front of them, about thirty yards ahead, was a giant grizzly bear. It was standing up on its hind legs, rubbing against a tree, which made it about twelve feet tall.

John said, "Just stand still. Don't move at all and don't show any aggression."

Cloe managed to make a joke, whispering, "I wish you would tell the bear not to show aggression."

The bear looked at them curiously, staring from one to the other. It did not look frightened at all. It dropped to all fours and opened its mouth and growled.

"I think it's just claiming its territory," John said as the bear slowly walked their way.

"I'm not going to stroke it," said Jack, trying to hide his fear, but he was not very successful. His voice was trembling; he was terrified. He prayed, *God, I've only just met Judy. Please don't end it all now.*

Suddenly there was a loud bang from behind them, and the bear stopped, reared up on two legs, and roared. It then dropped down, turned, and wandered away from them. Relief poured out of them. Their bodies had been so tense with fear. "What was that?" Jack managed to get out.

They turned around to see a ranger holding a rifle with smoke at the barrel. The ranger said, "It's a good thing I saw your car parked back there. You must not wander off down these tracks. These animals are very dangerous. If they are panicked, they will kill. Now, please go back to your vehicle. keep to the trails."

"We are very sorry, officer, and thank you for being here when we needed you," said John.

"That's my job, sir," said the ranger.

When they got to the car, they quietly assessed what could have happened. They spent the rest of the break on the main roads and did see plenty of animals by the end of the day. Jack was quiet for a long time, thinking how lucky they were. Finally, he said, "You know, that little incident makes me realize how much I like Judy. I thought for a short time there that I would never see her again. That concentrates your mind."

'You're right, Jack. I think it concentrated all our minds," said Cloe.

The following day they started the drive back to Seaward, a two-day trip. The landscape was again rugged and mountainous. Having left the rental car at the airport, they collected a commercial plane to fly them to Nome.

Cloe remarked when they arrived, "I love mountains; they make me feel nearer to God."

"That's because of your spiritualism, darling," said John.

"You're probably right. One of these days, I must climb a mountain and stand on the peak," said Cloe.

"I'll come if you don't want to go, John," said Ben.

CHAPTER SEVENTEEN

They did not have rooms booked in Nome, but there were only three hotels, and they are very basic. The town is tiny, the number of visitors passing through is small, as it is only accessible by plane or ship. There are no long-distance highways, and the summer season is very short. As they drove up Main Street, having rented a small runabout car, Cloe said, "I like the looks of that hotel." She pointed.

"That's fine, then," said John, "But they all look the same to me."

"That's because you don't see things as I do. The one we just passed is where Michael and Judy are staying."

Jack immediately perked up. "You can't see that," he said with a snigger. The truth was she could not see them. She had seen see a rental car in the car park and guessed the rest, but she wasn't going to let John know that. She liked him thinking she was psychic.

John turned into the hotel parking lot, and they checked in at reception for an unspecified number of days. The hotel was only half full, so there were plenty of rooms. Jack had made a note of the hotel where Cloe had said Judy was staying.

After a good dinner and wine, they all said they were ready for bed after the long drive.

In the morning, John knew he had to go to the bank to sort out the Don Wicker's deposit box. He was concerned as to whether the bank would accept his explanation for why he should have access. He decided it would be better if he and Cloe went alone; the bank might be more sympathetic then, as all they had was the note giving the finder the claim. *Will it be regarded as a will?* He wondered.

John and Cloe walked to the bank. They pass the bank that John and Jack had gone to on their last visit. The doorman was there again. John walked up to him, and he recognized John immediately. "It's good to see you again, sir," he said. "The bank you want is the rebuilt one further down the road. If you have any problems, ask to speak with Raymond. Tell him that George sent you."

"Thanks, George. We will certainly do that," said John, and then he and Cloe continued down the road to the new bank, rebuilt ten years ago. The previous bank had been started back in the mid-1800s.

They entered. This was a very modern bank; no old-fashioned doorman here. They went to the receptionist sitting behind glass; this was, after all, the year of the Covid 19 epidemic. John explained that they wanted to go to access their deposit box. She pointed them to a glass door at the end of the reception area, next to the tellers. They walked down and opened the door; this led down to a flight of stairs down to the basement. They walked down, and in the center of the room, a young man was sitting behind a desk.

"Can I help you, sir?" he said.

"Yes, please. We would like to enter our deposit box," said John as he handed over Don Wicker's key from the chest.

"Number 157," said the receptionist, and he opened his book of names and numbers. "This box has not been opened for over a hundred years, sir." The young man said in amazement, and he eyed John and Cloe suspiciously.

"That is correct. The box belonged to a Don Wicker, who died in 1900. We inherited the key this year," John said. Cloe left it to John to do the talking.

"Do you have the will of Don Wicker, sir?" the man asked.

"This is all we have. We purchased this in a chest at auction a few months ago. Don was a very lowly man, a miner. He would not have had a formal will," John said hopefully as he handed over Don's claim form.

The young man was in way over his head, and he knew it. "Can I ask you to wait for a minute while I see my manager, sir?"

"Certainly. Why don't you speak with Raymond? Say George sent us here," said John.

The young man was happy now that he understood that John knew his manager's name and left the room. Cloe whispered, "Is this going to work, John?"

"I don't know. You are the clairvoyant one." John laughed, although he did not feel happy.

The young man returned with an elderly gentleman, who introduced himself as Raymond. "Ah," said John, "George said we should ask for you."

"George, the doorman at the other bank?" Raymond said.

"Yes," said John. "We explained the situation, and he said to ask for you."

Raymond was pleased. If George approved, it was a point in these customers' favor. Otherwise, he might have turned them down without explanation. "So, what is the story?"

John told him the tale from start to finish. Although Don Wicker's death was long before Raymond's time, he did know about the horrid murder. He thought very carefully; this deposit box was something that the bank would like to terminate; there had been no payment made since its creation. According to the records, the bank had considered emptying it many years ago, but because of the circumstances of Don's death, they'd agreed not to do so and bear the cost. He looked John and Cloe up and down, trying to ascertain whether they were telling the truth; the story was very plausible.

He looked once again at both sides of the claim form. "I suppose I can accept this as a will. We are going back to the wild west days, and this is probably as good as it gets." He smiled, turned to the young man, and told him to take the customers into the deposit room and open the box.

"Thank you, sir," said John, and Raymond left the room. The young man showed John and Cloe into the adjoining room with one table and two chairs. Along the back wall were all the deposit boxes, dozens of them, all different sizes. On the left-hand side were the small boxes, and they gradually increased in size as you moved along until the one at the end of the row, which appeared large enough to hold a person.

"Please have a seat, sir and madam. I will get your box."

John and Cloe sat, and the young man moved to the boxes on the left, which was where John thought the box would be. The young man looked at each box's number, and then he started moving across the room. John was shocked; what would Don want with a large box? The young man got to the middle of the room before finding the correct number. He put the key in the lock; it turned as though it had only been locked yesterday.

The receptionist took out the box, carried it to the table, and set it down. "Here we are, sir. When you have finished, ring the bell over there, and I will come back. You will not be disturbed."

John thanked him, and then the young man left the room. "Well, this is it, Cloe. Let's open the box." They took the lid off, and the box was less than half full, which led John to wonder why Don had gotten such a large box.

On top of the box was a blanket. Cloe said, "It's a Native Alaskan blanket with a colorful design. It's beautiful." She held it up, admiring the design and feeling very emotional. "I can imagine Don buying this blanket for Sophie. She never received it."

Underneath the blanket was a glass jam jar. Its contents were evident from their gold color. "It's a jar of gold flakes, no doubt some of the flakes Don panned for. Not worth a fortune, but nevertheless valuable," said John. Also in the box were two keys on a ring. One was a mortice key to some door, and the other one, he did not know what it might be for. Cloe took them out and felt them wondering where they fit, hoping to get a signal.

"Well, what do you make of that?" John said as he made sure there was nothing left in the box.

"I don't know, John. I don't get any signal from the keys," said Cloe.

"Hold on a moment," said John, "There is another piece of paper here." He picked it up and was shocked."It's another mining claim. This one is in the Klondike. There is a map on the back, and it's not in Dawson, but further up the river."

"And look underneath it. There is a detective badge from the New York Investigation Agency. What is that about?" said Cloe.

John and Cloe look at each other. Surprise showed on their faces, which were now both profoundly wrinkled.

John studied the badge carefully. "It was issued in 1885 to a Robert Dogood. We need to investigate that name."

Cloe took it in her hand. "It's very heavy."

"I suppose you could use it as a weapon," John said with a smile.

They picked up the contents and rang the bell to bring back the young man. John said to him, "Thank you, sir. We will not need the box anymore," and he handed over the key.

They took all the contents of the box to their car, where Jack and Ben were waiting. John explained what had happened. He held the keys out to show them but could do not explain their purpose. Then he said, "Hey, wait a minute. This could be an old car key."

Jack laughed. "How could Don have a car key in this godforsaken town over a hundred years ago?"

"No idea, it's not the same as our car keys, I agree, but maybe. So, what would the other key be?" said John.

"Well, if you are right, the other key might be to where the car was stored," said Cloe.

"Good girl," said John, "I bet that's it."

"A bit far-fetched, I would say," said Jack.

"There were two other pieces of interest in the box," said John. "One is another mining claim in the Klondike, but this time out of town, in the hills. Maybe that fits your idea, Ben, about the gold coming from the mountains. The other item is the agency badge of Robert Dogood of the New York Investigation Agency." There was a general silence as all considered what that meant.

"At a loss for words, guys?" said Cloe. "We need to get onto the internet for that."

"Well, if anyone has other ideas, let's hear them. In the meantime, we should register mining claims for Cloe and Ben next to ours, Jack," said John, and he drove to the registry office.

On entering the office, Jack went directly to the map on the wall with the claims marked; the map was getting old now. It had been renewed about fifty years ago and had been hardly touched since then. He put his finger on the claims he and John had made earlier in the year, much further inland than Don Wicker's. "There were no other claims near ours when we came before," he said.

John came over to investigate, and sure enough, the area next to theirs had a claim marker on it. They looked at each other in disbelief. "You are right, and I bet I know who made that claim."

"There is still room on the other side for Ben and Cloe," John said.

They went over to the desk and pressed the button to summon the receptionist; there was very little passing trade. A young lady came to the desk, a different one than earlier in the year. She said, "What can I do for you today?"

"We'd like to make two claims, please. We were here earlier in the year and saw a different receptionist; she was very helpful." John handed over the certificates that had been given to them before.

"Certainly, sir. Where would you like the new claims?"

"Next to the ones we got before."

The receptionist looked at her computer map and saw that another claim had been made earlier that week. "The claim immediately north of yours is already gone. That's strange. It was only a few days ago. Does everyone know something we don't?" she joked. "But the two south of the others are available."

"They will do fine. Thank you. Interestingly, you said the claim north of ours has been taken. Can we ask who took it?"

"Well, I suppose data protection applies; on the other hand, these are public records. The claimant is Michael West. You do realize, I hope, that it is up to you to stake out your claims."

"Yes, we understand that. Thank you," said John.

He and Jack filled in the forms for Ben and Cloe, and the certificates were handed over. "There is one other thing. We have inherited the claim Don Wicker made in 1900." John handed over Don's claim note.

"That is fine, sir. Many claims changed hands that way in those days." The receptionist made a note in her records of the transfer.

"Before we leave, could you please show us the position of Don's claim?"

The receptionist searched through the computer files. "It's a good thing all the old claims were computerized twenty years ago. Ah, here we are. Let me show you on the large map at the back." She came around the desk and went to the wall map. "Here we are. It's this one at the back of the beach. I'll give you a map of the area and mark it on that."

"Thank you," said John.

She gave him the map, and then John and Jack left the office and sat down in the general reception area outside to consider the situation.

Back in the office, the receptionist thought, *What is going on here? Maybe I should register a claim myself.* And she did just that, registering three claims near John's.

Jack said, "Michael West and Judy, they must have come here directly from the ship and taken the claim. I thought I liked Judy. I feel abused."

Cloe was sympathetic. "Jack, maybe she wasn't involved or had any knowledge of what Michael was doing. Just be careful, that's all. We will see them again, be sure of that."

John nodded in agreement. "I think we should go down to see Don's claim. Cloe might get some vibes."

They left the office and headed down to the beach. Once there, they agreed it was impossible to get an idea of what the area was like in Don's day. The beach now was like any other up and down the country; there were no signs that miners had ever been there.

Looking at the map, John said, "This is definitely the spot." Cloe got out of the car and walked around. She wondered where Don's tent would actually have been; there was no way of knowing, and she could not get any vibes from the area. They got back into the car and drove back to the hotel.

Inside the hotel, they sat in the comfortable chairs in the lobby. John got out his laptop and did a Google search for "New York Investigation Agency." He learned that it had been established in 1850 and taken over by the Pilkington Agency in the 1920s. It had specialized in foreign business, particularly from Britain.

John then searched for "Robert Dogood." There were many results, but the timing on them told John it was not their man. "Try Agent Robert Dogood," said Cloe.

That produced a different result. There was an article in the local newspaper at the time saying that Agent Dogood had been on a case involving stolen gold from a mine in Wales. The suspect was Taffy Jones, an employee of the mining company. It was thought that Mr. Jones jumped ship in New York Harbor and headed out west to the Klondike. Agent Dogood had followed, but nothing had been heard of either of them again.

"Well, what do we make of that?" said John. "Did Don kill this agent?" They all shook their heads, not knowing, but they agreed they were not likely to find out anything.

That evening, Jack was feeling more upset with Judy. On his own, he left the hotel and walked down to the hotel where Cloe said Michael was staying.

Michael and Judy had just finished a heavy drinking session. Michael was particularly drunk, and when they got to their room, he sat in an armchair and quickly fell asleep. Judy looked at her phone, wondering if she should phone Jack and tell him that none of this gold business was her doing.

She looked at the phone screen, and Jack's name appeared. She got up, switched off the ringer, went to the bedroom, and closed the door. The phone was still bleeping, and she answered it.

Jack's voice said it all. "What the hell is going on with you? Can you come downstairs?"

"Okay, I'll be down in a minute," she replied.

Judy used the minute to wash her face, rinse with some mouthwash, and touch up her hair. She then quietly left the room, making sure she had her key. Michael was still well asleep.

She went down to the lobby and saw Jack standing there. She became very emotional when she saw him again, knowing that he was not happy with her.

"I'm sorry, Jack. This has nothing to do with me; I am just here to accompany Michael. Part of me wishes I had not done that now, but then I would not have met you, and you mean a lot to me." Judy tried to get close to Jack, but he stepped back.

He asked, "Why has Michael taken a claim next to ours?"

"I have no idea. He came to me when we were driving down her and said he wanted to make a claim."

"But he did not know we had one here."

"Truly, I know nothing of his business affairs. However, I know that he has just gotten out of the penitentiary in Calgary. Maybe it has something to do with that. Please believe me, Jack. He means nothing to me."

Jack stepped over to her, and they embraced. Judy said, "Text me anytime. It's probably better not to phone at the moment. I'm not sure how Michael will react. Look, I'd better go now. He was asleep when I left, but I should get back before he wakes up."

They kissed deeply, and Judy went back to her room. Jack walked to his hotel room feeling happier; he knew he was falling for Judy.

When Judy entered her room, Michael woke, and he was in a mood. He knew Judy had left the room. He said, "Where have you been?'

"Just out for a walk, Michael."

"More likely to see your new man

"Let's get one thing clear. I am here as your guest, no more than that, and I'm getting a little bored with it now and want to go home."

'You'll go home when I say so unless you are paying for the fare," Michael said aggressively. Judy was boring him now, but he didn't want her to have someone else.

"You know I don't have any money."

"That's why you need me, bitch." He got up to confront her, and she backed off, fearing for her safety—with good reason, as Michael threw a punch at her face. He hit her in the eye, which immediately swelled so that she could not see out of it.

"You bastard. That's the last time you hit me," Judy said, and she ran into the bedroom and slammed the door. She took her suitcase from under the bed and filled it with all her clothes and possessions. Struggling with the case, particularly as she could only half see, she walked right past Michael, who had returned to his chair, and headed to the door. She slammed it behind her as she left.

Once she was downstairs, she thought, *What am I to do now?* She did the only thing she could think of: she phoned Jack and said, "Jack, I am sorry to call you, but Michael has hit me, and I've walked out, I have nowhere to go." She was sobbing uncontrollably.

"Where are you?" said Jack.

"I'm walking along the street toward your hotel."

"Stay still, and I'll come and get you in the car. It's a small SUV," said Jack, who was sitting in the reception area with the others, having a drink.

"I've got to go," he said to them. "It's Judy. Michael has beaten her up. Can I have the car keys, John?"

"Sure." John passed over the keys. "You'd better bring her back here. I'll get her another room while you pick her up." He looked at Cloe.

Jack rushed out to pick up Judy.

"We'll look after her," said Cloe. "I liked the kid, and Jack does, too, I know. I don't know what the arrangement was with that Michael, but maybe we will find out more."

"I'm glad you feel that way, Cloe," said John. "I have an idea for the gold mines here. I think I half-mentioned it the other day, but we'll talk about it in the morning. I'll go and get another room."

Ben said, "Look, John, Judy had better move in with Jack. I'll take the extra room."

John smiled and nodded in agreement. Ten minutes later, Jack walked in with Judy.

Cloe stood and said, "Come here, Judy," and she embraced her. "John is getting another room. We know you two like each other, and Ben has volunteered to take the extra room so you can be with Jack if that's all right with you."

"Oh, you are all so good to me. Thank you." Judy looked up at Jack to make sure it was what he wants. He smiled at her lovingly, and she threw her arms around him.

John returned and confirmed that the extra room was booked. "I think the best thing we can do for tonight is get the rooms sorted and make it an early night. We can discuss things in the morning over breakfast."

They all went upstairs. The extra room was further down the corridor, and Ben packed his suitcase and walked down to it while Judy unpacked her case in Jack's room. When she and Jack were on their own, she held her face in his hands. "That's a nasty black eye you've got there," he said as he kissed it.

CHAPTER EIGHTEEN

The following morning, they met for breakfast at eight-thirty, but Jack and Judy were late. They looked happy as they walked into the breakfast room, holding hands.

"Well, we won't ask you two why you are late. You look as though you had a good night," said John. The couple looked at each other like lovers do. "We need to sort things out here, Judy. Please tell us your whole story with Michael."

Judy proceeded to tell them about her relationship with Michael and what she knew of his intentions, which was not much. She said, "He is a con man by trade, having spent many years in prison."

"He seems to know a lot about us," Ben said.

"I wondered about that as well. The only thing I can think of is that maybe he met someone in prison who knew you," said Judy.

Jack said, "You did mention that before. I wondered whether it was Edward Isaacs. He could easily have known about the mine claims."

John pensively nodded in agreement. "We should drive out to view our claims today," he said to change the subject so as not to embarrass Judy anymore. "I imagine you don't want to bump into Michael today, Judy, so why don't you stay here and decide what you want to do."

"Thank you, John," said Judy. "I don't want to interrupt your business here. I think I should go home. Will you take me to the airport, please, Jack? I don't want to meet Michael alone?"

"Of course," said Jack. "I will catch up with the others later."

"John, why don't you and Ben go to the mines? I'll stay with Jack and Judy," said Chloe.

'Good idea," said John.

"Come on, Judy. Let's get you packed," said Cloe, and the two women left with Jack.

John and Ben set off in the car to their claims, located up the river from the beach and in rural lands only used these days to graze cattle. Ben said, "This is much more likely to have been the source of the gold found on the beaches during the rush. The river would have washed the flakes away from the riverbank and washed them downstream to the sea."

John paced out the area and inserted some markers to separate their claims from Michael's while Ben walked along the river to see if he could locate a gold seam. "I have an idea," John said as he came over to Ben. "That gold we found in the bank safety deposit box, why don't we have it made into more recognizable nuggets? Maybe we can fool Michael into thinking we found them here. Perhaps he would purchase the claims from us."

'Worth a try," Ben said.

"Let's give it a try. I saw a goldsmith on the way up here. Let's go there."

They drove back down the valley and found the shops at the edge of town. One had a large sign outside saying, "Goldsmith." They parked the car, and John took the jar of gold with him.

Inside, sitting behind a workbench, was an older man with bushy gray hair. He was busy making a jewelry broach. He put down his blowtorch at an appropriate point, looked up, and said, "What can I do for you, gentlemen?"

John put his jar of gold on the counter. "Can you make these flakes of gold into nuggets, please?"

The old man walked over and picked up the jar. It was heavy. "You've had this a few years, haven't you?" he said as he took off the lid.

"Yes, it's been around for a hundred years, untouched," said John.

The elderly man looked at him. "You don't look like a prospector, so how did you come by it?"

"It belonged to a prospector named Don Wicker who was murdered in town in the year 1900."

"Don Wicker?" The old man laughed. "You don't know what this means to me. My grandfather, who started this shop, told me all about Don Wicker. It was a terrible business, but this was the wild west in those days. So, where did you get this?"

"It's a long story, but my wife purchased a chest at an auction that contained Don's claim form, and it said the finder was welcome to it. It led us to a deposit box in the bank up the road to make a long story short. This was inside the box, along with two keys."

"I can turn these into nuggets. I assume you want small ones, which would make about twenty. Do you have the keys with you?"

"No, my wife has them," said John.

"What do you intend to do with the nuggets?"

"Well, we are trying to collect things of Don's. We will take whatever we find back to his granddaughter in San Francisco."

"In that case, there will be no charge for this. Come back tomorrow, and I'll have it ready," said the goldsmith. "But just one moment. You said these flakes came from Don Wicker, the miner?"

'Yes, that's right," said John.

The goldsmith looked at John curiously. "This gold did not come from around here. Look, if you hold the jar to the light, you will see it has a reddish tinge. That means it could not have come from Nome or anywhere else on this coastline. This is rose gold, which only comes from specific areas. Look, I'll show you more clearly." The goldsmith opened the jar and emptied the contents into a dish. As he ran water over it, years of dust washed off, and the color of the gold changed to rose. "There, now you can see," said the goldsmith.

"Wow! Oh, yes, I see now," said John. He looked at gold pensively. *Then where did Don get the gold?* "Where would you get gold like this, then?" he asked.

"Abroad, definitely. The most common place is Wales in Britain, but they don't sell their gold generally, certainly not in Don Wicker's days. Had he or any of his friends been to Wales?"

"I would think it highly unlikely. He was a poor person without the means to get over the ocean."

"That's interesting. Anyway, I'll get it done for you. Come back in a couple of days."

"Thank you," said John, and they left the shop. John's mind returned to Taffy Jones, whose name they had found on the internet; he'd been from Wales.

John said, "We need to get an earthmover on site. I wonder where that gold came from."

And they went to a company that rented equipment and rented a mover for two weeks. It was delivered later in the day.

Ben said, "I'll move some earth around to make it look as though we are working." He spent an hour doing that, by which time, the site seemed a hive of activity.

"Well done," said John. The plot was set.

Cloe took Jack and Judy to the airport. Judy's eye was still swollen and black. She managed to get a flight leaving for Calgary in two hours. Jack paid for her ticket and stayed with her until the flight was called. Cloe left them alone to say their goodbyes while she went shopping for a little gift for John. She felt guilty that, while Don had purchased so many things for Sophie, she had not bought anything for John recently.

There had been no sight of Michael, much to Judy's relief. Before getting on the plane, she said to Jack, "I will pay you back the money for the flight. I know where you are. It would be nice to come down to the warmer climate in the summertime. When I get home, I am going to set about getting a real job. I think I am falling in love." They held hands and kissed, and then Judy slipped away quietly.

Jack felt miserable at Judy leaving and was glad to have Cloe's company. She could see that he had got the lovebug badly. She said to him, "Jack, I mean this kindly, but don't jump into anything too quickly. It might have just been a vacation romance; time will tell. On the other hand, she could be the love of your life."

Jack looked at her, knowing that she was right, and although he didn't want to hear it, he was grateful that his friends thought of him in that way. He moved close to Cloe and hugged her. "Thank you. I love your friendship. I don't know what I would do without John and you and all our adventures together."

They drove to the mining site. John and Ben were now digging up the soil on the rocky outcrop that ran along one side of the claim. The rock in this area was very porous; Ben could see that from looking. They had purchased some paint on the way to the site, and John was painting a very narrow fake gold seam on the face of the rock.

They both stood back and admired their work as the paint was absorbed into the rock; the seam looked very realistic. They left it at that for the moment and went back to digging up other areas of the claim.

Michael turned up at his claim. He was embarrassed about his actions with Judy last night; he guessed that she had gone to Jack, and they all knew what had happened, and no doubt, she had exaggerated, he thought.

When they saw Michael, John and Ben looked at one another, and John whispered, "I think we should not mention Judy unless Michael brings her up." Ben nodded in agreement.

Michael saw that Cloe and Jack were missing; this confirmed his thoughts. He went over to John and said, "I regret what happened with Judy, but I don't want that to destroy our relationship, as we have adjoining gold mine claims."

John took the opportunity to clear the air, saying, "Judy has flown home, and as far as we are concerned, it had nothing to do with us."

"Thank you for that. I must learn to control my temper."

"That is always a good idea," John said sarcastically, guessing that soon he might be the target of Michael's temper. "I think we have done enough for today, Ben. Let's go back and see what the others are doing." Ben smiled, knowing what was on John's mind, and they left the site.

On the way back, Ben said, "That was clever. You know he is going to search our claim, don't you."

John laughed. "You've got it."

On the way back, they stopped at the registry office. John went up to the clerk and said, "I am sorry, but I don't remember your name."

'It's Ronald. What can I do for you?"

"We came in a few days ago, saw your colleague, and registered other claims," said John.

"Yes, I have a record of it all here, sir," said Ronald.

"Please tell me, is there any tax to be paid on any gold found?"

Ronald scratched his head and laughed with John. "In truth, sir, no one has found any gold for a century, and in those days, there was undoubtedly no tax. When gold was found in the old days, it was recorded here. If gold is found today, I imagine it would be recorded on your annual federal tax forms. There has never been a local tax, but I am sure that if any large quantity were found today, the county would soon impose a tax! You know how politicians are."

"Do you have any record of a gold find for Don Wicker?"

Ronald studied his computer screen. "No, sir. Nothing recorded."

"Well, in that case, we should declare a finding for Don Wicker of thirty ounces. We found it in his bank deposit box. However, the goldsmith up the road said the gold did not come from here, as it is rose gold."

"That would have been a good claim. Don didn't enjoy it, obviously, as it was still in his deposit box. If the gold did not come from here, there is no need to declare it."

"Sadly, not. He was murdered before he could enjoy it."

"That happened so often in the old days, you know."

"Thank you. That is fine," said John, and then he and Ben left the office.

"There's one more thing to do, Ben, collect the gold nuggets," said John.

They drove to the goldsmith, who was standing outside his shop, talking to a neighbor. On seeing John arrive, the goldsmith walked over to him and said, "Come in. It's all done." Inside, he handed over the glass jar, but this time, it contained six gold nuggets.

"Excellent. Thank you very much," said John, and then he and Ben left the shop.

As they pulled into the hotel, the engine made a horrible sound, and the car sputtered and came to a stop. Ben said, "It's the transmission, I think."

John got out his phone and called the car rental company. "Hello, this is John Smith. We have the Nisson SUV. I am in Nome, Alaska, and we have a problem. I think the transmission has gone."

"One moment, Mr. Smith. Let me check up here." The line went dead for three minutes, and then the clerk returned and said, "Is it driveable, sir?"

"I think so, but only for a few miles."

"That's good. Can you please take it to Nome Autos on Main Street? I will tell them that you are coming. They will give you a loaner."

John hung up and said, "Let's go and get Cloe and Jack from the hotel, and we can go out to dinner afterward."

They parked and went into the hotel. By chance, Cloe and Jack were in the lobby. John explained the situation, and they all headed out to the car.

John was driving, and he said, "Can you put the car key in your purse so that we don't forget it?" Cloe did as asked, although it was challenging to find the space inside.

The car could only be driven at a snail's pace, but the garage is only a quarter of a mile up the road. It just about made it. They went into the showroom, and the owner, Justin Polanski, came to greet them, as he'd heard them drive into the service station. "That noise does not sound very good. You must be John Smith. We have been expecting you. That is definitely the transmission. We will put it right, and there is a loaner car for you."

They were just about to go get the loaner car when the owner said, "Oh, don't forget the key for the SUV."

Cloe said, "Yes, I have it," and she opened her purse, which was filled to the brim. She rummaged around inside but couldn't find the key. She started to take things out, putting them on the table. Suddenly there was a loud clang as the keys they'd gotten from Don's deposit box fell out and onto the stone floor. Polanski heard the noise and looked down at the keys before bending down to pick them up.

He turned them in his hand and held them up to the light. "That is interesting, " he said. "Do you mind if I ask you where you got this key from?"

"Not at all. It came from the bank deposit box of a miner from the late 1800s that we recently came into possession of," said John.

"Hmm," said Polanski. "Can I ask you to come with me, please?" He walked to a room at the back of the showroom.

John looked at Cloe with surprise, but they all followed.

"Let me explain," said Polanski. "These premises were built by my grandfather in the late 1800s. In those days, it was just a petroleum pump on the road; it was called petroleum in those days. There weren't many cars around then, but my grandfather thought a highway would be built to here. Sadly he was wrong, but he thought of cars as things of the future. How right he was. The trouble is he did not consider the road problem" He laughed. "There was a family argument over it, as my grandmother thought he was mad.

"Behind the pump, along the back wall here"—he indicated with his hands—"stood a row of twelve storage garages. They were rented to the local miners at the time. A few had cars, but most of the others were used to store mining equipment."

"However, it did not work out financially, and in 1930, when cars were more widely in use, my father, who had taken over the business by then, had the garages demolished and the existing building erected. The problem was that several of the garages still had vehicles inside that no one used, and the records were all gone by that time.

"My father had the cars removed, and he stored them in our other facility. These keys hanging on the wall here are the copies of the ones issued to the tenants." He pointed up at the keys, which were of the mortise type and all slightly different.

"I wouldn't mind betting that this matches one of those keys up there," Polanski said as he moved the key he'd gotten from Cloe along the line. "Here we are. It looks like a perfect match on number six." He went down to the desk below the keys, and from the drawer, he pulled out a ledger.

Opening the pages, he said, "Let me see. Garage six contained a Packard Runabout from the Packard Automobile Company of Detroit. That was a classic car and is very valuable today, particularly if it has not been used. There is a note here that my grandfather made saying the garage was rented to a Don Wicker."

"That confirms it. The key was found in Don Wicker's belongings. He was murdered here in 1900," said John.

"There is an asterisk next to the entry. Let me see." Polanski flipped to the back page, where there was another asterisk. "It says here that, as you said, Don was murdered; we had no way of contacting his family, so the car was kept as an exhibition piece until someone turned up for it. My father had a guilty conscience, as he put it, over the sale to Don Wicker. He knew that Mr. Whicker couldn't drive it home to San Fransisco."

Everyone was in shock, and not much was said. They just looked at one another in amazement. Finally, John said, "Where is your other facility?"

"I'll take you there in the morning if that is alright. It's not far. We will be glad to get it sorted out, to be frank," said Polanski.

"About ten o'clock here?"

"Fine, I'll see you then."

John and the others left the premises and went for an evening meal at one of the local restaurants. They were quiet that evening, having found so many of Don Wicker's possessions. John said, "We must get all Don's possessions back to San Francisco and Sofie. But before we do that, I think we should investigate this gold mine in the Klondike and see if we can find out about this Inspector Dogood."

"Agreed," said Cloe. "Let's fly to Dawson City. When we go down to San Fransisco, I think we should contact Gloria. She might like to come and film the situation."

John agreed.

CHAPTER NINETEEN

In the morning, they flew down to Dawson City. Cloe remarked, "Can you imagine Don traveling this distance in the 1800s, with no roads and on horseback?" she said as she looked out of the window at the mountains below. "That would have killed me," No one replied, but they all agreed.

When they arrived at Dawson City, they rented a car at the airport and John said, "Remember, we have two mine claims here already, but I think we should concentrate on the new one we just found. Let's call into the library and see if there is any record of Inspector Robert Dogood."

They kept their eyes open as they drive down Main Street. John said to Jack, "Not much has changed since we were here in the winter. The shops seem to have gotten back to normal."

"There is the library," said Ben, pointing.

John found a parking space and pulled the car over. They entered the library, and not knowing where to start, Cloe went to the receptionist and said, "We are trying to trace a person who was here in 1900. Do you have any suggestions as to where we should start?"

"If the person was a resident, then there is an electoral roll over there. Surprisingly, we did have records of residents in those days. This is Canada," she said, realizing that Cloe was American and that things were not so controlled in the wild west. "But if he or she were a miner or other transient, then we would not have any records. The old newspaper cuttings might give you something, but that is a long shot unless he or she was notorious. The reference section is through the archway."

"Thank you. We'll try the newspapers. He wasn't a resident."

They walk to the reference section, and all the old newspapers were neatly preserved in long lines. They took out those from 1885 to 1900. Fortunately, newspapers were weekly in those days. They spent the next hour going through each one. Cloe found one article that referred to Agent Robert Dogood from the New York Investigation Agency, who had come to Dawson in search of a miner named Taffy Jones. "This is it," she whispered.

The others stood behind her and read the article.

"What's the date of the newspaper?" said John.

Cloe looked "September 18, 1897."

John took out the issues for the next three weeks. They read through them all, but there were no further reports. There was an advertisement from the agency asking for any information about the disappearance of Agent Robert Dogood.

Finding nothing else of interest, they left the library. John said, "Let's consider what we know. Taffy Jones is a Welsh name, and the gold Don had likely come from Wales. We know the inspector was chasing Taffy, who must have had a link to Don because the inspector's badge was in his bank box. Did Don kill the inspector? I guess that the inspector was looking for Taffy because the gold was stolen from the Welsh mining company. We know the gold did not come from the American continent. Let's go and try to find this claim we found in Don's box."

"There is a sketch map on the back of the claim, but we need more information. Let's go back to the mining office," said Jack.

John laughed. "You just want to see that girl again. What was her name, Susan? But that is a good idea anyway."

They drove to the office, but a different receptionist was there, a man.

John handed the receptionist the mining claim. "Good morning, sir. We are looking to find this claim area. Can you help?"

The receptionist looked at the claim form, scrutinizing its authenticity. "No problem, sir. This seal on the document is genuine. Whether it still exists today is another matter. Much has happened in the last hundred years, and mining companies have just moved in, ignoring the old claims if the descendants cannot be found. Let's have a look at the map over here, and we can see where the claim is. Are you the beneficiary of Don Wicker?"

"No, but I can give you the address of his granddaughter." John wrote down Sophie's address, and the receptionist entered it into his records.

He led them across the room to a map on the wall. The office manager was watching through a window. "Here we are. Your number is 5634. Yes, here we are," the receptionist said, pointing to the spot. "This area has never been mined. It is at the apex of the hills between here and the village of Bear Creek. The area was occupied originally by the Han Indians. Let me think now. The tribe's name was Trondek Hwechin. Yes, that's it. I am told it was their name for the Klondike region. Most of that area is open space now, used by the horse riders. The Indians left before the gold rush days. There is a burial site up there, but I have never been. It was sacred to the tribe, and at one time, people said the area was haunted. That kept the locals away in those days. Now, as I said, it's just a riding area."

"How would anyone have gotten there in the 1800s? Since Don Wicker made a claim, he must have gone there," said Jack, acutely aware that Don must have used horseback.

"Let me have a look at a current map. I have one in my desk," the receptionist said, interested in the intrigue. He got the map and spread it out on a table. "Here we are. Look, this is the town here, and here is your claim area in the mountains. There is no road up there even today, but a path is recorded that runs along the river gorge; it's a bridle path for horses. If you go up there, be careful. There is a huge drop to the river and rocks below."

"Thank you, sir. You have been very helpful," said John, and then he and the others left the office.

John said to Jack, "I didn't want to say anything while we were in the office, but do you realize Don's claim is next to the two that we took out earlier this year when we dealt with Edward Isaacs?"

"Oh, is it?" Jack replied. "No, I didn't realize, and when we took out those claims, I didn't see there was one adjacent."

'I didn't, either. Do you think we were guided to those claims when we made them?"

"Who knows?"

"I know," said Cloe. "Of course you were. Everything we have done in this matter has been guided by someone or something."

John just nodded. Then he said, "How is everyone for riding?"

"Not sure I was made for that, but I'll give it a go," said Cloe. The men were all pleased. Ben was actually looking forward to it; he always fancied himself a cowboy, but he hadn't been riding since their escapades in Mexico.

"Good, then let's go to a stable," said John.

They drove to a stable, where they rented four horses for the day. The hostler made sure they were capable riders with a small test around his corral. He was happy to let them go out, but they did not tell him where they were going. The hostler gave them a map of the area, the same one they had seen earlier. He told them not to go into the mountains, as they were dangerous, but they took no notice; this was the sole reason for getting the horses in the first place.

The mining claim path was relatively straightforward at the start and signs were posted along the way. But as it started to climb, it became more difficult. They took their time with the horses, watching their every step. Climbing rocks is not natural for horses, with hooves as opposed to feet. It was a slow trek, but they enjoyed the scenery, thinking that this route must have been the one Don had taken all those years ago. It was pretty eerie somehow, and Cloe, particularly with her clairvoyance, could feel what Don must have felt. She could feel his apprehension as she got higher up into the hills.

John said to her, "You can feel something, can't you?"

She nodded. "I can. The higher we get, the more I can feel Don's apprehension about something. It is getting worse all the time."

When they got to the top of the hill, the path entered a clearing. In front of them was a beautiful copse of oak trees, ancient, with wide trunks. Cloe stopped by the trees, but John went to the side of the gorge and looked over. He, too, was thinking of Don. He knew that Don was likely to have killed the inspector. *This would be an ideal place*, he thought. *Dump the body over the cliff, gone forever.*

"I can feel something powerful here. It is giving me a headache," Cloe said as John walked back to her. She was holding her head as though directing the vibes. Ben and Jack got off their horses and tied all four together. John looked up and down the track in both directions, thinking.

"This would be an ideal spot for an ambush. Look how the view is unfettered in both directions. The trees would be ideal for a rifle sniper and would have been smaller a hundred years ago. Let's look around the wood. They left the horses and walked through the trees. The woods were not very deep and situated on a flat area before the hillside rose steeply again.

Once through the trees, they saw the cave ahead. Just outside was the pile of rocks. The skull was gone, and vegetation had grown over the rocks. The Indians no longer tended them. John said, "This must be the burial place that the receptionist referred to."

Cloe said, "I'm not so sure about going inside. These superstitions are powerful, you know."

"Why don't you wait outside," said John. He looked at Ben. "We need a flashlight, though."

Ben always carried a flashlight.

"Ok, I have one in my saddlebag. I'll go and get it," said Ben, and he ran back to his horse and got it.

Back in the cave, he shined the light down the pitch-back tunnel. There was very little natural light, as the trees blocked the entrance. They walked down the tunnel slowly, with Cloe leading the way. She was getting the vibes strongly now. Once they were well down the cave, they saw a skeleton to one side. John rushed to it and bent down over it. "This is the skeleton of an important person. Judging from its size, it's presumably male. And look; it is resting on the remnants of what I think is leather, probably a coat. The leather would take longer to disintegrate. My guess is this is Agent Robert Dogood."

"Is there anything in what is left of the coat?" said Jack.

John lifted a flap, and there was a sheet of paper under it. He picked it up. "Just this, but the writing is no longer visible."

As they think about their find, Ben shined his flashlight on the cave walls. "Look here," he said. He focused the light on a seam of yellow in the rock.

The four looked at one another. "Is that gold?" said John.

"My guess would be yes," said Ben. "Are you sure that mine claim covers this area?"

"That is what the receptionist said," said John, "but what are we to do about the body? If we report it, Don is likely to get the blame, but we must do something about this gold if that is what it is. Perhaps it is iron sulfide or pyrite, fool's gold."

Ben went over to the seam and touched it. "I think it's the real thing. I saw a similar-looking seam in a mine outside of Denver, Colorado, a few years ago on a trip with the school."

They all looked at one another, pondering what they should do. Finally, John took the lead and said, "I think we should leave things as they are for the moment. After all, it has been that way for over a hundred years. For old Sophie's sake, we don't want to get Don accused of murder. There really is no point after all this time, and Sophie won't last that long in any event. Let sleeping dogs lie, I say."

The others again looked at each other before agreeing. "That has to be best," said Jack, and then they rode back down the mountain to Dawson City.

Just before the mining office was about to close for the evening, the manager came out to his receptionist and said, "It has been a busy day back there. I'll be glad to get home for a vodka tonic tonight. By the way, did I see you talking to someone about the Wicker claim? I saw you pointing to it on the map."

He doesn't miss much, the receptionist thought. "Yes, sir. Someone came in with the original claim form. They were interested in seeing the location."

"I have been intrigued by that claim for all my forty years here. Why would this Don Wicker take a claim on his own so far away from everyone else unless he knew something? Yet no one has heard hide or hair of him or his family for over a hundred years. He would be dead now, of course, but it is strange. I have always thought I would go and see it for myself, but I never have because of the Indian connection, although they severed those links years ago."

"Should we go and investigate tomorrow, sir?" the receptionist said.

"Oh, I don't know. Technically, we would be trespassing."

After a pause, the manager said, "Well, I suppose it would be alright as long as we don't touch anything. Be here at eight and have two horses ready. We will then be back in time to open the office."

That evening, Cloe phoned Gloria, who answered immediately. "Glad we managed to get hold of you. I wanted to fill you in on what is happening here. We found the bank deposit box, and inside were the keys to a car that Don purchased before he died. We also found another claim form, this time for the hills outside Dawson City in the Klondike. We are there at the moment, investigating, and tomorrow we head back to Nome.

"We will see Don's car when we get back. We located the vehicle by chance at a service station. So much has happened to us by chance that I think there is more in it than that. I know Don is controlling events. We plan to take the car back to Sophie's house in San Fransisco, but we're unsure how we will do that. There are no roads out of Nome, and we are talking about an original motorized pram," Cloe joked.

"That is amazing," said Gloria. "I like the pram idea, but you are probably not doing it justice. The station here would want to be involved as a follow-up to the previous items. Ring me when you get back to Nome, and we will work something out."

After breakfast the following morning, they headed back to the airport, handing in the car rental, and collected a flight to Nome. The conversation on the way was entirely about the death of the inspector.

"Don't forget, Taffy was involved in this. In fact, he must be the prime suspect," said John.

On the way, he phoned Mr. Polanski at the service station, saying they would be back in Nome in a few days and would come and see him and Don's car then.

CHAPTER TWENTY

As arranged, the mine claims department manager was at his office at eight o'clock in the morning, and his receptionist was waiting there with two horses. They rode up into the hills alongside the Klondike River. The journey took a half-hour, as they took a shortcut along the water's edge that the assistant knew about. The manager was a competent rider and was unbothered by the drop into the gorge. His poor assistant was petrified, though. and just closed his eyes, letting the horse find its own way.

Once they reached the flat ground at the top, the manager laughed and said, "You can open your eyes now. We are at the top. I take it you don't like heights."

"Not a lot, sir," the assistant said sarcastically, as he could now breathe again. He looked around. "I haven't been up here before, sir."

"It's only been open to us for about thirty years since the Indians relinquished the burial site, which leads us to how and why Don Wicker laid claim to it in 1898. There doesn't even seem to be much up here other than a few trees, which, judging by their size, were here in Don Wicker's time. Doesn't that amaze you, son, to think these trees were here in a different lifetime?"

The assistant ignored the question, but he knew from the maps that there is a cave somewhere, and he'd brought a large flashlight with him, knowing that his manager wouldn't be bothered. He walked through the trees while the manager peered over the ravine. He wanted to see if he could spot a cave. The assistant was more successful. He found the Indian burial cave with the pile of stones outside.

He called out, "The cave is over here, Mr. Bonstein."

The manager rushed over, and they entered the cave. The manager had some knowledge of gold mines and the shallow seams that can appear in the rock. He took hold of the flashlight and shined it at the rock surface, scanning for the seam that he was certain was there. After half an hour, he became frustrated; he felt sure that the seam had to be easily visible. After all, Don Wicker had found it, and he'd known nothing of mining. Then they heard a crunch underfoot as one of them trod on a skeleton lying on the ground.

"What the…?" said the manager, who now directed the flashlight at the skeleton. They knew this was not an Indian who had been buried here; this person had not been buried at all. They looked all around, but there was nothing to say who it was. They guessed from the state of the bones that the body had been there for many years. Shining the flashlight all around, the manager suddenly saw what he had been looking for initially: the seam of gold. It was about nine inches deep and wound its way up and down the rock.

"Well, that is one for the books. Not only have we found the gold, but also the skeleton of someone who has been dead for many years. We need to get back to the office and report this now."

When they got back to Nome, John, Cloe, Jack, and Ben returned to the service station. Polanski had arranged for his people mover to be available. He said the car rental was not as bad as everyone expected and could be put right in a week; it was a half-hour drive to his other premises on the far side of town, an upscale car showroom where he used the three Victorian cars as showpieces.

"That's your beauty there," Polanski said with pride, pointing to the car in the window display. "It is in pristine condition. As the only model of its kind now in existence, it is very valuable."

Jack appreciated these old cars, and he said, "The Packard Runabout was far in advance of its time. Look at the quality." He glided his hand over the bodywork.

"Just look at that two-seater armchair. Can you imagine the pleasure of driving that vehicle over a hundred years ago, when it was unique, especially in the backwaters of Alaska?" he said, rubbing his hands over the leather upholstery.

"I don't think it has ever been used. There is no odometer, so we can't tell. Do you have the other key that was on the keyring?" said Polanski.

"Oh, yes," said Cloe, and she handed the key over.

Polanski put it in the ignition. "It fits just like Cinderella's slipper," he joked. "We will have to charge the battery. In fact, we will give you a new one and service the engine. It has brought us a lot of business, standing here all those years. We will miss it."

John whispered, "It's not my cup of tea, but then, I am a biker."

"You're a Sasanach," Cloe said, laughing at the term from her Scottish ancestry.

She tried to open the glove compartment in the front dashboard, but it was locked. " I wonder if the ignition key fits." She put the key into the slot and turned, and the door popped open. "There's something inside," she said.

Now everyone was interested as she removed a pair of white chamois leather gloves. "Don must have placed them there for Sophie. Look at the size, much too small for a man," said John.

Cloe could feel the quality of the leather. "Considering all the things Don did for Sophie, he must have loved her very much. How sad it is he could not tell her." A tear formed in her eye.

"But they are together now," said John, trying to comfort Cloe.

Taken aback by this, Cloe said, "Darling, I did not realize you thought like that." She leaned over and tenderly kissed him.

Jack was more impressed with the car, and he rubbed his hand down the bonnet. By now, he had caressed every inch of the car.

"We are going to have to transport the car down to San Fransisco. How the hell are we going to do that?" Just then, Cloe's phone rang, "It's Gloria," she said, and she answered it.

"Hello, Cloe," said Gloria. "I have spoken to my boss, and he wants us to be involved with the project. I am flying up to Nome later today, and we can talk about it then."

"Good, we look forward to seeing you again. We are staying at the Nome Hotel on Main Street." With that, Cloe disconnected the call. "ABC TV is coming up, Mr. Polanski. They have been following our exploits since our meeting with Don's granddaughter."

"Well, in that case, we will see what we can do. The publicity would be good for my firm. Times have been hard lately with this pandemic that has spread across the country," said Polanski. He drove them back to the other showroom to pick up their car. They then headed back to their hotel, and they sat in the lobby to discuss their plans.

John said, "I think Cloe and I should go back to San Fransisco with the car. We need to update Sophie on what we have found out. Maybe Gloria will go with us with the cameraman."

"That sounds good to me. To be honest, I'm happy not being on the television," said Jack. "Ben and I can carry on with things up here while you are away. We can dig up that site more with the digger."

Just then, Gloria walked into the hotel with her cameraman. Cloe was pleased to see her and rushed over to greet her. "A lot has happened since we last saw you, Gloria."

"Well, you have to fill me in," said Gloria. "Why don't you and I have dinner tonight? You can bring me up to date."

The two women booked a table in the hotel dining room. The three men were pleased, and they booked a table for themselves at the adjoining sushi restaurant.

At dinner, Cloe filled Gloria in about the bank deposit box and the keys they'd found inside, which had eventually led them to the car Don had purchased.

"How could he have afforded that in those days? The car must have been expensive, and we know he didn't make much from his mining," said Gloria.

'We have no idea," said Cloe. "He did have a jar of gold in his deposit box, but it was untouched. Maybe there was a second one we don't know about. However, the goldsmith up the road said the gold did not come from this continent, as it is rose gold. He must have acquired it from someone on his journey. Maybe he stole it."

"Hmm, I doubt he stole it. From my experience, if he did, he would have spent it. More likely, he got it from another miner who might well have stolen it in the past," said Gloria.

"Well, we also learned that Don became pals with a Welshman called Taffy. We know a private detective was looking for Taffy, and we think we found the detective's body in a cave in the Klondike. I say a body. It was actually a skeleton. We reckon it was Taffy who killed the detective," said Cloe, wanting to avoid any suggestion that Don had done it.

"What do you plan to do with the car? It must be one of the first cars ever made," said Gloria, ignoring the mention of the body. She did not want to go down that road, either. The purpose of the program was to boost Don's character.

"It is. We have checked," said Cloe. "It is a Packard Runabout. It only has one cylinder. Can you imagine that? The car is in immaculate condition; it has been in a car showroom since 1930 as a publicity stunt. The garage is happy for us to take it back to San Fransisco. That is where I thought you might come in. The present Sophie wants to turn the house over to a trust, as you know, and open it to the public. The car will be a real attraction, and Don and his Sophie will be reunited in spirit. I am sure that is why I have been brought into this with the little chest."

Gloria was quiet for a minute. Then, looking down at her dinner, she said, "You are deep, aren't you, but you may be right if you believe in such things. I'm not sure that I do. However, the TV station will want to follow this. You will need a transporter for the car, and we will need to go by ship to Vancouver There is no way such an old vehicle would make a California road trip today even from Vancouver. I wonder how Don thought he was going to get it home in those days. There wouldn't have been many gas stations, either. He must have had a plan."

"That is a very good point, Gloria. We were thinking of a transporter, but how would Don have managed it?" Cloe said.

They finished their meal and went back to the reception area, where Jack, John, and Ben enjoyed a coffee. Cloe said, "Gloria has come up with a good point. How did Don intend to get the car home? We know he had finished his mining prospecting once he signed the back of his claim form. He must have had a plan."

The three men looked at each other questioningly, but no one spoke. John ventured, "I have no idea. Maybe that's something we should look into, but where would we start?"

Ben said, "We should consider where he purchased the car. Was it from Nome Autos? Polanski might have some records that would help us."

Everyone thought that was a good idea. "In any event, we need to see Polanski tomorrow to finalize arrangements," said John. With that, they all went to their rooms. Their thoughts were on the question, *How was Don going to get the car home?*

CHAPTER TWENTY-ONE

Polanski called and invited them to come to his showroom at ten o'clock in the morning. "I have some news that I think will interest you."

At ten, they entered the Nome Autos showroom. John said, "This is Gloria Rowbottom and her cameraman from ABC Television, Justin. She has come to witness things and prepare a follow-up to her earlier program on Don Wicker."

"Glad to meet you, Mr. Polanski. We'll turn Don into a star by the time we finish these programs," said Gloria.

"We discussed how Don got the car to us in 1900, when it was the first of its kind," said Polanski. "So, I did some research into the old records of my grandfather. Fortunately, they have been kept, although I have to admit I have been going to clear them out every year. My grandfather was the dealer; it was the first car he sold. The Packard Company agreed to transport it here and then to wherever Don Wicker wanted. The Packard Company has been sold and merged many times since then, so we couldn't hold them to that or even prove it, but my company will take on that responsibility. Hopefully, we will get a little publicity out of it."

"Well, thank you for that. The car will make a good exhibit for the museum when it is set up," said John.

"I'm having the car brought over as we speak on the transporter," said Polanski.

A single-level transporter drew up to the building and honked its horn. Fortunately, it was a dry day, as the car was not covered. "So, this is the car," said Gloria. "It would do for a trip to the coast, would it?" she joked. "Let's get some shots of it being unloaded," she said to her cameraman. "Are the record books handy, Mr. Polanski? I want some shots of those as well."

"They are, but please, call me Justin," said Polanski.

He went to his office and returned with two large ledgers, beautifully bound just as they had been a hundred years ago. The cameraman filmed him as he opened the book to the relevant page. Besides the sale details, several notes had been written in the margins in pencil.

"Zoom in on the notes," said Gloria. "What is that? Wow, it says Don won the money to buy the car by gambling on the wheel of fortune!"

They were all surprised. " So that's how he got the money," said Cloe.

"By the way, don't worry about talking freely. I will edit all that out later and put a commentary over it," said Gloria.

"When can we head down to San Fransisco?" said John.

"You can leave any day," said Polanski. "There is a cargo ship that leaves here every day for Vancouver. The transporter will carry the car, and you can ride with the driver. You mentioned Don's relative is going to open the house to the public. We could drive the car through some towns on the way. Once we leave Vancouver and collect money for her trust. People are always interested in the original cars. That way, it would take about ten days. Gloria could come with you as well, filming on the route."

"Try and stop me," Gloria said with a smile. "I've been working on this from the start. I'm not going to let it go now."

They made arrangements for the transporter to leave the following day at ten o'clock. There was just enough room in the cab for John, Cloe, Gloria, and her cameraman, which would then be in order, Polanski confirmed. John said, "Jack and Ben, you remain here and carry on with the mine excavation until Cloe, and I return."

At nine-thirty the next morning, Gloria set up her television crew on the sidewalk adjacent to the transporter loaded with Don's car. She indicated to the cameraman to start rolling.

"Good morning, viewers. This is Gloria Rowbottom, reporting from Nome in Alaska. Today the 1900 car owned by Don Wicker, who was murdered in that year, sets off for its last journey to San Francisco, where it will go into the museum at the family home. We are following the procession. The car will be driven in certain towns to raise money for the museum once we leave Vancouver. Please come and support us if we are in your town. A list of the cities will appear at the end of my report."

They set off at ten o'clock, with the transporter in front and Cloe and John and then the television crew following behind. The dock is only a short journey, and the ship is ready for them to drive on. The weather was fine, so the ship made a good time on the trip to Vancouver.

Having left Vancouver, they were under their own steam, and on the journey down the country, they stop at the outskirts of ten towns. At each stop, the Packard was taken off the transporter, and John and Cloe drove through the city, waving to the small crowds that had gathered. Most of the onlookers seemed more interested in the television camera, and while waving madly, they threw cash into the bucket held by the cameraman's assistant.

The car could only move slowly, so the short journey at each town took about two hours. After three days of transport, they arrived at San Fransisco, having raised five thousand dollars on the way. They went straight to Sophie's house; she was aware of their arrival, as she had been watching the television broadcasts. The car was unloaded, and John went into the house.

"Hello, Sophie," he said. "I don't know if you have been watching the television, but we have found out much more about your grandfather in Nome. He did make some gold finds, and the car outside is the result. We believe he intended to drive it back to here before he was brutally murdered, but it wasn't to be. You can have the car put in the museum now. There are other items, too, a jar of rose gold and another mining claim in the Klondike, and we think there may well be a real gold seam in the cave."

"I don't know how to thank you. Although I always believed Grandfather intended to return home, I did not know that for a fact, but you have unearthed the truth. Thank you. You have allowed me to die a happy and contented person."

The camera was rolling the whole time.

"We were pleased to have helped," said John, and with that, he passed over the jar of gold nuggets. He didn't worry about telling Sophie where Don had gotten them, letting her think he had panned them from the river.

"Will you deal with the new gold mine claim? Sell it for whatever you can get and take ten percent for your trouble. The balance can be sent to the trust bank account," said Sophie, and she handed John the bank's details, along with the name and address of the other trustee, Rachel Goldberg.

"We will do that for you, Sophie. Fear not," said John, who suddenly noticed how much she had aged since they'd last seen her. It was as though she had accomplished her goal and was ready to pass on.

"There is one thing we need to do to complete the picture." Says Cloe.

"What's that?" Sophie says.

"We need to ut the two stones of Sophie and Don together." Cloe says, "We have kept them apart all this time so that you can see anything that happens. It may be nothing,"

Gloria says, "This part must be filmed although we may be disappointed."

Cloe has kept each stone in individual matchboxes, which she lays on the table. Opening them, she takes out each stone and places them on the table one at a time. Gloria is filming. At first, nothing happens, so Cloe moves one to touch the other. Still, nothing happens, but then the stones start to glow and get hotter and hotter, to the point where eventually they burn up, and the smoke rises into a plume, and then there is nothing.

The camera is switched off, and Gloria says, "Oh, my God, I don't believe what I just saw."

The others just shook their heads. Sophie says, "They are both happy now together in heaven forever."

They all left the house, leaving Sophie to her memories. That night, Sophie was in her grandmother's bedroom, sitting in the armchair, thinking, *Grandmother, I have made your request and established Don's innocence and that he did love you. You can rest in peace now, and I know I will shortly join you.*

Sophie drifted into sleep and did not wake up. She was found in the morning by her daily maid. Three days later, John found out from the trustee Rachel Goldberg that Sophie had passed away the night they left her. Cloe immediately phoned Gloria to tell her Sophie had died. Gloria had left Sophie simultaneously and went back to the television studios pending further developments, which Cloe had promised to inform her.

John and Cloe had made their way back to Nome with the transporter, going in reverse. Jack and Ben were waiting for them on their return. Saddened by the news of Sophie's passing, they went to the local bar and rose their glasses of Scotch to her.

John's phone started to ring, he looked at the screen, and it said 'unknown caller' John answered it. "Hello, this is John Smith."

"Good morning Mr, Smith. This is Chuck Bonstien from the mining registry office at Dawson City. I need to talk with you in private sir, this phone is not secure. Are you able to come into the office?"

John is concerned and reticent to answer, *has the inspector's body been found?* "I could be with you in two days, Mr. Bonstien."

"Very good then. I will see you on Wednesday." Said Mr. Bomstien and hung up.

"We have to go back to Dawson, Cloe, something has come up," John said.

"I hope they haven't found the body in the cave. Well, think further, it was nothing to do with us, was it? We can drive back tomorrow once we find out what has been happening in Nome while we have been away." Cloe said.

Jack said, "Not much has happened here. Michael has been around all the time, watching us as we have been excavating on the claim site. He has started to talk with us now, questioning what we are doing. I think he is bored with the exercise now, he has not done anything on his site."

"Just keep going, for the time being, let me know if there are any developments, I expect we will be away for a week. When we get back, we can decide where we go. Have you heard from Judy at all?"

"Oh, yes, we speak every night. I would ask her to come over if Michael wasn't here. I think this could be the real thing." Saud Jack.

Cloe jumped in, saying, "We are pleased for you Jack, it is about time you settled down, but don't rush into anything until you are sure."

"Let's go and have a look at the site." John said, "It rained heavily last night."

"Yes, we haven't been able to do anything for two days," Ben said.

When they finished their drinks, they drove up to the claim site, "It is very muddy. Good job, we have the boots in the back," said Cloe.

They spent ten minutes sloshing around in the mud when Ben said, "The surface looks different today, look, Jack, I think the rain has washed away a lot of the topsoil that we disturbed with the digger. What is that white over there?" he said pointing. They walk over and bend down over what looks like a large piece of white plastic.

'It's only plastic," says Cloe

"I don't think so, dear," John says as he bends down and clears away some more mud. "look, feel the touch of it. It's not plastic." Hesitant to say anything, John looks at the others, then says, "I think it is ivory."

"IVORY," says Jack, "But how......."

"I don't know, but while we are away, you two clear this part carefully when the ground dries out. We need to keep quiet about this. Look at the width of this tusk if that's what it is. If I am right, then this site needs to be fenced. And whatever, don't let Michael see it."

"Got you, boss. It should have dried ou by the time you get back, and we will keep it discretely covered," said Jack.

Over dinner that evening, John produced a book of historical animals. "Let's see what we have in here." Says John as he opens the book to elephants and their ancestors. He settles on one page headed Mammoths and moves his finger down to the drawing. "Look at the size of the tusks, they are enormous, compared to the present elephant, and you know how much the present elephant tusk is worth." They all read the narrative in amazement.

All except Ben, he has already gotten out his tablet, which he carries everywhere for occasions like this. He searches mammoth tusks, and he finds several entries. Besides all the offers to purchase the tasks, there is one which gives fundamental details.

"If that is a complete mammoth tusk, it would be worth a small fortune. It says here they fetch between $75 and $125 per pound weight, and they can be pretty heavy. Even if it is a partial tsk, the website says it is still worth considerable money." Ben says. "Do you think we should fence the site now?"

They look to each other in turns and settle back to john, who always takes the lead in these matters. "Maybe wait till I get back. We don't want to give any help to Michael on his adjoining site, do we?" Says John.

CHAPTER TWENTY-TWO

The following day, Cloe and John take a plane down to Dawson City. On the way, Cloe says, "Why do you think the manager phoned John?"

"I don't know. Maybe he has been to the claim site and found the skeleton. The police may be waiting for us when we arrive. On the other hand, they must know that we had nothing to do with the killing. The skeleton is ancient. We'll have to wait and see." Says John, but he hadn't convinced himself as yet, let alone Cloe.

The flight takes an hour and a half. Cloe is busy looking out of the window when the small airliner lands, searching for a police car with flashing lights. Nothing the airport looks deserted, as the plane taxis to the gate. They walk through border control unhindered. "Well, so far, so good." Says John, and they proceed to the car rental depot and rent a small SUV.

They drive to the mining claims office. On entering, the manager who has been watching for them through his glass screen comes out and says to his assistant, "I'll deal with this " and to John and Cloe, he says, "Thank you for coming so quickly, do come into my office, I have some good news and regretfully some bad." He said with a glum look on his face.

That relaxed Cloe in particular; they followed him into the office. "Let me introduce myself first as we have not formally met. I am Chuck Bonstein, and I have run this office for, let me see now, it must be thirty years."

"It's good to meet you, Chuck; please carry on." Says John.

"When you were here on the last occasion with the paperwork from Don Wicker's claim, I thought to myself I must look into this further. I always have been intrigued as to why we would have one claim so far away from all the others, made a hundred years ago, and then we have new claims made by yourself adjoining earlier this year. May I ask you why you did that?"

John glanced at Cloe and said, "My colleague and I were here to investigate the claim scam that went on at that time. You may recall the details it was in all the papers, and the criminal went to prison. We thought it would be fun to take out the claims further up the mountains, where undoubtedly the gold originated. At the same time, we were investigating the circumstances of Don Wicker's death a hundred years ago. We learned that Don had a claim adjoining our new ones all those years ago purely by chance." Said John.

"Well, as I say, I was curious, so I went up to the Wicker claim with my assistant after you left. I am not an expert, but I have studied gold seems, and I am sure that there is a sizable one inside the cave. As Mr. Wicker is no longer with us, I took the liberty of calling in an expert, and they have confirmed there is a seem running a considerable length of the cave. As your claim is adjacent, yours would likely have the same seem. You could well have been rich by now." Says Chuck with a smirky smile.

John interrupted him, saying, "Could have been? Chuck, what do you mean?"

Chuck's expression had changed, into despondency, "Well, yes, that is the bad news, I am afraid, there was a mix up when we registered your claim. We subsequently found it was already registered twenty years ago." Said Chuck trying to look upset.

John looks at Cloe, pretending not to know about the gold seem, but is suspicious of this sudden finding of a claim registration on the adjoining site. And he says, "That is amazing, isn't it, Cloe? Don Wicker's Estate will, of course, be delighted. I suppose we shouldn't grumble. After all, it was only luck for us, wasn't it?" He didn't, of course, mean a word of it.

Cloe just scowled at him.

"Did you find a skeleton in the cave?" says John wanting to clear the air to give him time to think.

"Oh yes, I reported it to the police, which in turn sent an expert, and it was established the skeleton was ancient. It was an Indian burial ground, you know, but it was surprising they would leave the body on the surface like that. The police said it was all history and did not want to pursue that matter further. However, the Royal Mounted Police said they would investigate further, and I am expecting their inspector to come this morning. They are aware you would be here today."

Cloe turned to John looking concerned and thinking, *what is he playing at. This is not like John.* John kept a stony face.

"By the way, as a matter of interest, who was our claim originally registered to?" John said to Chuck.

About time too! Thought Cloe.

"Let me check," Chuck said as he got up and went to a filing cabinet. He flipped through the drawer, although he knew exactly where the file was. "Ah, here we are, let me see, a Mrs. Audrey Croft," Chuck says.

"And do we have any more information about her?" says John.

"We have an address, as the claim was only registered twenty years ago."

'And her address is, Chuck? I would like to make contact with her to let her know there are no bad feelings." says John.

"I am afraid I'm not at liberty to give you her address because of data protection, but I can tell you she lives in Edmonton, Alberta. I will be contacting her shortly and will let her know you have no bad feelings." Chuck says.

"And the date of the claim is? Chuck."

"It says first of May, two thousand." Says Chuck.

"Hmm, is there any notes as to the reason for her claim? Has she made any attempt to excavate?" said John, knowing that she had not, as he was only there a few days ago.

"No, there is nothing on the file, to that effect," Chuck says.

At that moment, much to the relief of Chuck, John could hear the outside door is opened, and someone walked in the outer offer. John could hear the clump of boots. There is a knock on the inner door, and Chuck looks up to see the officer come in. The police officer holds his finger to his mouth, indicating that Chuck should keep quiet.

"Well, what have we here then? Says the officer in an official way, making John and Cloe turn around immediately.

"Oh, my God!" says John, and he stands up to greet Inspector Albert Jones of the Mounties. "It is good to see you again, Albert." And they embrace.

"When I heard that this dead body business involved you, I had to come over and see you." Said Albert.

"I am so pleased you did, although you frightened us when I heard the Mounties were involved in a death of over a hundred years. This is my other half, by the way, Cloe."John says, introducing Cloe.

It's good to meet you, Cloe. The better half, no doubt." Says Albert. "John and I had an adventure earlier this year, right in this town, would you believe?"

"Good to meet you as well, Albert. John told me all about your escapades." Cloe says.

"There is no problem with the skeleton. As you say, it is over a hundred years old, we had I checked, and the local police investigated. They don't think it was an Indian, although it was found in an old Indian burial site. Some bright spark investigated on the internet and came up with the idea that it was a private detective from a New York agency that went missing a hundred years ago. That is all history now, and the file has been closed, but I wanted to say hello. I hear you are involved with a claim at the cave." Says Albert.

John wonders whether Albert is entirely honest. He obviously knows more than he is letting on. "The cave claim is not ours. It belongs to the Trustees of Don Wicker, whom we are acting for. We have been investigating Don Whicker's death, who was murdered in Nome, Alaska, in 1900. Strangely enough, when we were here in the spring for fun, we took a claim on the adjoining lot, although, at that time, we did not know of Don's claim. That only came to light recently when we went to his bank deposit box in Nome." John says.

"That is a coincidence, but lucky you, your claim will no doubt be valuable as well," Albert says.

"There's more; I'll come back to the claim in a minute. A Michael West has been following us for two months. He also took out claims here and in Nome. Somehow, I think there is a connection with our friend Edward Isaacs."

"Michael West?"Albert says with an '*I told you so smile*.' "Before I left, I investigated all the recent claims filed here and Nome. To be honest, other than Don Wicker, there are only yours and this Michael West."

John picked up immediately that Albert found their claim and not Audrey Croft. Albert continued, "I dug deeper into our friend Michael, and it appears he was in the same prison as Edward Isaacs, he was only released earlier this year, but months after Edward went to the prison. Is he causing any problems for you? I have no jurisdiction in Alaska, of course, but I could always call in Josh Young from the FBI. Michael West is a Canadian citizen. Michael West is the other reason I came to see you today. I believe he carried out a bank robbery in Calgary ten years ago. Fresh evidence has come up pointing to him."

"He's not causing any immediate problems to us. I think he is just watching what we are doing, hoping to make some money out of his claims," John says.

"Well, it certainly seems as though you will do well from your claim. I gather gold has been found in the cave."

"There was a mistake over our claim; according to the registrar here, it was already registered to someone in Edmonton," John says, and he notices the registrar's face has turned a bright red, and he makes a nervous cough.

Albert is shocked as well; his expression dropped, but he says nothing.

Chuck comes into the conversation, glad that the Inspector had not taken the question of Audrey Croft up further. "I have many contacts in the mining industry, although not much for gold. I can't remember when the last gold mine was established here, but the news has gotten out, and I have received an approach from Klondike Mines Ltd. They will, I am sure, make a good offer."

"I will need to speak with the trustee of Don's Estate, but I am sure she will want to sell." Says John.

"Leave it with me then. I am happy to act as a go-between." Says Chuck.

"Happy to do that, Chuck. I am sure the company will pay you an introduction fee." Says John to make sure Chuck knows he is not a fool.

Coming back to Albert, John says, "What do you plan to do about Michael West?"

"Well, extradition would take a long time, and to be honest, we don't have the necessary evidence as yet," Albert says, looking expectantly at John.

John smiles. "Come on, out with it, what do you want me to do?"

They all start a nervous laugh. "I thought if I flew you both back to Nome in the company helicopter, we might be able to entice West to come back with me unofficially, so to speak," Albert said. At that moment, John's cellphone, which was lying on the desk in front of him, started ringing. He leaned forward and was just going to switch it off when he noticed the name on display was Josh Young.

Josh is John's contact and employer at the FBI. He is hesitant, but Albert says, "I think you should answer it," seeing that John is considering switching it off.

John picks up the phone and says to Albert, "You knew this, didn't you?"

Albert says with a smile, "Maybe."

John answers the phone and says, "Hello boss, this is a surprise."

"You don't sound shocked." Says Josh, "You will remember the help that Inspector Albert Jones of the Royal Canadian Police gave us earlier in the year with the scam of Edward Isaacs."

"I do indeed, and surprisingly he is sitting next to me now," says John.

"Oh, I'm a bit slow phoning then."

"Okay, Albert has told me about his plans. Are you saying you would like me to help him formally?" Said John.

There was a moment's silence, John knew he had put Josh on the spot, plus the FBI would have to pay him. "Right, let's make it formal, usual rates of pay. Give the Inspector all the help you can, please."

"Will do, boss. Thanks," and John discontinues the call.

"Well, it seems we are to help you, Albert," says John,

"Let me speak to the trustee about the mine" John dials Rachel Goldberg's number, and she quickly answers. "Hello, this is John Smith. We spoke regarding the Wicker Trust. I am now with the claims manager at the klondike site, and he tells me that there is an interested party who may purchase the claim. Frankly, it would resolve matters for all of us and produce a nice income for the Trust. Are you happy that I ask him to open negotiations, and we will see what the outcome is?"

'That would be very acceptable, and thank you for your help and interest, John. Of course, you must take a fee." Says Rachel

"On this occasion that will not be necessary, I am pleased to help. I will be in touch shortly," He switches off the phone and then to Chuck. "Are we done then, Chuck? I will leave it to you to negotiate with the mining company. We would like to sell our adjoining claims as well, although that transaction must be kept separate."

"I understand and will be in touch in due course. The mining company may want to do some more inspections and tests." With that, Albert, John, and Cloe leave the office. Outside they discuss the plan forward.

Albert says, "I do not want to let Michael West know I am a police Inspector, not that I have ever met him, but

I think it would be better if I use a different name. Perhaps you could bring me to Nome to look into your Claims there. I could be a mining consultant. Michael would not know what one of those is, but neither do I. I'll just bluff my way through things."

"What name do you want to use?" says Cloe.

"How about James Dogood? Does that sound American.?"

John laughed, "That should work, Albert, or let's get into this by calling you James now."

They all laughed, and James said, "The helicopter is in the airport if you collect your belongings, we can leave straight away."

"We're ready, James." Says John getting into the spirit of the new personage. "We didn't bring anything with us, but we have to return the car to the airport." They ride around the corner where the small airport is situated. As a Mountie, James has a unique access point avoiding any crowds at the front entrance. They are at the government gate within ten minutes, and once James shows his identification, they are shown through and walk out to the Airbus H145 helicopter sitting on the tarmac.

The pilot is sitting in the cockpit waiting for the Inspector to return. The doors are opened, and they get in. James instructs the pilot to go to Nome in Alaska. "We need special permission to enter the USA airspace." The pilot says.

"It's all arranged. Get onto the control tower, and you will get approval.?

'Yes, sir," and the pilot calls the tower, who permit him to take off to Nome.

"The FBI has approved the operation, sir. Homeland Security is involved. And you are free to take off when you are ready." The Tower officer says. The pilot gently starts up the rotors while the passengers get seated and strap in. Once the rotors are at the right speed, the pilot lifts the craft off the ground, and it heads north to Alaska, climbing high over the mountains

"The weather is perfect for the flight." James says, "You never know in this region," and then he carries on, "I wanted to say John, that business of your claim being already registered needs looking into. As I said, I checked out before my trip here, and it was definitely registered to you. I smell a rat."

"Thanks, James, that is exactly what I thought as well. We need to look into this, Mrs. Audrey Croft."

"Well, if you need my help. Let me know." Says James.

Two hours later and they are losing height, getting ready to land at Nome Airport. John has phoned Jack to pick them up at the airport. "I won't go into details now, but there are some developments, and you will meet an old friend.' John leaves Jack in suspense as he goes to their rental car and leaves for the airport. Everything is close together at Nome, and he is at the gate in ten minutes.

Jack looks to the sky and can't see a plane except for the helicopter that is just landing. *Are they coming by copter?* He thinks, and soon his question is answered as John and Cloe walk to the gate.

"Thanks for picking us up, Jack." John greets Jack as they walk through the gate. Formalities are few here.

"No problem, it's good to see you again, Albert, but you are far from home."

"Good to see you too, Jack. I fill you in, in the car on the way to the hotel." Says James.

In the car, James says, "As of now, I am James Dogood and not an inspector with the police. I am really here to apprehend, or perhaps I should say, kidnap Michael West and take him back to Calgary to stand trial for a bank raid and murder some years ago. It was a bad event, one of the guards was shot. We got the three bandits, but I always thought one had gotten away. It has recently come out from one of the other criminals, and the finger points to this Michael West. I have never met him, and he hasn't seen me. " Says, James.

'But why not simply extradite him, James?" says Jack

"Too long a process. It is easier just to bundle him into the helicopter and fly home with him. We have FBI approval of the operation, well I suppose I should say they will turn a blind eye. That is why you and John are involved." Says James.

"Sounds like something Josh Young would organize." Says Jack.

James laughs, "You both know your boss don't you?"

"What's been happening with Michael since we have been away." Says John, "By the way, there were no problems in Dawson, except James thinks we killed the body of the skeleton they found." General laughter ensues. "No, seriously, that cave looks as though it does contain a gold seem, and there is an interested mining company who hopefully will make an offer for Don's claim. The Claims Manager is dealing with it on our behalf, and I have spoken to the Trustee for Don's Estate. She is delighted. I don't think she wants to get too involved with negotiations." Says John. "There was an issue with our claim adjoining Don's. The manager said there was a mistake, and that particular claim was registered to an Audrey Croft, twenty years ago."

"That sounds suspicious to me." Says Jack.

"And the rest of us, Jack, but we will look into that further once we sort things out here." Says John.

"Good," says Jack. "Michael has been very quiet, Ben and I have been to the claim site every day, but we have not seen Michael. The weather was rough yesterday, so we were unable to unearth anymore. Ben is at the hotel waiting for us. He had a bad headache this morning, too much drink last night."

They were back at the hotel in minutes, and James checked in. The hotel has plenty of rooms available. Ben is sitting in reception waiting for them to return, and he is introduced to James. "How's the head, Ben? I hear it is sore this morning." Says Cloe.

'It's a lot better now, thanks. Tylenol works wonders." Ben says, wondering what James is doing with them and how much he knows.

Jack says to John on the quiet, but very embarrassed, "I am missing Judy a lot, we speak on the phone every night. I think I am in love. Do you need me here any longer? If not, then I would like to fly to Calgary to see her. I hope to convince her to come to Nashville with me."

"Jack, I am delighted for you. You go; we can handle things here." Says John.

"Thanks, pal. I'll fly off tomorrow." Jack says.

CHAPTER TWENTY-THREE

The following day Jack has spoken with Judy, and she is delighted that he is coming to Calgary to see her. He had told Judy that Michael is still in Nome. She sounded pleased, knowing that she did not want to see Michael ever again. Having packed his bag, Jack heads to the airport and gets the last available seat on the plane to Calgary.

John has explained James's position to Ben, and all four of them drive to the claim site. John sees that it is just the same as he left it. He is surprised that Michael does not appear to have taken any action, as his adjoining claim is also untouched. " I will pretend to be a gold mine strategist." Says James.

John smiles. "Are you that technical to get away with that?"

Now it is James's turn to laugh, "In my job, you have to be a master at everything, or at least have enough information to bluff your way through it."

Having ridden up to the claim, John walked over the site. The ivory is still as he left it. James says, "You know what that is, don't you?"

John smiles once more, "We have an idea. What do you think it is?"

James gets down on the ground and feels the ivory. "I would say without question it is the task of a Mammoth. The predecessor to the modern elephant. They occupied these regions before the ice age. The tusk will be anything around ten or fourteen feet long and usually curved more than a modern elephant. They are precious, worth about a hundred dollars a pound weight, and they are pretty heavy."

"You do know about your animals, don't you." Said, Cloe.

"Let's get to work and slowly take out the earth surrounding." Says Ben.

They get down on hands and knees, kneeling on rugs they had brought with them, and gradually cleared away the surrounding earth, and it was no time before the whole tusk is visible. Ben is very impressed with the size. He measured it as twelve feet long and curved almost into a circle. It was too heavy for two of the men to lift out of the ground.

"Let's get the earthmover." Says John, and he walks over and drives the CAT machine back to the tusk. They were just going to load on the tusk when Michael walked on to one end of the site.

"That's Michael West." Says John, indicating him with a nod of the head. James casts a discrete but beady eye on the villain as he walks toward them.

"I've not actually seen him before, only photos we have on the file." Says James as he sizes him up. He is a larger man than he had thought, he must allow for that when they kidnap him.

"Good morning, Michael," John says as he arrives with them. "This is James Dogood, he has come to help us in our deliberations of what we are to do here. Maybe you should employ him as well for your adjoining site."

James puts forward his hand, and Michael takes it. "It's good to meet you, James. Maybe we can do some business." Michael says. James acknowledges that with a smile.

"What have we got here then?" Michael says, looking down at the Mammoth tusk lying on the ground, now fully exposed,

"Well, it's not gold," John says sarcastically.

"A tusk, but it's huge, might be worth something," Michael says.

"Perhaps," John says, not wanting to give anything away.

Being professional, James did not want to say anything to his supposed customer in front of Michael, so He said, "Are you staying at the other hotel in town?"

Michael replied, "Yes, I intend to be there a few days more if you want to come and talk with me."

"I will do that, be assured, Michael." Michael got the message that he is not welcome at this moment and left them to go back to his hotel.

John said, "We need to get some serious help to excavate this site. We have found one task the other, to the dead animal must be below it, and it is too much for us to excavate. Let's go to a builder and get the site fenced off."

James says, "I'll leave that to you guys. I am going to sus out the situation with Michael West." And he leaves the others to go and check Michaels's hotel out.

Joh, Cloe, and Ben travel to a local builder and arrange for fencing to be put around their claim site. The builder says, " Excuse me for asking, but why are you fencing it? That site has been empty for decades. There can't be any gold there, or is there?"

John laughs, "No, there is no gold, at least not the type you mean, but we have found a mammoth tusk buried, and presumably, there may be more."

The builder is quiet for a minute, clearly thinking."You know, I have always been interested in those creatures. I checked up many years ago and found that they roamed this area over ten thousand years ago. I formed a local restoration club, and they would love to help you excavate the site."

"We'll take you up on that and give the organization ten percent of whatever we make on selling the ivory or whatever else we find." Said John, only too pleased to get the help that he didn't have to pay for upfront. They shake hands on the deal, and the builder said he would have six volunteers on-site tomorrow while h erected the fencing.

"That was a good deal," John said to Cloe after they left. "I have something else to do tonight back at the hotel." Cloe is intrigued but does not say anything as they head back to the hotel.

Back at their hotel, John said to Cloe, "We need to check into this Audrey Croft."

"I'm glad to hear you say that John. I thought you were just going to accept the situation."

"As if I would, I am confident this is a scam by the registrar, but we need to prove it,"

"Let's see what we can find on the internet. Chuck Bonstein said she lived in Edmonton, didn't he?" John says as he gets out his laptop and types in the name Audrey Croft and Edmonton. There are several entries, but none that looked like the person they are looking for.

Then Cloe says, "What about that one, and author of historical fiction?"

"Well, I agree it's the best we have got here, but then our lady might not be on the internet. There is an email listed. Let's send her an email pretending we are Gloria Rowbottom from the TV company. If Audrey is a writer, she will jump at that introduction." John says.

"It's worth a try." John opens up Gmail and gets an email that would be appropriate for Gloria Rowbottom and drafts an email to Audrey pretending to be Gloria. The email says that she has been reading some of Audrey's books and would like to do an article on her, in particular, her lifestyle and what she has been doing in her life. Gloria asks Audrey to phone her assistant, Cloe, for a chat and then gives Cloe's number.

John punches in to send. "Now we just wait and see. When she phones, see if you can get around to the gold mine somehow. You are good at that."

Cloe keeps watching her phone. "A watched kettle never boils, you know." John jokes, but after an hour, Cloe's phone rings,

"Good afternoon, this is Cloe Taylor, assistant to Gloria Rowbottom," Cloe said in her best speaking voice.

"Hello. I am Audrey Croft, the author. Gloria said, you would like to interview me," said Audrey.

"We would indeed, Audrey, if I may call you that. We have been following your career and see you have written six books. Have you been interviewed before?" Cloe says.

"Not really. How does the interview go?"

"Well, I will ask you various questions about your books and your general lifestyle; that's what a television audience wants to hear. The personal details, things you have done or expect to do. Anything that is unusual, different from most people. That sort of thing, so please tell me everything you can think of when I ask you a question. If it works out well, we will send a cameraman to you to take some pictures."

Audrey fell for it hook line and sinker. Cloe started by asking general things, which did not lead in the direction of Klondike.

"How about family, Audrey? Do you have children or siblings?" Cloe said, hoping to lead Audrey in that direction.

"My parents have passed now, so I am all alone, as I don't have a husband anymore, and we had no children." Cloe thought she was going down a dead-end, and she realized that Audrey would have loved close family, but then Audrey said, "I do have a brother, but I don't see him much unless he wants something."

"That's interesting, and what's his name?"

"William," Audrey said.

There was a moment's silence when John and Cloe looked at each other knowingly. John had a sheet of paper and was busy writing. *Have you seen him recently?* And Cloe asked the question.

"No, we don't communicate much. There was a falling out a few years back over a silly family thing. You know how it is. We haven't spoken since." Audrey said.

"Oh, that is sad, so where does he live?"

"He's in Dawson City. He has a government job there of some description. I'm not really sure exactly what he does." Said Audrey. Now John is smiling. Cloe then asked her various questions about her writing to make the conversation sound genuine and then finalized by saying, "I'll write things up, and if we need to photograph you, we'll come back to you." Cloe disconnects the call.

"That's it, I became concerned for a moment when she said her brother's name was William, but Chuck might be a pet name," John says, "Chuck forged everything. That's my opinion. We'll get James or Albert as he has gone back to his real name to investigate. I think our friend Chuck will be joining Edward Isaacs!"

"I think I may have messed up, John." He looked at her and raised his eyebrows. "I should have got the surname of her brother. She was married so that it would be different from her brother. We need to get the connection with Chuck established."

John thought about it and agreed, "Why don't we get Jack to call on her as the cameraman that you mentioned to her? He could do some fishing around. I wonder how old she is."

"I know what you are thinking." Cloe said, laughing, "I think Jack is sorted with Judy."

"Worth a try, though." Said John, and he picked up his phone and rang Jack. "How do you feel like a drive to Edmonton?"

'That's about three hours from here!" Jack says in frustration. "What do you want me to do."

"Cloe phoned this lady who now has our mining claim in Dawson City pretending to be Gloria Rowbottom's assistant from the TV company," Jack could be heard laughing. "Don't laugh; she did a good job, but it turns out she has a brother named William, but we suspect it is the same guy at the Registry Office, who called himself Chuck, but we need to prove it. Cloe said she would send along a cameraman for pictures."

"I suppose I'm the cameraman?" said Jack.

"You got it, Jack. Hire a video camera to make it look authentic, take lots of pictures, see what you can find out. We need the connection to Chuck. Can you do it?"

"Okay, see if you can do it for tomorrow. Judy is out for the day. Let me know if Audrey can be there, and I'll need her address." Says Jack.

"Will do, brother," says John.

"You've not called me that before."

"I know, but it seems right. I don't have a real brother."

John disconnects and gets Cloe to phone Audrey again as Gloria this time, so she has to put on a false accent, and she is delighted that Jack, the cameraman, is coming tomorrow, and she gives her address. Cloe told her it would be around lunchtime and disconnected the call.

"She fell for it hook, line and sinker," Cloe says to John.

John then pones back to Jack. 'It's all arranged. You are to go there around lunchtime tomorrow." And he gives the address. "Remember, Audrey may not know anything of this. In fact, I suspect she doesn't. It may be just Chuck's scheme. Don't forget the camera."

CHAPTER TWENTY-FOUR

The following day at six-thirty, Jack sets off in Judy's car, on the scenic drive to Edmonton, he had found on the internet a shop in Edmonton that would hire the equipment he needed. He arrived in plenty of time, giving ample time for his shopping when he hired a Television style portable camera for the day to make his call seem authentic.

He found the address of Audrey Croft quickly with the app on his phone. The house is a relatively simple two-floored house of brick, with a tiled roof. It is probably about forty years old, Jack thought, and it was well kept on the outside. It did not look like the standard of a house one might expect of a gold miner.

There is a dog fence around the house, which concerned Jack a little, but then he saw a small corgi dog come shuffling around the front of the property as soon as Jack opened the front gate. He called out to the dog, "Here, boy." Holding his hand out in friendship, but not wanting it to be bitten off!

The dog is friendly, much to the relief of Jack, as the dog comes bounding over and licks Jack's leg. Jack typically has an aversion to dogs, after the time he was attacked by one in Mexico several years ago. It left him having to have very painful rabies shots. This dog is more sociable and rubs his head against Jack's leg, wanting to be petted. Jack rings the front doorbell, which played the Westminster chimes.

The door is opened by an attractive red-haired lady in her thirties. Audrey was expecting Jack, the camera gave it away as to who he is. "Come in," she says in a friendly manner. Jack thought, maybe too friendly, but then she is nicely dressed in a multicolored floral summer dress.

Jack explained to Audrey that he is there to photograph her so that the conversation with Gloria can be played over the camera work. "I need to photograph you in as many positions and areas of the house as possible to make it enjoyable to our viewers." Jack thought he was doing an excellent job of convincing Audrey to be open.

"That is fine." She says as she looks into a wall mirror behind her and adjusts her hair, then she looks at her dress in the reflection, and she undoes the top two buttons, revealing a slight neckline. "Is that better?" she says.

"You really look fine, Audrey, if I may call you that." Says Jack.

"Please do." She smiled.

Jack found out that she had been married, but her husband had left her many years ago. After that, she had turned to writing. "Do you have a family? I don't see any photos around the furniture," Jack said.

"Not really, we did not have any children, and my parents are both dead now. I do have a brother, but we don't speak, and I haven't seen him for …. let me see, it must be fifteen years," Audrey said.

"Oh, that is interesting Audrey, any gossip is always good. What's his name?" Jack says, and then continues, "Do you have any photos of him? If you do, it would be good to have them on view for the video." Jack said.

Audrey is getting a little concerned about why Jack wanted photos of her brother, and it showed on her face, which Jack picked up on, and he said, "I say that because viewers like to know about a family existence, and it is good to have a photo around if there is one. It helps to sell books, you know."

Audrey seemed to accept that agreement "I want to sell books, I find that very difficult, I don't like to ask friends and these media companies charge so much. I went to one some time ago, but that did not work either.

She went to a drawer in her sideboard. "My brother's name is William. I am sure I have one in here somewhere. I don't know why I kept it, but then perhaps someone was telling me of an occasion such as this." and she pulled out an old photo in a frame. "Here we are," she said.

"Let's put it on the sideboard on view." Jack saws that the photograph had the names of Audrey and Chuck written across it in ink. Jack then took a video of Audrey beside the photo of her brother. Then zoomed in on the brother to get a good picture. Jack said, "I see the photo says, Audrey and Chuck?"

"Yes, although his name is William, he preferred Chuck." Said Audrey.

Jack couldn't remember what Chuck Bonstein looked like or if he had actually seen him in the past, but he knew this is what John wanted.

Jack spent the next hour taking lots of shots of Audrey in different positions. All the time, Audrey was flirting with Jack for the benefit of the film. Or was it? When Jack thought he had enough film, he said, "It is time to leave. I have a long journey back to Calgary." Audrey seemed disappointed, almost like she wanted Jack to stay.

Jack made his goodbyes and left Audrey standing at the doorway as he went to his car. He took the camera back to the shop, having first taken out the memory card of the recordings. He then had the long drive back to Calgary, where Judy is waiting for him. He had phoned John on the way to let him know his plan worked out perfectly, he had a photograph of Audrey's brother, and he would bring the recording over to him in a few days.

Back in Nome, the excavations of the claim site are progressing well. The restoration club has sent its older members, those retired gentlemen, and ladies, out to the site each day. They are gradually revealing whole animal skeletons. It is a slow process as they mark each bone to be collected by the local museum for reassembly. John has agreed they can have one set of tusks.

So far, there are twelve sets of tusks that are revealed and taken out slowly, not to damage them. John has made contact with a dealer and sold the complete batch. Arrangements are made for that company to send a ship to Nome to collect them. John has made a substantial donation to the Restoration Club for their help.

Michael West has been watching developments and thinks his site might have mammoths buried under the ground as well. He fences off his site, and the Mounty Inspector sees this might be his opportunity to act. He bumps into Michael one day at the site and gets into a conversation.

"I see that you are fencing off the site. Are you starting to excavate?"

"That is the idea, having seen what is going on next door, these tusks are worth more than gold." Michael laughs.

"Well, maybe I can help you. Mining for gold is similar to mining for artifacts." James says.

"Why don't you come to my hotel tomorrow at about seven in the evening and we'll have a drink in my room. It is more private than downstairs. It's room 230." Says Michael.

"I will definitely be there. It is time I got down to some work." Says James, but the sort of work he means is not what Michael has in mind.

James meets John and Cloe for a drink in their hotel bar that evening, and John tells James what has been happening with Jack in Edmonton.

"It sounds to me that the likelihood is that Chuck Bonstein is the brother of Audrey, but I can easily check that out through records." Says James. "Look, I need your help tomorrow. We'll make a trade if you help me get Michael West out of the country, I'll help you with this gold mine situation in Dawson.'

"Fair enough, what do you want me to do?" says John.

'Michael has asked me for a drink to his hotel room tomorrow to discuss mining for mammoth on his site. I have checked out the rear of his hotel, and there is one of those fire escape metal staircases. If you can be at the bottom with your car, I will bundle Michael, who will be unconscious, into the car. We'll drive him to the airport to the helicopter, which will be waiting, and I'll fly him off to Calgary for questioning. It will be good to get back to using my proper name." said James.

"It will be good for us too, but we'll carry on the pretense for the moment. Tomorrow will be fine, just ring me five minutes before you want me to pick you up. What time are you going for the drink?" says John.

"Seven o'clock, I suspect it will take an hour to get him loosened up, in time for the knockout blow." Says James.

"Why don't we drive around the back of the hotel now just to familiarize me with the layout?" John says.

"Good idea John, bring Cloe as well. Always good to have a lady with us in case we are stopped." Says James. They finish their drinks and head out to the car. Ben is not with them tonight; he has gone on a date with one of the waitresses.

Michael's hotel is not far along the road, and traffic is light. All the cars are local as there are no outside roads. "Turn right here, John, besides the hotel." Says James. As John turns, he can see the hotel is more extensive than he thought.

It is an old hotel, and John laughs as he says, "Maybe it is this large after the gold rush. People were expected to come here. Fat chance." John drives along the rear of the building and comes to the staircase in the center. "Is this the one?"

"Yes, this is it, I have already checked, and I can get to the staircase from Michael's room in seconds." Says James.

'Excellent, I'll be here when you phone." John says, and they drive back to their hotel for another drink.

The next day, John makes arrangements to receive the ship in port, coming to collect the mammoth tusks. The museum also comes to collect its complete skeleton. John says to the driver, "You can collect anything from the site now. The bones are of no use to us, but science might like them. We are finished with the site as of today. The remaining tusks will be shipped later today. "When John gets back to the hotel, he says to Cloe, "I think I should take my contact card for Josh Young, just in case there is a problem tonight at the airport."

"Yes, you should. You know there is always something with you," Cloe says, and they both laugh at that.

That evening with everything sorted at the claim site John, Cloe and Ben eat early at six. John has finished by seven. He is always a little anxious when doing undercover work. James has arrived at Michael's hotel room and shown in. James is a scotch drinker, and he can handle a few, so when Michael asks him what he would like. James replies, "Scotch, please."

Michael is not a big drinker; he sometimes surprises himself, a criminal who does not drink, but tonight he joins James in a whiskey. They spend the best part of an hour chatting. The scotch is having its effect on Michael, he has almost forgotten why James is there, but he has to admit to himself he likes this drink now.

At seven-fifty, Michael pours two more scotches and excuses himself to go to the bathroom, Just the opportunity James needs. He pulls out a sash of sleeping drug and puts it in Michael's drink. He swills it around quickly, and it dissolves. Michael returns and slowly sips his drink. James is slowing down now for the task in hand.

Michael has stopped talking and settles back in his chair, and his eyes just seem to close, as though he had no control of them. He does not care anymore. James says nothing as Michael is sound asleep. James quietly says, "Are you all right, Michael?" There is no reply.

James takes out his phone and rings John, who says, "I'm on my way."

John says to Cloe, "It's go time," and he leaves her, going to the car, and heads off to the meeting place. When he gets to the staircase and looks up, he sees James carrying Michael over his shoulder in a fireman's lift. Michael looks passed out. They open the rear door and place Michael on the seat, careful to make it appear to anyone looking through the window that he is resting.

They drive off to the airport and go to the security gate to avoid ordinary passengers. John says, "We should be alright here, but I'm surprised there is a guard on the gate." James does not respond.

The guard at the gate steps out in front of the car, holding his hand in the air for them to stop. John winds down his window. "Good evening, sir, your papers, please."

"What papers are those, officer?" says John.

"This is a private entrance for government authorized personnel only. The main entrance is to your right, over there." He says, pointing.

"But we are here on FBI business, officer'" John says, and he gets out his FBI identification card and shows it to the officer.

"But this is an informant's card, sir, not an employee card."

"Please phone Agent Young at the number on the card. This is an official FBI operation in cooperation with the Canadian RMP." John says.

"One minute then, sir." The guard says as he goes back to his sentry post and picks up his phone.

"Something must be afoot to have a sentry on duty tonight in this godforsaken hole!" John says as he watches the guard speaking on the phone. The guard puts the phone down, and John says, "Now we will know how important we are" He is getting hotter by the minute.

"Very well, sir, that all seems in order. You may proceed." Says the guard, and he stands back as John pulls away. He thinks to himself, *what is our country coming to?*

John drives over to the waiting RMP helicopter, and in the darkness, Michael is carried out by James and put in the plane. He calls back, "I will be in touch when I get back to sort out the other matter."

John watches as the helicopter takes off and heads towards Calgary. He then drives back to the hotel, as he goes out, the guard salutes him, as the guard thinks *that's one that won't be back.*

Inside the copter, James has put on his Inspector's uniform and returned to become Albert Jones. Michael is beginning to wake up, with handcuffs on. He lifts his hands in disbelief, as his eyes are just coming into focus.

He can see the inspector, and says "What am I doing here?"

"We are going back to Calgary, Mr. West, oh and by the way, you are under arrest. Anything you say may be taken down and used in evidence." Says Albert.

"You kidnaped me. I was in Alaska, USA, not Canada. You have no jurisdiction here." Says Michael.

"You volunteered to come back to Canada with me, sir. You wanted to resolve the past crime of a bank raid, where a guard was shot. You told me it was playing on your conscience," Said Albert. Michael knew he had been duped and fell back to sleep, under the influence of the drugs, thinking *I don't have a conscience.*

An hour before they were due to arrive in Calgary, Michael woke up again. This time, he is coherent. He is still handcuffed, and he is also tied to the helicopter's frame with a leash. It was the only thing Albert could find at short notice.

"How did you get to me over the bank raid?" Michael says.

"Take my advice Mr. West and don't say anything until you have seen your lawyer." Said Albert.

"But I need to know," Michael says.

"A man that fitted your description was seen by many witnesses coming out of the drain system further down the road. We were able to put two and two together. Plus, it's one thing for a fellow criminal to keep quiet initially, but things change very rapidly after a period in jail." Said Albert.

Michael knew at once that one of the other crooks had shopped on him. *I can't go to jail again, and this time because a guard was killed, they will throw away the key,* he thought to himself.

"We are approaching Calgary now, Mr. West, so brace yourself for landing." Says Albert.

"What would you care?" Michael says.

The police helipad at Calgary is on top of a five-story building on the edge of town. It is still nighttime, and Michael can see that searchlights light the pad out of a window. The pilot slowly reduces height and brings the copter to a standstill on the roof, with a slight bump. The rotors are switched off, and Albert says, "It's time to leave. Can you walk?"

"Just about, but no thanks to you. My head feels like it is on fire."

Albert gets up and opens the door, lowering the steps. He then goes back inside and takes the leash off Michael that held him to the fuselage. Michael is still handcuffed, but he gets up slowly, deep in thought. Albert indicates that he should walk to the door and down the steps. Albert follows him out. There is no room for them both to get out together.

Michael is standing on the asphalted roof now as Albert walks down the stairs. Michael's mind is made up. Much to the surprise of Albert, Michael takes off in a run. There is nowhere to go, and he knows it, but Albert takes off after him. Michael seems to have got a second wind, and Albert is still in shock at Michael's reaction.

Michael is now coming to the edge of the roof and takes a flying leap over the low parapet wall. He tumbles to the ground five floors below, still handcuffed as he splats on the sidewalk. He made no sound on his way down, and now Albert is at the wall looking down. He is concerned, thinking *I'll get the blame for this.*

Several officers have come out of the building, and Michael is declared dead. Seeing what had happened, the helicopter pilot walked over to Albert and said, "Maybe it's for the best. At least we won't have to pay to keep him in prison for the next thirty years."

Albert said nothing, he is still concerned a prisoner in his custody committed suicide during his watch.

CHAPTER TWENTY-FIVE

Albert spent the next two days handling all the questions of the investigation unit as to how the prisoner was in Alaska, a foreign country when he was arrested. Albert kept to the story he had told Michael. Although his superior was not entirely happy with the explanations, she had to admit that this was one criminal out of the way, without any expense to the country. The papers were filed away marked 'Death by suicide.'

On the third day, Albert phoned John to tell him what had happened. "Give me a few more days, and I will come to Dawson City with you to sort out Chuck Bonstein."

"That's fine, Albert. We will clear things up here. We are almost done." Said John as he put the phone down before calling Jack. "Hello Jack, are you alone?"

Jack wondered why he said that "Yes, Judy is out shopping."

"That's good. I have to tell you some news that might upset her. Michael West is dead. He killed himself while trying to escape capture in respect of a bank raid some years ago. I'll explain more when I see you. How are things going with you and Judy?"

"Very well, actually. I hope you are sitting down because Judy and I have decided to settle down in Nashville. The old singleton won't be so for long. From talking this situation out with Judy, I don't think she will be distressed at hearing Michael is dead." Said Jack.

"That's fantastic news Jack, I am so pleased for you settling down. We will have a few drinks on that when we meet. Everything is tied up here in Nome, we have sold about fifteen mammoth tusks for a good sum, and they have been removed. Albert has agreed to help us sort out Chuck Bonstein in Dawson, which will be the next project, before heading back to Nashville. So far, it has been a productive summer financially for us all. Are you and Judy flying direct to Nashville?"

"No, if it's alright with you, I will come back tomorrow to you, or I can meet you in Dawson. That will give Judy time to sort her move out, and you might like some extra help in Dawson."

"Sounds good to me. Why don't you meet us in Dawson? Flying is easier for you then. Say the day after tomorrow. We can use the same hotel as before." says John.

"Will do, boss." Says Jack, and he disconnects the call. Judy is pleased with Jack's decision. She still cannot believe her luck in finding Jack, who seems to be so honest and open.

"Why don't you take my car and drive to Dawson? It's a nice drive over the mountains, at this time of year." Judy says.

"You know, I'll do that. I've flown the Rockies but never driven them. I'll leave tomorrow and take the two-day drive. That will give you plenty of time to sort things out here, for our new lives in Nashville." Jack said with enthusiasm, he is looking forward to their life together.

The following day early, just as the sun rises over the surrounding hills, Jack gets into Judy's car, having loaded his suitcase. "Wait a minute, I want another kiss before you leave," Judy says, and they embrace, kissing tenderly.

Jack drives the car out of the parking space and heads off to Dawson, following the route on GPS.

In Nome, John and Ben have cleared up everything. John thanks the Restoration Club for its help and tells the leader they can have anything they find in the ground at their mining claim site. They are delighted with that outcome and are confident they will find other relics in the future.

John and Ben go back to the hotel where Cloe has finished packing. John arranged flights for the three of them later in the day. He looks at Cloe, and says "Do you think we have done all that don wanted?"

"I think we have. I do not get any visions anymore. I think he and Sophie are at peace now together." Said, Cloe.

"Yes, but we still have to sort out Don's mining claim in Dawson." Said John.

Cloe is quiet for a moment, "Don is not concerned about the gold now. He does not need it anymore. He just wanted to sort things out with Sophie."

"Let's go then," John says as he walks out with their suitcase and meets Ben with his outside. "The plane leaves in three hours, and we have to take the car rental back."

They are at the airport in plenty of time to hear the announcement that the flight to Dawson City is boarding. Having passed through passport control, they went to their gate and boarded the plane. Before takeoff, John phoned Jack, "We're on our way should be in Dawson in about two hours."

"That's great. I am driving in Judy's SUV, will be in Dawson later in the day. So there is no need for a rental. I have got the video recording with me." Says Jack, as his signal goes, having gone around the mountains.

John, Cloe, and Ben checked into the hotel they used previously; the receptionist said, "It's good to see you back again, sir. We have the same room as last time."

"Thank you," John says, and "We'll need two singles, oh and Inspector Jones will be joining us at some point."

"That will be fine, sir. We have plenty of rooms available at this time." The receptionist says. They go to their rooms and unpack, just as John's phone rings, the screen says Albert Jones.

"Hello, Albert, how are you?"

'I'm fine, thank you, I've sorted out Michael's death with the authorities and will come to Dawson about the claim manager. I assume you are there now." Says Albert.

"Yes, we have just arrived, and Jack should be joining us later today." Says John.

"I will see you tomorrow morning then." Says Albert as he disconnected the call.

Later that evening, after their dinner, Jack arrives and joins them at the table. "I'm starving." He says and orders a dinner while John fills him in on what has been happening.

"I can't wait to see your video of Audrey. Do you think she is Chuck's sister, Jack?"

"I'm sure she is, but I'm not so sure she is in on this scam." Says Jack.

After dinner, they go to John's room, The video is on a memory stick, which Jack puts into his laptop, and they watch the video. "there is the only photo I could find of Audrey's brother, and that is twenty years old according to her." Said Jack.

"How old would you say she is, Jack?"

"Well, I thought in her early thirties, I know what you are thinking, I thought the same. Chuck must be fifty years old at least, from what I remember of him that day we initially met him. There is a big difference in ages, which could point to them not being siblings." Said Jack. To which both John and Cloe said "Hmm" and nodded their heads.

"Hopefully, Albert will be able to come up with something definite tomorrow. Let's have an early night, to be fresh for the morning. Let's meet at breakfast at eight-thirty," Cloe said, and the others left for their rooms.

Inspector Albert Jones walks into the dining room at breakfast, resplendent in his formal attire, and joins them for breakfast after his long drive. They exchange details on what has been happening, and Jack tells Albert about the Video.

"You pretended to be a TV cameraman?" says Albert laughing in pretend shock. "You are getting as bad as me. Let's see it after breakfast. I hope you didn't ask her to undress." Albert says.

"Certainly not." says Jack, "although I don't think she would have minded."

Cloe says, "You men! you all think the same, that we can't wait for you to get your pants down."

They all look through the video again, and Albert made the same comment about the ages but added, "The girl or the boy could have been adopted, of course."

"Good point," said John.

"Can I borrow your laptop for a minute, Jack, please? I want to go into government records and check out the pair of them."

Jack hands over his laptop, and Albert says, "Now you do not know what I am typing in!" as he gets online to the records site. "The registrar calls himself Chuck Bonstein; that's not a common name, but there is no one registered here in that name." he deletes Chuck and rechecks. The program comes up with six people in the Yukon. "This is the interesting one WILLIAM born 1965." Albert chicks on that name, and it enters another record.

"Bingo," Albert shouts out. "He has an adopted sister named Audrey in the year 1987." He looks around at everyone who looks gleeful. "We need to pay a visit to William or Chuck."

Albert rubs his chin, "Why don't John and I go alone? We don't want to make Chuck panicky at this moment. We need to make him admit his crime. It will be easier that way." They agree, and John and Albert set off the registry office. On entering, Chuck can be seen through his glass screen that he is in the office. There is no receptionist on duty today, and Chuck seems quite relaxed at the moment.

He comes out to greet them. "Good morning, Inspector and John. It's good to see you again," he says, lying, and now John can see that he is not so relaxed. He looks very nervous and is obviously wondering what they are doing here.

Yes, it's good to be back." Says John. "How are you getting on with the negotiations with the mining company over the two claims.

"Slowly." Said Chuck, which is true. He has been pushing the company every day for a decision, he even offered a bribe to the person handling the matter, but that brought no further activity, but now Chuck is more concerned that John is still referring to both claims.

"You do realize I would not be able to discuss the second claim, as that is with Audrey Croft." Says Chuck, who became panicky when Albert said in a formal police voice.

"That remains to be seen.".

Chuck did not respond, but Albert said, "I think we should go and inspect the two claims, John." Chuck is now openly panicking, stumbling over his words.

Chuck says, "Is this some sort of formal investigation, Inspector?"

"Everything I do is a formal investigation, Mr. Bonstein, but I am sure you have nothing to worry about. You only oversee the registration of the claims and are not personally involved. Are you?" says Albert pointedly.

"Precisely, Officer." Now Chuck is getting formal. "Shall I come with you?"

"If you like Chuck, it is a free country." Said Albert.

They all go to the stableyard, hire three horses, and ride to the top of the mountain. It is a pleasant morning for riding. John is enjoying the breeze, but he turns around to look at Chuck, who is riding behind them, and he can see that Chuck's face is getting redder.

When they get to the entrance to the cave, they descend from the horses. They look down the cave; with the aid of Ben's flashlight they brought with them, Albert Whispered to John, "Thank goodness for Ben, the flashlight is essential."

There seems little interference in the cave. They go out of the cave to the adjoining claim site, which is still in the mountain range, and already there is some excavation of the rock happening. "Has Audrey Croft suddenly turned up then after twenty years? Asks Albert.

"Yes, I contacted her with the good news last week, and she came here immediately and instructed workmen to investigate her site." Says Chuck, feeling he had answered that question well.

"How old is Audrey Croft Chuck? She is a fortunate lady." Said John.

"She is about thirty-two."

"And when did you say the claim was registered?" Albert says.

"Um, I think it was twenty years ago." Says Chuck.

"That would have made her twelve at the time. Too young to register a claim in her own name," said Albert.

Now Chuck is really perplexed. He had not thought of that. *Why didn't I register it as a trustee?*

Albert took out of his pocket a sheet of paper with a photograph on it. The one he printed off from the video that Jack had taken. "Is this Audrey Croft?" said Albert showing Chuck the picture.

"It looks like her, but I'm not sure. Where did you get it?" said Chuck

"Never you mind. I have to put you on notice, Mr. Bonstein, that this now becomes an official investigation. I believe that you have falsely registered this claim in your young sister's name to exclude the genuine registration of John Smith and Jack King made earlier this year. This is extortion and theft and will carry a substantial prison sentence if proven. It will help your case if you choose to take Queen's evidence and admit your crime. The sentence would then be reduced." Said Albert.

"Am I under arrest? Inspector."

"Not at the moment. You are free for the time being while we build up your case. We will be interviewing your sister in the next few days. After that, if she confirms the situation, you will be charged." Says Albert. They ride back to the village, with Chuck twenty yards behind, deep in thought. He knows that he does not stand a chance. His sister has not spoken to him for twenty years, they had a falling out over their parents. She will not protect him.

John and Albert go back to their hotel. Cloe, Jack, and Ben are waiting for them in the reception lounge. "How did it go?" Cloe says.

John looks to Albert, "Ok, I'll tell her. We think it went very well. We confronted Chuck at the claim site. I offered him a deal if he admits what he has done. He is definitely guilty, but he will get a lower sentence if he admits it now, without the need for an expensive investigation." Says Albert.

Albert's phone rang, "Hello, this is Inspector Jones. How can I help you?"

"This is Chuck Bonstein" there is a pause. "You are right. I did register the claim in my sister's name after Smith and King made theirs. You will see I get a reduced sentence, won't you? I realize I have been stupid, and I am very sorry." Said Chuck.

"That is your best action Chuck I will tell you that we have already been in touch with your sister. I will be over to your office in a few minutes to formally charge you." Said Albert.

"Will I be arrested?"

"Not at this stage. I do not regard you as a flight risk. You will be on police bail at this stage. Who knows, if this is your first offense, you may not even get a prison sentence." Says Albert, who had put his phone on speaker so the others could hear but now disconnected.

"It looks like you will be gold miners after all, but I suggest you deal with the mining company direct now. I'll go and charge Chuck and come back for this evening. We can have a good meal together before I head back to Calgary tomorrow.

That evening over their meal, Albert says, "I misunderstood Chuck. When I got to his office earlier, it was cleared out. His assistant said Chuck had rushed back earlier in the day and told him to delete the registry regarding Audrey Croft and that he would not see him again."

"Doesn't surprise me. " said John.

Albert smiled, which said it all. "You crafty old so and so." Said John.

Cloe's phone rang. She went to turn it off but saw the name Gloria Rowbottom on the screen. "It's Gloria. I'll take it outside," she said as she left the table.

"Hello Gloria, How are you doing?"

"I'm fine. I wanted to check the situation with you guys now that the Don Wicker thing is finished," Gloria says.

"It's not quite finished. Did we tell you about the gold mine claim in The Klondike?" says Cloe.

"Well, while Don was here, he took a claim high in the hills, a body was found in a cave of an old Indian burial site. The body dates back to the time Don was here. John and Jack, purely by chance, made an adjoining claim earlier this year for fun. It turns out that the cave has a rich seam of gold." Says Cloe.

"That's lucky for you then if you have next door."

"You know us. Nothing is that easy. The registrar deleted our claim and falsified the entry twenty years ago to his sister, Audrey Croft." Said, Cloe

"You are joking. I had a phone call the other day from an Audrey Croft, saying that I had phoned her. I told her she was mistaken. But now I am wondering if it was you." Said, Cloe.

Cloe had to smile, "Yes, sorry, we had to use your name to get in touch with this lady. Why don't you come up and see the final installment to the Don saga?"

"I'd like to. This has been a fascinating experience that I will never forget. Let me speak to my boss to try and get a few days off. I'll come back to you." Cloe switches off her phone and goes back to the table.

"Guess what." She says, "Audrey croft phoned Gloria after Jack's interview. She is going to try and come up. We'll be here for a few days, won't we?"

"Yes, we need to see this mining company." Said John.

Jack spoke up and said, "Can I leave that to you, John? I'd like to get back to Nashville and help Judy move into my apartment.'

"Of course, you get off to her. We'll clear things up here now, and to be honest, Ben. You can head off as well. There is nothing for you to do now. When we are all back home, we will share out the spoils."

The following day Albert, Jack, and Ben head home in their cars. John rents a small Compact car as there are only two of them now.

CHAPTER TWENTY-SIX

There is a call from Gloria, which came to Cloe's phone saying she would be with them later in the day. John contacted the Klondike Mining Company and told the representative that they must deal directly with him on both claims, now that they had confirmed gold in the cave. The representative had heard of the deception of Chuck Bonstein and was happy. He had not got on well with Chuck. He explained that although gold was confirmed in both claims, there is still some time needed to ascertain the quality and the quantity. He assured John he would be in touch with offers for both claims within a month.

Gloria arrived in Dawson that afternoon with her usual cameraman. John and Cloe took them to the site of the cave, and the cameraman started filming as Gloria said into the microphone, "*Good afternoon, viewers, this is Gloria Rowbottom reporting on the final stage of the Don Wicker saga. I am at a cave above Dawson City. John Smith and Cloe Taylor have only recently discovered that Don claimed this site before heading to Nome in the late eighteen hundreds. Inside the cave, the skeleton of an unknown person was found recently.*

The police have established the skeleton would have been dated to around the time Don was here, but they have filed their papers as the matter is well over a hundred years ago. Now it is established that the cave contains a seam of gold, and the Trustees of Don Wicker will shortly receive a cash bonus for the continuance of the museum in his honor.

The question is did Don kill the person and then take the claim hoping no one would find the body. Or did someone else do the deed and Don was covering up for them? We will never know, and I leave it up to you to make your own judgment, having seen all the facts that we have unearthed over the past few months.

The End

BOOK REFERENCES

The Mexican artifacts and Drake's treasures are from their experiences in *From a Jack to a King*.

The attempt on the president's life and Carrie and Alexandra appear in *Revenge Is Mine*.

John Smith and Cloe appear in *From a Jack to a King* and *Daylight Robbery*, and John Smith and Ben are in *Revenge Is Mine*.

Ben appears in *Revenge Is Mine* and *From a Jack to a King*,

Agent Josh Young appears in all the above and in *The Clone*.

Lightning Source UK Ltd.
Milton Keynes UK
UKHW020342280721
387881UK00008B/509/J